M000284755

HIGHLANDER'S VOW

Called by a Highlander Book Six

MARIAH STONE

Stone
Publishing

This is a work of fiction. Names, characters, places, and incidents either are the products of the author's imagination or are used fictitiously. Any resemblance to actual persons, living or dead, businesses, companies, events, or locales is entirely coincidental.

© 2021 Mariah Stone. All rights reserved.

Cover design by Qamber Designs and Media

All rights reserved. This book or parts thereof may not be reproduced in any form, stored in any retrieval system, or transmitted in any form by any means—electronic, mechanical, photocopy, recording, or otherwise—without prior written permission of the publisher. For permission requests, contact the publisher at http:\\mariahstone.com

Whatever our souls are made of, his and mine are the same.

— Emily Brontë, Wuthering Heights

PROLOGUE

E ilean Donan Castle, 1301

HER BETROTHED WAS COMING FOR HER.

Catrìona Mackenzie strained her eyes, focusing on a single black spot among the frenzy of moonlight sparkles on the loch. That must be the boat.

That must be Tadhg. The lad she loved. The lad who would change her life.

Midnight wind gusted hard and cold, whining and wailing in the slits of the castle gate behind her. She straightened her shoulders, her stomach squeezing in nervous anticipation. Not daring to look away from the spot, she sprinted down the path towards the jetty, gravel rustling under her feet. Guards be damned, she'd wanted Tadhg to see she was right there, waiting for him.

She let out a shaky breath, clutching the small wooden cross under her cloak. Tadhg had made it for her. *Remember, yer mother is with God*, he had told her. *She and God are watching over ye.*

1

Tadhg...her sweet lad.

Nae, not a lad.

A young man who reminded her of a golden wolf. His piercing green eyes always alert, watching from under long eyelashes the color of wheat.

He'd be her husband later tonight...

Her father, chief of clan Mackenzie, had been negotiating her marriage to a rich nobleman, Alexander Balliol, for almost a year now. Tadhg was just a poor clansman, the son of a warrior.

But he would give her a lifetime of love and save her from the destiny of being a prized possession.

Her late mother's destiny.

That is, if her father didn't find her here, outside the castle walls at night.

A shiver ran through her as she imagined the enraged bull of her father running at her, his red fists ready to strike—and no one around to protect her. Her older brother Angus wouldn't know where she was. And Tadhg...

If Father saw them, he'd kill Tadhg, surely.

She let go of the cross and touched her dagger tucked behind her belt. Angus had taught her how to use it so that she could protect herself against Father if he wasn't there to shield her.

She felt like someone's eyes were on her back, and the soft hair on the nape of her neck stood up. She looked over her shoulder and at the looming black castle wall. Up there, she knew, night guards were huddling in their cloaks.

Her back as tense as a bowstring, she waited, never taking her eyes off the boat. It grew bigger as it approached, the silhouette of the man who rowed the boat slouched as the oars rose and fell. The wind grew stronger, tugging at her skirt and flapping her cloak. Needles prickled her hands from the cold.

Black clouds advanced from the north, just as she had hoped, to swallow the moon and the light and let her escape into the darkness.

When the boat got closer, she noticed there were two

figures, not one. One of them was big—much too big for Tadhg. The other one could be Tadhg...

Her pulse pounded hard in her temples as she watched the oars dipping into the water and the boat rocking on wild waves. As the first gushes of icy rain hit her in the face, the big man turned to look over his shoulder. The wooden planks of the jetty shifted from under her feet.

The big, meaty face, swollen and somber, the black brows over deeply set eyes like two windows into hell.

Kenneth Og Mackenzie.

Father.

A thick cloud swallowed the moon, and the boat dissolved in the dark wall of rain.

Her head swimming, she stared into the blackness, trying to see who the second man was. *Oh, Lord, please let it not be Tadhg...*

The boat thumped against the jetty, and she saw that the other man was Laomann, her eldest brother.

Father turned to her. "What are ye waiting for?" he barked. "Tie the boat. Since ye're the only one on the jetty."

Laomann threw her the line and she rushed to grab it. Tying it to the cleat, she strained her eyes, trying to see if there was another boat.

But all she saw was black rain.

Father and Laomann climbed onto the dock. Father shoved her shoulder, pushing her towards the castle. "Come, nae use for yer betrothed if ye're sick."

She walked alongside them, numb and cold. "My betrothed?"

She glanced at the misty lake. The sky was completely black now. Did she have any choice? Surely if Tadhg did come for her, he'd find a way to get inside the castle or pass her a message. He was a clansman after all. And Father had no reason to suspect him.

"I finally got him to agree to marry ye. Alexander arrives in a sennight," Father said. "Their man just appeared in Dornie to inform us of his agreement and let us prepare."

Alexander's name was like a heavy stone around her neck.

Laomann's gaze was on the ground, his shoulders slumped, a mournful frown on his face. What did he have to mourn?

Over the last few years, Father had refused every single marriage proposal until he'd started negotiating with house Balliol.

"Finally, 'tis happening. Ye'll be marrit to a royal bloodline. Yer children will have claim to the Scottish throne. They may even throw the Bruce's line one day."

Chills rushed down her spine. She thought of the man in his forties who already had five grown children, all older than she. On his visit to Eilean Donan, he'd stared at her so coldly that her neck prickled.

Tadhg could still come. He could still save her.

Slamming his fist against the heavy gate, Father turned to her. "Thanks to this match, I'll rise higher than any Mackenzie before me." As the door opened, he added, "What do ye say, is yer father the best matchmaker, or nae?"

She said nothing.

They passed through and marched across the quiet inner bailey; the only sounds were the slurping mud under their shoes and the murmur of rain.

Father kicked at a bucket standing by the timber house with a thatched roof. "A royal bloodline!" Splashing their feet with water, the bucket flew through the air, dashed like Catrìona's hope. "Smile, lass," he added, threat palpable in his voice.

If the bucket had been a promise of what he'd do to her if she didn't obey, Catrìona understood the message and pressed out a smile.

"Ah," Father said. "Better. Isna yer father the smartest man alive? All ye have to do now is do yer duty as a woman and give yer husband a son."

As they entered the warm, dry main keep, Catrìona was shivering, but not from the cold. Under her father's heavy gaze, she climbed the stairs to her bedchamber. When she closed the door behind her, it sounded like the door of a dungeon.

Her breath rushing in and out in ragged bursts, she ran to the window and stared into the darkness, trying to see another boat. But sheets of rain lashed at her like a whip, blinding her view.

A small knock at the door made her spin and she closed the shutters.

Her maid, Ruth, stood in the doorway with a tallow candle. Her sweet, round face was full of worry. "Mistress, what happened?"

Catrìona shook her head, blinking away unwelcome tears. "Why didna he come, Ruth?"

The lass hurried to her. She placed the candle on the windowsill and took Catrìona's hands in hers. Their warmth burned Catrìona's freezing skin.

"Did something happen to him?" Catrìona whispered. "Was he hurt?"

Ruth gave her a kind, supportive smile. "Have faith. We'll wait. He may still come."

Catrìona nodded. "Aye. I should pray. I canna go to Dornie and find him, and I canna do anything else."

Ruth squeezed her hands. "But ye can ask God for help."

Catrìona nodded, hugged Ruth close, then released her and dropped to her knees by her bed. She began praying, whispering fiercely, her hands clutched together so tightly they were soon numb.

She lost track of time.

Morning light colored the rough stone walls of her chamber in pink and orange. The storm had passed, she realized when birdsong seeped through the closed shutters.

"Mistress!" A voice made her jump. She turned to the door— Ruth stood there, eyes as wide as two moons.

She rushed into the room, her freckled face white. She helped Catrìona stand up. Catrìona's knees ached from having spent the whole night in prayer.

Ruth's eyebrows knit together in a sad expression. "Ye didna even sleep?"

"Doesna matter. Any word from him?"

Ruth lowered her eyes and sighed. "I just went to the village, mistress."

Catrìona grasped Ruth by the elbows and shook her a little. "And?"

"His da's house looks abandoned. The door was open. The swineherd, their neighbor, said they left last night before the storm."

The world under Catrìona's feet shifted.

Just left... Nae a word.

The man she loved didn't even have the courtesy to tell her he didn't want to marry her after all. She let go of Ruth and held on to the bedpost, her heart ripping apart, her feet heavy and sinking.

And now she'd have to marry Alexander Balliol. She was a means to an end for Father and she'd be the same for Alexander.

The storm hadn't stopped Tadhg. He must have gone to look for fortune elsewhere.

Because if he really loved her, he would face whatever stood in his path to be with her, to rescue her.

He didn't love her. Her only use was as an object to move her father forward politically.

Her mother had been right.

She would be better off becoming a nun.

CHAPTER 1

E ilean Donan Castle, end of July 2021

"YE KNOW, PEOPLE DO DISAPPEAR IN THE HIGHLANDS."

Detective James Murray glanced at Leonie Peterson, a sweet, plump woman in her fifties, who walked alongside him towards Eilean Donan. At the end of the long bridge, the castle grayed against the brilliant blue sky like a vision from the past.

Tension creased the space between Leonie's eyebrows. He understood her concern.

How could two people disappear in the museum, under the noses of other visitors and in plain view of security cameras? Was there more danger to visitors? Was she or any of the employees under suspicion?

Rogene Wakeley, a recent Oxford University PhD graduate, and her eighteen-year-old brother David, both Americans, had visited Eilean Donan two weeks ago and hadn't been seen since.

Given it had happened in a medieval castle, with its thick walls, dark corners, and old furniture, people could easily imagine ghosts, faeries, and spirits. But his childhood and adolescence had taught him logic and simple psychology was the answer to anything that appeared strange, magical, or required faith.

"People disappear everywhere," James said noncommittally.

The quiet around him pressed against James's ears. Birdsong echoed from the sapphire surface of the loch splotched with yellow, orange, and green seaweed. Somewhere in the distance, a few cars rustled past on the A87. The moss green and yellow hills of the Highlands around them were mirrored in the still water. The air was so crisp, so fresh, and even the fishy scent of loch and algae were refreshing, invigorating.

As if his lungs were rebelling against the clean air, James craved a cig. He reckoned he had time for a few drags before they reached the castle. He fished the pack and his lighter out of the pocket of his gray suit jacket.

Bloody hell, only two left.

Leonie shook her head. "But here, 'tis just unexplainable..."

He stopped and lit up, the first drag already loosening the tension in his chest and sending his head into a pleasant spin. Leonie frowned at him as many nonsmokers did. Resuming walking, he puffed out the smoke, part of him regretting how the smell shielded the scent of nature. "There's always an explanation. It's just the matter of finding it."

"Do ye have an idea already? I mean, ye and I both saw it on the footage with our own eyes. They went into the castle, down into the cellars—which they were not supposed to do!" She gave a firm shake of her head. "And never came back."

The grayscale security footage James had seen back in the Oxford Police office and again today in the management building on the other side of the castle showed Rogene and David Wakeley first in the queue to buy their tickets. Then the siblings had purposefully marched down the bridge to the castle —not looking around and enjoying the view like regular tourists.

Rogene, dressed practically, wore a big travel rucksack that looked stuffed as though she was preparing for days out in nature. The car she'd rented had been reported by the rental company about a week after she'd arrived here from Oxford with her brother. She'd have a big fine to pay—if she ever returned.

James exhaled a stream of smoke. "I can't share any ideas I have, unfortunately."

"Right," said Leonie. "I understand that. Only, the young woman disappeared once before, on the night of the Fischer wedding, didn't she?"

"Yes."

"And yer lot looked for her then, too."

"Yes. When she came back, she claimed to have been with a man she met on the castle grounds that night. Angus Mackenzie. That's what she'd told the police."

But none of the Angus Mackenzies James had contacted had ever met Rogene.

And yet, based on her careful preparations combined with her huge rucksack, Rogene seemed to have known she was going somewhere forever this time. Another interesting fact was that she was pregnant, and the date of conception coincided with her absence in May.

She seemed to be prepared for a long trip, and not for taking her own life as her note had suggested. He doubted very much that a pregnant woman would prepare her suicide so meticulously.

Even his sister, Emily, who had recently lost her fiancé, had told him the baby she was expecting had become the light of her life.

Leonie's lips puckered like a raisin. "I dinna know an Angus Mackenzie. But the island grounds are accessible to the public even if the castle is rented for a wedding."

"Right."

As they approached the gatehouse, James looked up the tall walls. An odd thought occurred to him—how would it feel to stand atop the wall with a bow in his arms, string taut, arrow pointing at an approaching medieval enemy? He hadn't held a bow and an arrow since he was fourteen years old, but it had been an important part of his everyday life when he'd lived in the Unseen Wonders cult. Archery had been his stress relief and a means to help provide his mum and sister with food since the age of eight.

Leonie unlocked the door within the portal of the gatehouse and pushed it open. As they passed through, they entered a small, quiet, sunlit courtyard. Brown-gray walls loomed at him from all sides. The biggest building was the main keep, with a stone staircase leading to a heavy door on the first floor.

James threw the butt of his cigarette on the cobblestone-paved ground and stepped on it to put it out.

Leonie glared at him. "Do ye mind throwing that in a bin, please?"

Inwardly cursing at himself, James leaned down and picked up the butt. "Sorry. Long night. Didn't mean to disrespect history."

He threw the butt in the bin.

Leonie sighed and gestured at the keep. "This is where Rogene and David went. The main keep."

"Great."

They proceeded through the courtyard towards the building, where Leonie unlocked the arched door.

Inside, a small hall stretched straight ahead. Leonie gestured to their left where, down a short flight of stairs, was another large door. "This leads to the Billeting Room where wedding receptions are held."

She showed him down the small hall where they came to a barrier familiar from the security footage, with the sign Staff Only. Leonie pointed at a watercolor painting on the wall next to them. It showed a medieval castle on an island, with massive walls and four towers.

"'Tis a reconstruction of the castle the way it may have

looked in the fourteenth century, in the time of Robert the Bruce."

"Interesting..." James muttered. "And this tower right here would be one of those?"

She pointed at the widest tower. "Aye, this has always been the main keep."

He gestured to the door. "I'd like to see where Rogene and David went."

She walked down the hall. "Oh, aye, of course."

"Any idea why someone might want to go down there?"

"She's a historian, so I suppose she was especially curious. She and her colleagues did find Bruce's letter hidden in the wall, after all."

Right, Rogene and her friends Karin and Anusua had found a letter Robert the Bruce had written to King Edward I where he'd stated his intention to give up his fight and his throne. The letter had been quite a shock for the historical community and had made Rogene's name. Her career was booming. One more reason not to disappear or end her own life.

Leonie opened the barrier and unlocked the door. As she flicked the switch, light illuminated narrow stone stairs leading down. James followed her, breathing cold, wet, moldy air.

He had a strange sense of uneasiness as he descended. This reminded him of something, something he'd desperately wanted to forget. A private farm, the old Victorian cottage among the woods and abandoned oat fields. The scent of wet dust, of woodsmoke and the warmth of the fire that had desperately tried to chase the ever-present cold away. His mother, crying yet again, huddling in the corner of an old cottage.

It's just an old castle, that's it. Just another case to solve, another bit of chaos to turn into order. Another presumed mystery to bust open and take apart.

As the stairs opened into a long, broad hall with furniture covered with white protective sheets along stone walls, James's phone beeped.

It was a text message from Emily.

The consultant can squeeze me in today for the scan.

He exhaled a small sigh of relief. He'd insisted she go for an ultrasound because the baby had been moving less for the past few days. She was thirty-nine weeks pregnant, and told him she wasn't worried. But James was. She was almost at her due date. He couldn't let her lose her baby on top of everything else.

He typed, *Great. Call me. Good news or bad. I'll come straight back to Oxford if you need me.*

Her fiancé, Harry, a firefighter, had died in the line of duty six months earlier, and James was the only support she had. He'd held her that day as she'd sobbed into his jacket, and had vowed he wouldn't let her face being a single mother alone. He'd be there for her like he'd always been.

He put the phone away, looking around. It smelled like mold and wet earth and something flowery—lavender?

Dim lamps on the walls illuminated the space that brought the cold deep into his bones. James walked into the middle of the room and stopped. Covered furniture and a couple of cupboards stood in alcoves along the wall. There were two doors.

James looked around. "What could be of interest for a historian?"

Leonie pointed at the single door at the end of the hall. "Over there, there's an ancient rock with a Pictish carving. 'Tis nae so interesting for most, but a rare find for a true historian."

"Let's go there first, then."

James's sense of uneasiness intensified the closer they came to the ancient door with cast-iron hardware. As rusty, metallic gnashing of the key in the keyhole echoed off the walls, James had an urge to reach out and stop Leonie. As the door opened, pitch darkness breathed earthy, cold air into his face. But with the flick of a switch, James was looking into a large space with an arched ceiling and rough stone walls. A pile of rubble and rocks lay to his right.

A phone rang angrily, disrupting the dead silence and chasing James's uneasiness away.

"Sorry," Leonie muttered. "My son's calling. Are ye going to be all right in here?"

"Sure. No worries."

"Just please don't go near that renovation site."

The search team had checked the rubble for bodies, he knew, so they must have reinforced the ceiling to prevent it from further collapse.

"Cheers."

As the door closed behind her, James was glad to be able to check things without Leonie's watchful eye. He looked for hair, a dark blotch indicating blood, a piece of paper—any sign that the missing pair had been here. Rogene must have checked that Pictish rock.

He approached the rock and crouched to look at it closer. There were three wavy lines and then a straight line and a hand-print. He didn't know the meaning of it, but he could imagine it had some sort of religious connotation, perhaps. Maybe a Pictish shaman had carved them to worship some sort of an imaginary god.

Anger and revulsion came over James at the thought. He was the product of such delusion, he and Emily both.

And his mother had been the victim. Fanaticism was danger-ous. Believing in all things "miraculous" and "beyond under-standing" was dangerous. His mother's sad descent into alcoholism and despair was proof. James's damaged psyche was proof. Millions of pounds that people had paid to the leader of Unseen Wonders, Brody Guthenberg, was proof.

The scent of lavender and freshly cut grass tickled James's nose. Leonie must be back. He looked over his shoulder, but the door was still closed.

And yet, a shadow on the floor lay three feet away from him. As he turned around, he saw a woman in a dark-green hooded cloak standing a few steps away. She was smiling at him, her eyes sparkling.

How had he not heard the door open and close?

He straightened, tensing. "Are you with Leonie?"

"Nae." She cocked her head, studying him.

"Then I'd like for you to leave, please. This is a police investigation."

"I may have, as ye humans say these days, information ye're looking for," she said with a sweet, pleasant voice. She had a pretty face with full lips and freckles.

Ignoring the odd "ye humans" expression, he frowned. "What information?"

"I ken where the people ye're looking for are."

He cocked his head, astounded. "And who would you be?"

"My name is Sìneag."

"Detective Murray. Criminal Investigation Department."

He waited for her to spill her information, but all she did was bite her lower lip as if attempting to hide a smile. The single light bulb buzzed quietly above their heads.

He blinked. "Well? Where are they?"

She gestured at the Pictish stone. "Back in time, through that rock."

Right.

James sighed. "Is this supposed to be funny?"

She walked a half circle around him, but no sound came as her feet hit the packed-dirt floor. She wore the strangest perfume, something that brought the image of someone scything lavender on a hill. How strange it was that he could smell her before she appeared. Perhaps she had been hiding here before he and Leonie entered.

"I kent ye wouldna believe me. Ye're one of the most difficult of them all."

"I don't want to be rude, but if you don't have anything to contribute to the investigation—"

She stopped, and light from the bulb fell on skin that seemed as smooth as polished stone. "I do. The rock was carved by the Picts to open a tunnel through the river of time."

James looked over his shoulder at the rock. There wasn't enough light to see all the details. Darkness seeped from the shadows cast by the stones and rubble. "Right."

"I told this to Rogene."

His head turned to look at Sineag so sharply, his neck clicked. Sineag was practically beaming at him.

He asked, "You saw her here?"

"Aye. Twice. On the night of the wedding. And two weeks ago."

He blinked and took a step towards her, trying to see any signs of a lie, a twitch of a muscle, a touch of the nose—anything. But she only looked at him with a sweet, calm smile.

"And David?" he asked.

"He was with Rogene."

"What were they doing here?"

Her eyes sparkled with excitement for a moment, two brilliant small flashes, like diamonds catching the light. He must have imagined it. "Rogene was on her way to Angus Mackenzie, and David was trying to stop her."

"Where is Angus Mackenzie?"

"She's with him. And so is David."

"Where?" he practically yelled.

Darkness seemed to intensify around Sineag. "Do ye believe in love, Detective Murray?"

He let out a long sigh. "Sure. I believe in love. Love is a powerful tool of manipulation."

She narrowed her eyes at him. "Oh, ye'll have such a journey. I canna wait to talk to ye at the end of this. Angus Mackenzie has a sister, Catrìona, a sweet lass, and the love of yer life."

He couldn't stop a laugh now. "The love of my life?"

"Aye. Listen. Leonie is coming back. Ye must hurry now. If ye put yer hand in the handprint, the tunnel will open and ye can go through there to find Rogene and David."

He stared at the rock. A tunnel that opened—maybe she meant some sort of a secret tunnel. Leonie had told him the castle had plenty. That was how they must have left the island without anyone noticing. He knew there was always a logical explanation. Every magic trick had science behind it, and this was the logical explanation for Rogene's and David's disappearance.

He sank to crouch by the rock again and looked at it from different sides. But he couldn't notice any indents or other indications it could move.

And then, as though some sort of mechanism had switched on neon lights, the carvings started to glow. Just like he thought. A carefully prepared trick.

"Just put my hand in the handprint?" he asked.

"Aye. And think of Rogene, David, or Catrìona."

Why did he have to think of anyone? He didn't even know Catrìona. Something told him there was a trick, that he was trusting the strangely dressed woman too easily. But he was close to uncovering the truth—he could feel it.

He put his hand into the handprint and pressed into the rock, thinking that maybe it worked like a button or something that you had to push in.

But the moment he touched the cool surface, an invisible force grasped his hand from all sides and glued it to the rock.

Only, he couldn't feel the surface anymore. Instead, there was empty air, wet like fog. And suddenly everything went pitch black, and he was falling and falling and falling, like Alice through the rabbit hole.

Until he stopped feeling anything.

CHAPTER 2

E ilean Donan Castle, end of July 1310

CATRÌONA STARED INTO THE EYES OF THE MAN SHE'D THOUGHT she'd never see again.

The man she had once loved still looked like a golden wolf, but leaner, more muscular, a creature who fought to survive. He stood in the inner bailey next to Catrìona's youngest brother, Raghnall, who was holding his bloody side and looking at her with concern. There was blood on his shoulder, too. A guard was supporting Tadhg from the other side as one of his legs was wounded, bent, and bandaged. Tadhg was dressed in the clothes of a simple Highland warrior: *leine croich*, a heavy, quilted military coat, which was torn and bloodied, and clearly old. A woolen cloak hung from his shoulders and a sword was in the sheath at his waist.

Was she *truly* seeing Tadhg? He was blurry, as were the tall curtain walls surrounding them and the timber buildings within the inner bailey.

Angus's wife, Rogene, holding her by her elbow, whispered, "Who is he?"

A gust of fresh morning wind brought the scent of loch water and cleared Catrìona's head. She stood straighter as her vision returned to normal. "The only man I've ever loved. My betrothed..."

Tadhg's ear-length blond hair was dirty and hung in strands plastering his forehead. Part of his short beard was caked in dry blood.

"Yer who?" Angus growled from Rogene's other side. Though he was the middle son, he'd been the family's protector her whole life. Until a couple of months ago when Euphemia of Ross had kidnapped him. Catrìona, Rogene, Raghnall, and a few trusted men had sneaked into the Ross castle to rescue him. Men on both sides had died in the ensuing battle.

Angus deserved to know the truth, but she had no time to explain now. She was a healer, and before her stood a patient who needed her.

Commanding her heart to calm down, she marched to Tadhg and put her arm around him to support him from the other side. He stared at her with one wide eye, blinking.

Laomann, who had become laird after their father's death in 1304, frowned at her with a strange expression of guilt and concern. There was something familiar about that, something she may have seen on that night, nine years ago.

Raghnall said to him, "Is it all right with ye, brother, if Tadhg stays here until he gets better? Ross men attacked on my way back from clan Ruaidhrí and he saved my life. Euphemia isna going to leave us alone."

The Earl of Ross's sister wanted to claim Mackenzie lands because the clan hadn't managed to give their overlord the full tribute, due to the costly Wars of Scottish Independence. At Euphemia's request, Angus had become engaged to her to save their lands. But he'd broken off the engagement when he'd fallen in love with Rogene Wakeley. Now Rogene was his wife and pregnant. Euphemia had sworn to destroy the clan, and the attack on Raghnall was probably just a start.

"Of course," said Laomann. "Stay, Tadhg. Ye need help, too, Raghnall."

"I'll help ye get better," Catrìona said to Tadhg with more feeling than she intended. She told herself it was something she'd say to anyone who needed her healing skills.

"Thank ye," Tadhg said, his breath scalding her face.

His voice was different from how she'd remembered. Raspy, low, and deep... The voice of a man. Not a boy.

She needed to look at Tadhg's and Raghnall's wounds quickly. With the help of the guard, she guided Tadhg to the keep, and Raghnall followed them. Always at odds with Laomann, Raghnall had wanted to go to Father Nicholas in Dornie village for treatment. Catrìona was grateful she'd managed to convince him to stay in the castle. Though she would never say so, she knew more about healing herbs and treatments than the priest and wanted to ensure her brother didn't get rot-wound.

As they were passing the great hall on the first floor, Raghnall said his wounds weren't dangerous and he was first going to eat and have a stiff drink, and slipped through the large arched door into the hall where a few servants stirred and rose to their feet. She needed to treat Tadhg first anyway, so she didn't protest.

When they stood on the next landing before the door to her bedchamber and the one to the guest bedchamber, she told the guard to go ahead and help Tadhg to get onto the bed. She went into her chamber to get her medicine basket. She glanced at one of her chests where her good gowns were, and a sinful thought crossed her mind, that she wished she wasn't dressed in a simple, homespun dress that resembled a sack for barley.

No. She wouldn't wish she was beautiful for Tadhg. Such thoughts shouldn't concern her anymore. After all, she would go into the nunnery at the end of summer.

She returned to Tadhg's chamber. Ignoring his green gaze burning her, Catrìona marched to the bed he was lying on.

With her heart slamming against her ribs, she placed her medicine basket on the bed. Laomann followed her in, and she glanced at him, surprised. The deep concern on his face made her straighten her shoulders.

"There's nae need for ye here, brother," she said. "I've treated plenty of injuries before, and I'm sure there's much for ye to do to prepare for the Highland games."

"Highland games?" asked Tadhg. "When are they?"

"In about two sennights," said Laomann. "I wasna sure about your idea, Catrìona. But I suppose if we manage to earn enough coin to pay the rest of the tribute, 'tis the most peaceful solution."

"Aye," said Catrìona. "It is also a good chance to build our alliances. The Cambels, the Ruaidhrís, the MacDonalds that are coming are strong and will help us against Euphemia if we need them, I'm sure." Catrìona glanced at Laomann. "Go, brother, there's much to do. I'm fine."

Laomann shook his head, appearing resolved. It was an expression Catrìona didn't see often on her older brother. "I'm nae leaving ye alone with him."

Without looking away from her, Tadhg said, "I'm nae stranger, Laomann. Ye taught me to fight on swords, remember. We grew up together. Ye dinna need to worry about me and Catrìona."

Catrìona disagreed. Her hand holding a clay jar with a poultice shook and the cover rattled.

God help her, she didn't want to look at him. She was afraid she'd burst into tears or want to claw his eyes out. The first was weak, the second unchristian.

He'd betrayed her and left her. Did she not deserve a word of explanation? She had been ready to abandon everything for him —her clan, her brothers...

"I'm nae worried about being compromised, brother."

Tadhg's gaze could have burned a hole in her skin. She'd need to meet his gaze eventually, as he clearly had some sort of injury under the bandage that covered his eye. But for now, she'd just concentrate on his ankle. Blood was seeping through the poor, dirty linen dressing. She took out scissors to cut it.

The muscles of Tadhg's ankle stiffened. "Are ye nae marrit?"

An invisible fist twisted her stomach, and a wave of anger hit her face. The handle of the scissors cut into her palm and her knuckles whitened. With a strange satisfaction, she noticed Tadhg's eye dart to the sharp edges of the scissors.

Good. Be afraid, ye betraying bastart.

But as the thought crossed her mind, she knew she was wrong to think that. God forgive her, she'd just sinned. She should be kind to the wounded man in front of her.

Well, she'd have her whole life to pray for absolution of her anger.

Catrìona took a deep, cleansing breath. "I'm nae marrit," she said, looking straight into his green eye. "And I'll never be."

She sat down on the edge of the bed and leaned over Tadhg's ankle. She slipped one blade between the bandage and Tadhg's leg and cut it.

Tadhg went completely still. "Why nae?"

Laomann stopped pacing. "'Tisna yer concern."

Tadhg didn't even look in his direction. "Ye were supposed to marry Alexander Balliol."

Ignoring him, she crumpled the old bandage, and forced herself to take longer, deeper breaths. Tadhg was a patient, and she was his healer. She coudn't make any mistakes.

The bandage revealed a gash on the outer side of Tadhg's ankle. She'd seen wounds like these before many times—a sword wound, by the looks of it. The flesh around it was purplish, and blood was still slowly oozing from the depths, filling her nostrils with a metallic scent.

His hand lying on the blanket shifted towards her. "Ye are so pale, and so thin, Catrìona..."

Why do ye care?

She was pale and thin because she was fasting. She deserved this penance after she had broken the commandment not to kill in that bloody chamber to save Angus from Euphemia's claws.

The worst was, deep down, she didn't feel as repentant as she should. Instead, she felt powerful, grateful to have protected her family.

Pushing the grim thoughts aside, she concentrated on the wound she needed to clean. She rummaged in her basket, looking for the waterskin of *uisge-beatha*. Reeds scratched her hands as she moved jars, pouches, and wooden boxes around.

Where was it? She couldn't see it. Tadhg clouded her mind. She must have forgotten to put it into the basket.

She stopped, a sharp reed biting into her palm as she clutched the edge of the basket. "Alexander Balliol died on his way to the wedding. And I'm never going to marry because I'm going to become a nun."

He blinked. *"A nun?"*

There, she'd said it. A strange sense of liberation opened up space in her chest. He had no power over her, not anymore. She belonged to God. Why should she care if Tadhg had ever loved her? Or if she was unlovable for any man?

She noticed a waterskin on the belt of Laomann's tunic. "Ye have yer *uisge* with ye? May I have it?"

Laomann handed her the waterskin. "Aye, of course."

To Tadhg, she said, "'Tis going to hurt."

She uncorked the waterskin and poured a little on the wound, the sharp scent of alcohol pinching her nose. Tadhg sucked in a breath as she patted his injured flesh with a clean linen cloth.

"How's yer father, Tadhg?" asked Laomann.

Tadhg grunted. "My father's dead."

Catrìona looked up at him. "I'm so sorry."

"Thank ye, it was a long time ago. Nine years."

Laomann started pacing the room, fiddling with his fingers. "Nine years?"

"Aye, right after we left Dornie."

There was something in his voice she couldn't discern— sadness, pain, bitterness? It was impossible to tell from his set jaw, his facial muscles so tight it seemed his weathered, tanned, golden skin could burst.

She shouldn't go there, should leave the past alone. She'd just decided to let herself be free from him.

Tadhg's eyes narrowed on her. "What ye dinna ken, is why."

She swallowed a tight, painful knot in her throat. "Why?"

Laomann hurried to loom over the bed by her side. "'Tis time to stitch him, sister. Look, he's bleeding again."

As if in a dream, she looked down at Tadhg's ankle— Laomann was right, more blood was gathering in the gash and slowly flowing down Tadhg's skin. With shaking hands, she went into the basket and found her wooden box of hooklike needles. She took a long thread of catgut and, on the fifth attempt, put it through the eye of the needle.

Laomann was right, this wasn't the time to turn over the past. Mayhap she should never even try. But part of her was dying to.

"Here." She passed Laomann's waterskin of uisge to Tadhg. "Drink as much as ye can. Ye'll need it."

With his eye dark on her, a special meaning in his gaze that she couldn't discern, he took the uisge from her.

"Light a candle, Laomann," Catrìona said as she leaned over the wound. "I'll need all the light we can manage."

Laomann did as she asked and placed a candle in a large bowl by her side. Then he resumed pacing the room behind her. With the candlelight illuminating the gash, she could now see better where to pierce the needle.

Now be a healer, and forget everything else. Here's a patient God has given ye, and 'tis yer responsibility to help him. 'Tis how ye serve God.

As Tadhg obediently drank uisge, she pinched the sides of his ankle together and pierced them, dragging the needle through.

She worked quickly, under Tadhg's stifled grunts. When she was finished, he mumbled something, then closed his eyes and let his head hang over his chest. He began snoring. She took Laomann's waterskin from Tadhg's limp hand and handed it back to her brother.

A servant put his head through the doorway. "Mistress, Finn Jelly Belly arrived, asking for ye, if ye need any herbs or roots."

Catrìona beamed. "Finn is here?"

Finn Jelly Belly was a traveling herbalist and healer. He'd come every year to Eilean Donan and stay for a few days in Dornie, selling herbs and treating people.

Laomann's face flushed. "Finn is here?" he growled with his brows drawn into a single line.

Catrìona rose from the bed. "Be kind, brother. He may have something better for Tadhg and for Raghnall. I still need to treat him, though his wounds look less dire than Tadhg's." She put the old bandages and her jars and pouches into the basket. "He always learns about new treatments and new herbs, so he may even take a look at Tadhg, as well."

Laomann sighed and walked to the door. "He isna going to stay here while I'm laird."

"Good grief, Laomann," Catrìona muttered.

But Laomann had already stormed out of the room, the servant following him. She sighed and blew out the candle. She should go into the underground storeroom to fetch some herbs she could trade with Finn. Looking around the chamber, she tidied up a bit and then put a blanket over the wheezing Tadhg. Sadness squeezed her heart tightly.

But what she was sad about—the lost years with Tadhg or the loss of her belief in love—she didn't know.

CHAPTER 3

E ilean Donan Castle, end of July 1310

JAMES SAT UP WITH A JERK, STARING INTO COMPLETE darkness.

His head spun. What the hell just happened? Blinking, he shook the headache away. The damp air smelled like dust and earth—just like it had a moment ago, before he fell through the stone.

Fell through the stone? What was he, a child? Believing in magic would be like going back to Brody's cult.

But how could he explain the sensation of falling through? Must be just a dizzy spell, nothing more.

He needed light. He retrieved his phone from the pocket of his trousers and pressed the button. The screen wouldn't light up.

"Bloody hell!" James muttered.

As he brushed the screen with his thumb, he felt cracks.

Great. How would his sister reach him? He looked around,

trying to see through inky darkness, but couldn't even distinguish a shadow.

"Sìneag?" he called. When only his own echo responded, he called again, "Leonie? Anyone?"

Nothing.

Then a thought struck him. He had the lighter! The one time being a smoker paid off. He found the lighter in his pocket, took it out, and flicked.

No flame.

He flicked again and again, but it didn't work. With a curse, he shoved it back into his pocket. He'd need to move by touch.

Where the bloody hell was Leonie?

"Leonie!" he called.

His voice echoed around him.

Slowly, he moved towards where he thought the door must be. A few tentative steps, and he stumbled. Pain shot through the side of his head when he landed on a pile of rocks. Something sharp pierced his suit jacket with a ripping sound.

Cursing, he scrambled to his feet and carefully shuffled forward, searching with his arms in the darkness. After what felt like an eternity, he touched something rough, hard, and cold.

A wall! One hand tracing the stones, he walked with the other hand in front of him. He bumped into chests and barrels smelling of alcohol.

Odd. He didn't remember any chests or barrels. This felt like a different place.

Time lost all meaning as he kept going. After a while, his left hand, which had been tracing the rough wall, sank into an empty space—and then reached wood.

He felt it with both hands. Wooden planks, iron hardware...

A door!

He found a cold, round, iron handle and pushed the door, but it didn't move.

He pulled it.

It didn't budge.

Fury, mixed with desperation, raged in him in a burning red wave. He grabbed the handle with both hands and shook it, rattling it back and forth, roaring, growling, yelling.

Suddenly, he wasn't a man of thirty-one. A CID detective who investigated murders and disappearances.

He was an eight-year-old boy, locked in the house his mother had been renting from Unseen Wonders, banging on the door. Mum had left him to do something with Brody Guthenberg because Brody had time for her—something in Brody's bed. Behind him screamed his five-year-old sister, probably more scared by James's banging and screaming and crying than anything else.

That, he remembered, had been the first moment in his young life when he'd realized something was very, very wrong in the world he'd been born into.

Now, he didn't know how long he'd been banging on the door in this darkness. Had he gone mad or was he really hearing the blissful grinding of a key in the keyhole. He went completely quiet and still, not believing his ears.

Then the door opened, and the light of a flaming torch blinded him. Now accustomed to complete darkness, his eyes hurt as he peered through the open door.

She was blond, with long, curly hair streaming down over her shoulders. A pretty face with eyes so big and so blue they looked like forget-me-nots peered up at him. Her skin was translucent and delicate, full lips parted in surprise. She was dressed in a simple brown dress that reached the floor and looked like a long burlap sack. Despite her pale skin, a pink flush was forming on her cheeks. She was thin, so thin, he wanted to offer her something to eat. And standing there, staring at him in disbelief, with fire casting a dance of light and shadows on her face, he thought she must be a vision from somewhere beyond.

Reverence came over him. His plea had been answered, and an angel had opened the door and saved him.

Only, she wasn't an angel. And he was just disoriented and

probably in some sort of shock—perhaps he'd banged his head against the rocks harder than he'd thought.

He cleared his throat. "Cheers for letting me out. Leonie must have forgotten about me..." He received a confused frown from the pretty stranger. "Sìneag, too."

She winced in confusion. "Who are ye?"

He pushed past her into the dark space behind her. "Detective James Murray."

The light from the torch turned and illuminated the walls and the large hall. He turned to her. "Any chance we could switch on the lights?"

"*Switch on—*"

Over her other arm, she had a woven basket, just like bloody Red Riding Hood on the way to her grandmum. Only she didn't look like a lost girl—thunder and fire were dancing in her eyes.

"A bloody light, is all. Where's Sìneag?"

Suddenly, the fire in her eyes turned into alarm. "I dinna ken who Sìneag is, or who ye are."

Her alarmed expression transformed into doubt, then settled into a fiery resolve. With a lightning-fast movement, she retrieved something long and sharp and held it out like a knife. It was hard to see in this light, but it looked like scissors made of simple iron, rather big and rough, and...medieval. It looked more like a torture implement than anything else.

Great. He'd scared the woman.

He raised his hands in a gesture of submission. "Look, there's no need to be scared. I'm a policeman. Here's my warrant card, I can show you." He slowly went to the inner pocket of his suit jacket.

"Dinna move."

He sighed, lowering his arms.

She looked him up and down. "Where do ye come from and why are ye dressed like that?"

With a frown, he looked down at his suit. Certainly, he wasn't wearing a medieval costume, and he spoke with a regular English accent, whereas she spoke Gaelic.

Wait a second...

He blinked.

Gaelic? He'd never learned Gaelic. How did he understand her?

Moreover, *he* spoke Gaelic, too.

How?

"I'm from Oxford," he slowly pronounced the words, hearing Gaelic coming out of his mouth. "How can I speak Gaelic, do you know?"

Her face straightened. "Would ye prefer to speak Latin?"

"Latin?"

What was going on in here? Sìneag had said stuff about time travel. The torch, the woman's dress, the basket, the Gaelic were odd, but he knew better than that. This woman was probably working with Sìneag in some sort of historic reenactment.

He wouldn't get involved in this game. He shook off his bewilderment. "Look, miss, I'm investigating the disappearance of two people. I don't mean any harm."

She frowned. "Who disappeared?"

"Rogene and David Wakeley, they're sister and bro—"

She lowered her scissors. "Rogene and David disappeared? Nae, that canna be right. I just saw them riding off with Angus this morning."

He became very, very still. "Angus Mackenzie?"

"Aye, my brother."

The ground shifted under his feet, the only sound in the dark underground room was the crackling of the fire on the torch.

Although he could already guess the answer, he asked, "And you are?"

"Catrìona Mackenzie."

Catrìona Mackenzie. The woman who, according to Sìneag, was supposed to be the love of his life.

The shock of that realization tightened his throat, and he

stood frozen, staring at her beautiful eyes, too big on her thin face.

After some silence, Catrìona narrowed her eyes at him. "Are ye a Sassenach?"

Good grief, the ice in her voice could freeze him. "I'm English, yes."

She tightened her grip around the scissors. "Ye must go with me to my brother."

"Your brother? Look, if you only find Leonie, she'll tell you everything. Or if you call the Oxford Police. The museum must open soon."

Staring at him like he was talking gibberish, she raised the scissors and pointed at him. "I wilna have a Sassenach threat in my castle. Move."

He sighed and did as she told him. It was not like he was afraid of the medieval-looking scissors. He could easily unarm her if he wanted. But he didn't want a confrontation. Not unless it was absolutely necessary.

They went up the stairs, which looked the same as when he'd climbed down them with Leonie.

But when he passed through the open door on the ground floor, he stopped.

There was no narrow corridor with watercolor paintings on the wall.

Instead, he was looking into a square storage room. Crates, barrels, chests, and sacks crowded the space, and swords, spears, axes, and shields hung on the walls, along with helmets, chain mail coifs, and some sort of long, heavy, quilted coats. There were no windows, and the interior was illuminated by four torches in sconces on the wall.

Wasn't this supposed to be a small hall leading to the arched entrance door, and just before it, a turn to the right where the Billeting Room would be?

This wasn't funny anymore. "Where the hell am I?"

"Ground floor of the main keep." The cold, sharp metal edge of the scissors pressed into the back of his neck. "Keep moving."

He walked, stunned. The main keep, that's what the building was called. "Of Eilean Donan?"

"Of course."

As he moved past the crates and the weapons, his mind raced to find an explanation. This must have been a different exit and a different room. Perhaps there were several ways in and out of that underground area. Then why did the feeling of being trapped press at his gut again?

Because it looked real. Someone must have gone through the effort to build a reconstruction of the fourteenth-century fortress. He'd seen something like this done before. One of his ex-girlfriends liked reality TV and had made him watch this series where they put people into a reconstructed Victorian town, somewhere in England, and had them live there for a couple of days, completely immersed. No phones, no electricity, even the loo was dug out. He'd never understood the appeal of living without running warm water, food refrigeration, sanitation, and other modern-day conveniences. But people tended to romanticize the past.

Was this some sort of a reality show, too? He looked around, searching for the dark circles of camera lenses. He saw none, but they were probably hidden somewhere in the corners, walls, and furniture, like nanny cams.

She gestured at an opening around the corner of the wall where he'd seen stairs leading up. "This way, Sir James."

"Where is this leading to?"

"The great hall, where my brother is right now."

"Angus?"

"Nae. Laomann, chief of clan Mackenzie."

James's breath pumped in and out of him quickly. He didn't want to go anywhere else where a door could stop him from leaving. There wasn't supposed to be a clan Mackenzie here. The castle had belonged to clan MacRae for hundreds of years by now—that was one of the things Leonie had told him in her brief tour.

The chill in her voice could freeze him into an ice sculpture.

"Great," James said, climbing the narrow stone stairs. He needed a cig. "Okay if I light up?"

"Ye what?"

He stopped on the landing, took out the pack of cigarettes and his lighter. She stood by his side, staring as he showed her the pack.

"Okay if I smoke?" he said.

When she didn't reply, he took out his last cigarette and put it between his lips.

"What are ye doing, Sir James?" she said, alarm in her voice.

He put the pack back into his pocket and retrieved the lighter. Bloody hell, if it wouldn't work again...

He flicked the lighter. Fire appeared on its tip. Oh, thank—

But before he could bring it to the tip of the cigarette, Catrìona gasped, crossed herself, and took several quick steps back, her eyes as wide as if he'd just produced the flames of hell.

The emptiness of the dark stairwell gaping below her, she balanced on the edge of the step, waving her arms.

Reacting instinctively, James threw out his arm, grasped a fistful of fabric, and yanked the girl to himself. Absorbing the impact, he wrapped his arms around her. She was panting, her eyes big and shiny and sparkling. She was nestled in his embrace, and he didn't remember anything feeling so right.

"You all right?" he asked, unable to let go of her or look away.

She looked so pure. Her skin completely free of makeup, her features delicate and gentle. That image of her, coming to his rescue down below, like an angel casting away the darkness, came back.

She blinked, frowning, then pushed against his chest. He let go.

"Aye."

"Sorry," he said.

Straightening her dress, she scowled at the lighter that now lay on the floor. "What was that fire? How did ye make it?"

He picked up the cheap orange plastic lighter and the broken cigarette that had landed in the corner. His urge to smoke was gone, replaced by his raging pulse. He put the cig back into the pack, making a note to throw it into a bin when he saw one.

"Ah, come now," he said. "I know you need to follow a script or something, but could we at least skip the bit where I need to explain how a lighter works?"

"But I dinna ken—"

"Could we please go?"

She straightened her shoulders and put her hand out. "Only if ye give this to me."

She was dead serious, standing with an air of such authority that his instinct was to hand the lighter to her.

He chuckled. "Are 'modern' props not allowed?"

"Sir, ye are talking in riddles I dinna understand. But I wilna be distracted, and I wilna allow demons in my home. This is a home that worships the one true God."

Demons? Did she believe he was a sorcerer or something?

James would have laughed had he not been so astonished. He, who'd fought tooth and nail against the cult his mum got sucked into... He, who was the biggest skeptic and a police detective to boot... He was accused of casting *magic*?

But Catrìona, adorable in her seriousness, took out her scissors again and pressed the sharp edge against his throat.

"Give yer *demon* to me or, by God's bones, I will spill yer blood."

He frowned, searching her face for any signs of acting, any incongruence—a twitch of the eye muscles or a barely noticeable rising of a corner of her mouth...

Nothing.

Not that he was afraid of a woman with a sharp object—he knew exactly how to unarm her—but he didn't want to risk a conflict before he was sure of his location. His priority was

Rogene and David, and how he could get the three of them out of this madhouse.

He placed the lighter in her hand. "Here you go."

As his fingers brushed against hers, a charge of hot electricity ran up his arm, stealing his breath. She clearly felt it, too. Her pupils dilated, making her irises darken to a navy blue so deep he lost his breath.

Just twice in his life he'd been close to feeling what a true miracle felt like. The first time was when he'd seen his newborn baby sister. He was only three years old, and it was one of his earliest memories. He remembered being called into a room of their cottage on the cult compound. Three women surrounded his mum, who lay in a bed smudged by blood and cradled a bundle in her arms.

When he'd seen Emily's pink, swollen face, the tiny fingers, he'd felt light, warm, and so open he could encompass the world.

The second time was when the police had raided the compound and he'd seen Brody Guthenberg being handcuffed, and he'd known his mum, his sister, and the three hundred other men, women, and children living on the compound were free.

This, with Catrìona, was the third time in his life. The sensation was weightless, wide and broad and tingling, and he couldn't look away or take his hand off hers. This felt right. This felt like, finally, he'd arrived. He couldn't explain it with his logical mind, but something in his heart knew it all made sense.

Catrìona snatched her hand away. "Dinna touch me again," she whispered. "Do ye ken what the punishment is for sorcery?"

"No."

"'Tis death. So if ye dinna want me to tell my brother about yer love magic or whatever yer demons are doing with me, dinna lay a finger on me."

CHAPTER 4

Catrìona stared at the strong muscles of James's broad back moving under the thin cloth of his strange and elegant attire as he climbed the stairs. His touch had left the sweet sensation of being struck by a small but powerful lightning bolt.

That, combined with guilt that she had threatened someone with a weapon yet again, confused her. What was wrong with her? She was still doing penance for killing all those Ross men back in Delny Castle, and now she had threatened another human being again?

But she couldn't let harm come to her clan, even though it might cost her her soul.

Male voices coming from the great hall grew angry. *Oh, nae.* Was Laomann getting heated up because of Finn or because of Raghnall? As Catrìona entered the room, she saw Finn Jelly Belly leaning over Raghnall's shoulder and stitching it. Laomann sat at the long table together with several other warriors and ate a chicken leg with ferocity.

"...and dinna tell me that what ye gave me was an accident," said Laomann through a mouthful.

Raghnall laughed. "Sorry, Finn, friend, but I dinna believe it, either."

The large, square space was semidark, lit from four slit windows. Fire played in the large fireplace around which Catrìona's family had spent many evenings. Two embroideries showing burning mountains, the crest of clan Mackenzie, hung above the fireplace, and Catrìona's heart sang with pride every time she saw them. *I shine, not burn* was the clan's motto, and it always gave her strength and spoke straight to her soul.

Finn Jelly Belly had always been a large man, ever since Catrìona had known him. Altogether, he looked like a big white leech, with a stomach that wobbled as he walked, reminding one of a sack of meat jelly.

Raghnall added, "Finn wanted to heal your red, itchy skin."

"But I never wanted a limp cock!" cried Laomann. "I couldna lay with my wife for a year."

The warriors around the table chuckled in their cups. Even the servant who was pouring ale into Laomann's cup whitened, straining to keep his face straight.

The only one who wasn't amused was James, who eyed the room with a frown. As she stood next to him, his scent reached her—something strong, like smoke but more pungent. He smelled as if he were a shaman from another world who dealt with pagan magic and burned herbs that didn't exist in hers. That and a sort of pleasant mixture of perfume and his own earthy, manly musk.

That scent did something to her—something warm, and beautiful, like she was in a hot bath, aching for something she shouldn't.

She forced her mind to return to what was happening around her.

Finn chuckled. "But yer skin is healed. How could I have kent yer manhood is so sensitive to a wee licorice root."

"Aye, Laomann," said Raghnall. "Ye didna have to spread the bad word about Finn around the whole of Scotland."

Finn Jelly Belly's face grew stony, his large lips pressed in a thin line as he pierced Raghnall's flesh and her brother sucked in a sharp breath.

"I have been chased away from villages all around Kintail," Finn said. "Everyone said I was going to give them limp dicks. That I was a sorcerer and brought demons with me and would curse innocent men."

Finn made a knot and bit the thread off with his teeth. Catrìona threw a quick glance at Sir James as he frowned even deeper looking at Finn. His eyes were so dark brown in the semi-darkness, she could sink into them and never find her way back home. He was strange and handsome and...different. So different his face, illuminated by the white-orange light of the hall, would be forever burned into the back of her mind. The square jaw, straight nose, and high cheekbones. He had warm eyes the color of buckwheat honey, a broad mouth, and full, sensual lips. Barely noticeable freckles dusted his high cheekbones. His hair was cropped short—she rarely saw hair so short on men—and his chin bore a stubble of three or four days.

His accent... He spoke Gaelic, but it reminded her of a few Sassenach warriors she'd met over the course of her life, though it wasn't exactly like them. He wore the most delicate, intricate, and impractical clothes she'd ever seen. A tight jacket that hugged his muscular frame with strongly built shoulders in the form of a perfect triangle, some sort of broad breeches that went to his foot, and a white shirt with a high collar and buttons.

Laomann turned to her. "Sister! What are ye doing, listening to this? 'Tis nae for an unmarrit maiden to hear talk of male problems."

Male problems... She'd never believed any rumors that Finn could be a sorcerer. She'd known Finn her whole life and he, like she, used herbs in God's way. To heal people and help them. And she'd never heard of licorice root causing any problems with...well...

Heat scalded her cheeks as she thought of the male organ

she'd seen only a handful of times when she'd had to treat a wound near the groin or needed to wash an unconscious warrior. She'd wondered if they used it in the same way that animals did, if it got harder and—

She shook her head once and made sure to look at Laomann with reproach. "I am a healer, brother. I ken how the male anatomy works."

She was a single woman in the great hall, surrounded by two and a half dozen men, and every single one except for Finn looked uncomfortable. Good.

Only Sir James watched her with an amused appreciation and respect.

"Who is that with ye?" said Laomann, looking James over with a frown.

Still shirtless, Raghnall stood up, suddenly alert, his piercing dark eyes on James, one hand casually lying on his sword, which was on the table. Following Raghnall's reaction, the rest of the men became alert as well: some laid a hand on the hilt of their sword, others put their food down on their trays, a few stood up from their benches. She had let the scissors fall to her side before entering as she knew the great hall would be full of armed men.

"Sir James Murray tells me he's looking for Rogene and David. It seems he's from Oxford."

"Oxford?" said Raghnall. "Are ye a Sassenach?" The hostility in his voice was obvious. He'd fought the wars against the English with the Bruce.

"I'm an Englishman, yes," said James calmly.

Raghnall turned to Laomann. "We must throw him into the dungeon. I have lived in England and ken yer lot. I lost enough friends and sword brothers to the Sassenach bastarts. Come on, brother, ye're the *laird*. Don't be a ninny like ye always were. Command it!"

The word "laird" came out bitter, like an insult, and Catrìona winced. She couldn't stand this animosity between her two brothers. It wasn't Laomann's fault Kenneth Og had chased Raghnall away from the clan when he'd been a lad barely old enough to fight. They hadn't seen Raghnall for years—even longer than she hadn't seen Tadhg. He had returned last winter with Angus, and she wanted to welcome him back into the family. Only, Laomann hadn't made him an official clansman yet. He always had followed their father's directives, and he seemed inclined to continue doing so even after the monster's death.

Laomann scowled at Raghnall. "Dinna ye tell me what I should or shouldna command. Ye're nae our clansman nae more."

Silence hung in the hall so thick, the crackling of the fire sounded like claps of thunder. Everyone held their breath. The warriors stilled, pieces of bread or cups of ale halfway to their mouths.

Raghnall inhaled loudly and let out a sigh. He glared at Laomann from under his brows, his eyes like two storm clouds.

"I am nae a clansman, hey?" Raghnall said, his voice rumbling. "Then why do I bother to protect the clan?"

The edges of Laomann's mouth crawled down in a bitter grimace. "I think I ken why ye came back. And 'tis nae because ye're looking out for our interests. 'Tis because ye want a certain estate that would have belonged to ye had Father nae chased ye away."

Raghnall's face went blank. Catriona's heart ached. She knew Raghnall must want a home after years on the road, doing who knew what. But he wasn't a calculating man. He was her brother, and he loved his siblings, even though she hadn't seen him since she was a lass.

"A pitiful man chased me away all those years ago. My only crime was that I kept defying him, and yet ye're the one who's still punishing me for it." He sighed and shook his head. "I'm nae the enemy." He pointed at Sir James. "He is."

Laomann narrowed his eyes at James. "Why *do* ye look for Rogene and David, Sir James?"

James made a sweeping gesture with one arm. "Because their friends and family are looking for them."

Laomann rubbed his stomach with a grimace of pain. "But I thought...I thought Lady Rogene's lands were burned and pillaged by the English."

James sighed. "Whatever you want to believe for your games, mate."

"Games?" said Laomann. "The Highland games dinna start for almost two sennights. Lady Rogene will be there with David and Angus."

Raghnall tsked. "Why would ye tell him that? He's the enemy."

Laomann winced again and, instead of replying, gulped ale from his cup.

The Highland games required a lot of preparation. The messengers to the various clans and tenants were supposed to be sent out today.

"I'm not the enemy," said Sir James. "At least not yet."

Raghnall picked up his dagger and moved towards Sir James like a wolf who wanted to sniff potential prey. "Oh, aye?" her brother said as he stood before Sir James. "And what does that depend on?"

"On how well Rogene and David Wakeley are. Whether they are kept here by force, whether they are healthy, and whether they want to come home with me."

"'Tis what he says," Raghnall said, his dark eyes intense. "How can I be sure 'tis yer true intention, Sir James? Yer way of speaking, yer clothes, yer manner are very strange. We have nae proof where ye came from and if ye are dangerous or nae."

Catrìona could say something about the "lighter" now, but something within her hesitated. She didn't trust him, nae. But if she told Laomann and Raghnall about the sorcery, she would condemn Sir James to death.

She couldn't. She had taken enough lives already, and she had been holding the scissors to his throat, which already went against her penance. But she just couldn't let a potential enemy walk around the castle.

It was enough for her to have to pray for her soul for the rest of her days.

"He is dangerous," she said suddenly, her voice low and emotionless. "He is a Sassenach and we shouldna trust him."

He looked at her with wide eyes. She met his gaze, and despite her animosity, a wave of excitement rushed through her.

A similar one to when he had saved her from falling down the stairs. He'd held her in his arms, and she had felt as though every drop of her blood, every part of her was coming alive. She'd felt like a snowdrop stretching her petals to the sun, right after God's first warm sunrays melt away the snow. Like there'd been a string somewhere so deep within her that she'd had no idea it existed. And just with one touch, this stranger, this...sorcerer... had played it.

And, God's blood, she loved the sound it made.

What else was this but magic? Magic that was condemned by the church and by law as it endangered the well-being of people and endangered God himself.

She turned to Laomann. "Lock him up, brother."

Laomann stared at James for a long time, then sighed and turned to the men at his table, a grimace of pain still distorting his face. "Take him to the dungeon."

As men advanced on him, Sir James's expression changed to stunned panic. They dragged him down the stairs, and regret pinched her stomach. She told herself he needed to be locked up until they knew who exactly he was and what he was capable of.

When he was gone, she thanked God he wasn't in her proximity anymore.

Nothing had felt so powerful as what he made her feel.

Not even her faith in God.

CHAPTER 5

"Ye're burning up." Catrìona pressed the back of her hand against Tadhg's forehead.

He closed his eyes. "Hmmm. This feels nice, Cat."

Cat. He used to call her that when he'd been her betrothed.

She snatched her hand back, making the light cast on the rough walls from the candle by the bed jump violently. Tadhg's room was completely dark aside from that one candle, and when he opened his eyes again, they were glossy and as dark as a stormy sea.

"Dinna move away, Cat. Please."

She shifted on the bed, reaching down to the jug of water she'd brought with her. Throughout the day, in between taking care of the chores in the castle, she'd come to bring him food and check on him twice. He'd still been asleep the first time but had been awake the second. She hadn't lingered with him longer than she had to. He'd seemed fine both times.

Finn Jelly Belly had sold her an exotic plant he'd called olean-der, which grew in the Mediterranean and was good for skin problems, such as Laomann's. She'd also bought powder of carob tree's bark and fruit for digestive issues. For convenience, she'd bought dried black currants because she was out, and they were good for Laomann's runs. Laomann had felt unwell the whole day, suffering from an upset stomach, so she'd made him a fresh tisane of black currants and carob.

She'd come to check on Tadhg before she retired for the night, only to discover him turning for the worse.

She poured water into a cup and brought it to his lips. "Drink."

He raised his head slightly and took the cup, brushing her fingers with his—as hot as embers.

"And dinna call me Cat," she said. "'Tis Lady Catrìona to ye."

He gave her the cup and fell back on the pillow. "Aye, Lady Catrìona. I'm nae yer betrothed or yer husband, after all."

She stood up to check the wound on his head but froze. "And whose fault is that? I waited for ye. I snuck out of the castle and stood, risking everything, staring into the darkness, ready to be yer wife as we agreed."

The words, surprisingly charged with hurt, poured out of her. Despite the resolve to let this go, to forget he was ever supposed to be the biggest part of her life and remember that God was now her path, the pain was still there. And now that she could see her tormentor right in front of her, something came undone within her.

"Ye did?" His consonants were slurpy and long.

With the candle in one hand, she leaned over and shifted the edge of the bandage over his eye to look at the wound. "Aye, I did. Like a fool. Why couldna ye have mustered the courage to come and tell me ye'd changed yer mind?"

Thankfully, the wound looked fine—swollen, of course, but not enough to indicate any rot brewing.

"Because I didna change my mind," he said.

She stepped back, the candle's flame flickering violently from her sharp exhale. "Then why did ye leave? I was told ye and yer da were gone."

He let out a long breath. "'Tis because yer father found out about us. He came that night to kill me."

Catrìona's world shifted and she had to sit back on the bed. "How did he find out?"

"Laomann had heard us talking."

Catrìona's fist clenched around the skirt of her dress. So it was not because of Tadhg. It was because of Laomann.

Tadhg kept talking. "They came that night into our house. I was getting the horses ready for ye and me. I never told Da because he'd never have let me go against his laird. Yer father unsheathed his sword, yelling for me to come out. I came out of the stables, ready to fight for ye. Fight for us. God's bones, I'd have died for ye if I had to."

Catrìona was split in two. One part of her didn't want to know, didn't want to hear any of that because it wouldn't change anything, because it was better to believe she was never supposed to have a secular life. That this was God's will, for her to serve Him.

But the other part, the sinner in her, the simple woman who had once hoped to have a husband and children, longed to hear what he had to say. Longed to know that he hadn't rejected her after all.

Tadhg winced as he pushed himself up the pillow, attempting to sit up. A visible shiver ran through him—probably the fever chills. "But my da interfered. He stood between yer father and me and demanded to know why his laird was attacking his only son."

"Yer da had always been one of my father's favorite warriors."

"One of the most loyal ones, aye. Yer father yelled that I had planned to kidnap ye and marry ye without his consent. That he considered it treason against him and against the clan. That the only punishment for that was death."

"'Tis exactly what I was afraid of," Catrìona whispered as the worry and the excitement of nine years earlier whirled within her, stirring up the feelings and hopes she'd vowed to forget on that stormy night.

"Aye. Well. Only my da didna let Laird Kenneth Og touch

me. He raised his own sword against his laird, the man he'd sworn to serve and protect. He broke his word of loyalty. He did it for me."

And, indirectly, for her.

"They fought," Tadhg said. "And yer father wounded mine. He'd have killed him, but Laomann begged him not to. He asked him to just let us go, for all the service and good that my father had done over the years for him. Yer father told us to leave and to never come back. I couldna leave my da wounded, or I'd have come for ye, anyway."

A noticeable tremor passed through him, no doubt from fever and painful memories, and Catrìona's heart ached.

"We left. We went to clan Ruaidhrí as Da had distant relatives there, but on the way he got rot-wound. In a few days, under the endless rain of the Highlands, he died."

Something warm and wet rolled down Catrìona's cheek as she remembered Tadhg's father—as golden-haired as his son, a strong warrior with a kind smile and sad eyes. She'd always liked the man.

"I'm so sorry, Tadhg," she said. "He's with God now."

His Adam's apple bobbed. "Aye, I ken. As yer ma is. Both the victims of a tyrant."

She nodded. There it was, that connection again, the reason she'd fallen in love with him then. He'd been so kind to her and prayed with her for her mother.

"After I buried him right there on the slope of the mountain where he'd died, I turned back to Eilean Donan, determined to get ye back, to find a way to get ye out of there, away from him."

Her hand shot to her neck, where her cross was. Sadness passed through his expression. They both knew what it was. The cross that hung from her neck wasn't the one Tadhg had given her anymore.

"But when I was almost there, I encountered a group of Mackenzie warriors who hadna heard about my father and me being cast away from the clan. They told me yer wedding with Alexander Balliol was in a few days."

"Oh," said Catrìona, tears blurring her vision, her chest hot and aching.

He reached to his own tunic and held his cross in his hand. "Ye were nae mine nae more, that ye didna love me. Because ye told me ye'd never marry without love. So I knew that ye must love that other man."

Her cheeks wet, she shook her head. "When you didn't come, when you left, I thought you didn't want me. What did it matter after that who I marrit? My heart was too broken to give to anyone. My father had arranged that marriage with Alexander Balliol, but Alexander died on his way to Eilean Donan."

"I had thought ye betrayed me, Cat."

She inhaled sharply at the nickname but couldn't bring herself to correct him again. It hadn't been his fault, or hers, that he didn't come for her as he'd promised.

It had been her father's, all along.

"I didn't," she said.

Her heart beat fast. She'd been wrong; he had wanted her. The question was, what should she do now with this information?

He shivered again, his heavy eyelids closing and opening slowly. His forehead was even warmer.

"Good Lord, Tadhg, ye have a high fever. I'm going to make ye compresses. Lie down."

He did so, and she opened her medicine basket and found a clean linen cloth. She soaked it in the jug of water and put it on his forehead.

"Ahhh..." He shivered all over and pulled the blanket up on top of him.

"I have the yarrow and white willow bark tincture for fever." She went into her basket and found the clay bottle. She poured the tincture into the cup and brought it to his mouth. "Here, drink this."

As he drank and winced from the bitter taste, she sat back down on the bed. "I'll need to examine yer thigh, Tadhg."

"Aye, Cat."

She pulled the blanket up and lifted the dressing. Yes, that was the reason for the burning. The wound looked too swollen and too red. A pimple of yellow crust had formed on it, and as she pressed on it, he groaned in pain.

"I went back to clan Ruaidhrí." He kept talking through a clenched mouth. No doubt it was the fever shivers making him clench all over. "And stayed with them all this time. I traded on their ships and saw much of the world. Galicia. France. Norway. Orkney Islands. Thank God I encountered Raghnall. He'd have been killed by the Ross men." He looked up at her. "Thank God I encountered ye again, Cat."

She froze with the used linen cloth in her hands.

"Pray with me," he said, his voice coarse. "Like back then. Pray with me, please."

She swallowed hard. "I need to take care of yer wound, it doesna look good."

He leaned back. "Then I'll pray for the both of us."

Catrìona patted his red flesh with a fresh, moist piece of linen to clean it.

"O God, who by the grace of the Holy Ghost," he murmured, "hast poured the gifts of love into the hearts of Thy faithful people..."

Putting fresh honey and bear fat on a new piece of linen, Catrìona whispered the words along with him, the connection to God lightening up her whole being.

"... grant unto all Thy servants in Thy mercy health of body and soul, that they may love Thee with all their strength..."

With a smile on her face, feeling strength returning to her body, she put the fresh bandage on Tadhg's wound.

"...and with perfect affection fulfill Thy pleasure; through Jesu Christ our Lord."

"Amen," they said together, only Tadhg's eyes were closed.

His "amen" was weak, as though he'd just managed to whisper the word before he fell into an oblivion.

Catrìona sighed with relief, her spirits lifted, her hopes up. Did she really know Tadhg? What was behind this handsome, weathered face? He was, quite possibly, the man who understood her best in this world.

It seemed that circumstances had torn them apart nine years ago. Should she regret her choice to become a nun?

She pulled the blanket over Tadhg and put the medicinal supplies back in the basket. She'd better sit and wait until his fever diminished. As she settled into the chair by the window, watching the candle flame flicker in the slight draft coming from the slits of the shutters, she wondered if she loved him still.

How would she know? There was a warmth in the middle of her chest when she looked at this golden wolf. The dull ache at the memory of the lost love and trust. She felt safe with him again. Now that she knew why he'd really disappeared, the familiarity and the security were back like a warm cloud.

But the heat, the excitement, and the attraction she had felt nine years ago wasn't there. Not for Tadhg.

Not like it was for Sir James.

Nae! How could she be so fickle with her heart? How could she feel anything for the man she'd just met when her betrothed had returned to her?

Any feelings but pity for the man who was the enemy, the man who might be a sorcerer, were condemnable.

And even more importantly, she had already promised her heart and soul to God.

So she should just shut off anything she felt for Sir James and for Tadhg.

She should forget them both.

She would belong to God soon.

CHAPTER 6

"**D**inna think ye can do any of yer magic," said Catrìona
as she appeared in the darkness of the dungeon like a
vision.

A wall of iron grating separated them. The torch in the
sconce on the wall behind her made her hair glow like gold in the
sun. James squinted at her beautiful face illuminated by another
torch in her right hand.

Catrìona's jaw was set, her big eyes like two sapphires—hard
and blue. High cheekbones protruded from her rosy cheeks, but
whether they gained color because of the torch or something
else, he didn't know.

James stood from the cold wooden bench. "I don't do
magic."

Arching one eyebrow, Catrìona pointed a dagger at him with
her left hand. "This time, I wilna use scissors."

James's jaw worked. He looked at the basket hanging over her
elbow. How long had he been in the dungeon? One night?
Twenty-four hours? With no clocks and his phone dead, time
was like this giant swamp around him, sucking him in, drowning
him.

Like back when he was a little boy. He remembered the

house he'd been born into, the rough walls, the old wooden furniture, smelling sweet and dusty, like stale honey.

His mother, skinny and pale, her long chocolate-brown hair swaying as she tried to untangle James's hands from her home-spun skirt. "Mummy needs to go do things... You have to stay. James, let me go!"

She sank to her knees in front of him, her brown eyes so shiny from mania, they looked feverish. "What are you good for, you little bastard? What did I give you life for if your father still doesn't acknowledge me? Stay here, I said, and stop whining."

She took his hand and firmly yanked her skirt out of his fingers, the movement painful as it burned his skin. As the door shut with a bang, and the draft put out the single candle, the room plunged into darkness. He could hear four-year-old Emily start crying from where she sat on the single bed. Desperate for his mother's love, desperate for her to save him and stand up for him, James ran to the door, and began rattling the handle, bang-ing, irrationally calling for help. But who would come to him if his own mother wouldn't?

He'd needed his mum to be a mother and not a brainwashed groupie.

It hadn't been the first time she had locked him and Emily in the house to go see Brody, but it was the first time she had been so nasty with him, the first time James had realized what that meant.

It didn't matter now. It shouldn't. He was a thirty-one-year-old man.

Only, the rough stone walls, the darkness, the smell—all that triggered demons crawling from the inky black corners of his psyche. He knew with his rational mind this was immature. What was he afraid of, the lack of light?

But there it was, the desperation, the helplessness, the pain of rejection, like a weight on his ribs that he'd carried with him through his childhood and adolescence until his mother's death.

Once the cult had been shut down, she had quickly slipped

into alcoholism. One Christmas, she had left his grandparents' house, already drunk, and walked to the single pub in town that was still open. But it was one of the coldest nights in over fifty years, and she probably got cold in her short, fake fur coat. She must have wanted to lie down and sleep.

She'd been found the next day curled up in a corner just a few yards from the pub, covered with snow.

His chest clenched. If he'd ever needed a smoke, the time was now. But his last cigarette had been crushed when he'd kept Catrìona from falling.

Trying to keep his voice level, he locked eyes with her. "What will it take for you to let me out?"

She frowned. "Sir, if ye're offering pounds..."

"Sure. Pounds. Money. How much?" He went into the inner pocket of his suit jacket and took out his wallet.

But when he opened it, he hung his head. "Bloody hell..."

No banknotes. In this world of bank cards and mobile payments, who needed cash anymore?

She came closer to the grating and eyed the wallet with a curious apprehension. "I would thank ye not to curse, especially as ye're taking out yer things. How do I ken 'tis nae a demon ye're casting?"

James scoffed and held out his wallet to her. "Look at it if you want. There are just my bank cards and my identity card as well as my police warrant card. Take the wallet if it's valuable enough for you. Real leather."

She leaned a little closer, and with a careful frown, studied the shiny leather. "Aye, it looks valuable and rich, just like yer clothes. But I wilna touch it."

James shoved it back into his jacket and crossed his arms. "All right. So I don't have money. What else can I offer you so that you'll let me out?"

Catrìona cocked her head. "I'll ask the laird to release ye when I ken ye're nae a threat to my clan."

"I'm not."

"That remains to be seen."

James sighed and leaned against the crossbar of the cage with both arms. At least the dungeon was somewhat spacious. Granted, there was nothing in his small possession except a chamber pot and a bench, but he didn't lack space. The floor was packed dirt, the walls were part carved rock, probably from the island, and part rough stones and mortar. One wall was made of wooden grating. Since the air was humid and still, he'd hoped for some rotten wood, but the wall had held no matter how hard he'd kicked it.

The barren cell made his one-bedroom flat seem quite grand. He missed the simple but comfortable wooden furniture he'd bought from the previous renter, a sixty-year-old nurse who'd lived in the flat because she'd worked in John Radcliffe Hospital for thirty years and had moved out because she'd finally retired. All he needed, really, was a bed, a kitchen, and a bathroom. He didn't even own a TV, and his previous short-term girlfriends had complained about having to watch movies and TV series on his laptop.

The thought of a laptop seemed as odd as thinking of aliens.

"I came to care for yer wound," Catrìona said. "I'm a healer, after all, nae a jailor. And I also brought ye food and water."

James touched his head where blood had caked. "Oh."

Someone had brought him dry bannocks and water many hours ago, and he was already hungry. That must have been last night. Despite the lack of windows, his body told him it must be morning.

"Thanks," he added.

"I will open the door and come in, but ye wilna touch me or make a move, especially nothing magical. If ye do, I will slit yer throat. Ye wilna be the first man I've had to kill."

Her eyes shone so fiercely that he knew she was serious. She'd *killed* people? That sounded so...so out of the reality that he knew, that for a moment, he did believe he had traveled back in time. He didn't hear things like that every day in Oxford, even as a policeman. He might be trapped in the cell with a murderer. That thought unsettled him even more.

No, she was just a talented actress, that's all. Got fully immersed in her role.

"Sure," he said. "No magical tricks."

She nodded, put the torch into a sconce on the opposite wall, and retrieved a giant iron key.

As she opened the door, she pointed the dagger at him again, and the blade glistened, reflecting the torch fire. "Sit on the bench."

Her sapphire eyes glinted. What a strange, determined, beautiful woman. She held the dagger well and looked like she knew what to do with it.

"Sir James..." she added, a warning in her voice.

He chuckled. "Sure."

As he walked to the bench and sat on it, he was considering all the ways he could free himself. He could disarm her—he'd had to disarm a few hooligans with knives in his line of work. He'd need to stop her from screaming her throat out.

She put the basket on the floor and with one hand, opened it and retrieved a half loaf of bread and gave it to him. For a moment, his mind went blank and he forgot all thoughts of escape as the aromatic scent of a freshly baked bread reached his nostrils. He realized how hungry he was. He took it and bit into the loaf. It was a barley bread, crude and simple but delicious.

"Thanks," he said again through a mouthful.

"Keep still," she said as she leaned over his temple, studying it, the dagger still pointing at him.

"You know," he said. "It's pretty bizarre. You're supposedly a doctor and you're holding me at a knifepoint. Isn't that a little contradictory?"

She stopped and met his gaze. Then chuckled and, for the first time since he'd met her, smiled.

He stopped chewing, stopped moving, stopped breathing. The smile was broad, and sweet, and so beautiful he wanted to take a picture of her. Suddenly she'd become the third, and brightest, source of light in the dungeon.

"'Tis a jest, aye," she said and gave a little giggle. Then her amusement disappeared. "I wish the patient wasna a threat to my family."

James swallowed and resumed chewing. She touched his cut with her fingers, and he winced as sharp pain pierced him.

"I need to clean this," she said. "Ye dinna want any rot there."

"Cheers. If you have a simple antiseptic, that should do. I don't think it's anything serious."

She frowned. "Antiseptic?"

"Ah, right. You're probably not supposed to know the word. Who are you supposed to be, anyway? The healer of the family?"

She crouched in front of him, took out a waterskin and poured water into a bowl. Then with an experienced gesture, she moistened a clean cloth and gently dabbed at his wounded temple. He winced as pain pierced him.

"Aye, I am the healer of the family."

"Herbs and such, I assume. How did you come to be one?"

She shot a quick, doubtful glance at him as though deciding if he was mocking her. "I...I had to be one. Someone had to care for my brothers' and my mother's bruises and broken bones."

He went completely still. That sounded like domestic abuse. "From your father?"

She shrugged with the shoulder of the arm that held the dagger. "Aye. From my father."

"Bloody hell... Sorry you had to go through that."

Her dabs became gentler, weaker. "Hell... 'Tis where my father must be now."

So her father was dead. At least she wasn't in danger anymore from this violent man.

"Healing is a useful skill these days, I suppose," he said. "Someone always has something, don't they?"

"Aye, 'tis what I want. To be useful. To help. Is nae better place for me than the nunnery."

He hadn't thought she could shock him again, but there it was.

"The nunnery? Are you a nun?"

She sent him an amused "Where do you come from, the forest?" expression. "Nae, I'm nae a nun yet. But I will go to the nunnery in preparation for that at the end of summer."

"Right. Why at the end of summer?"

She looked at him again, as though deciding whether she should tell him or not. "I suppose there's nae harm in telling ye. Our father died six years ago and Laomann became the laird, I already knew I wanted to be a nun. But Laomann had asked me to wait. He was to be marrit to Mairead, and they've been so happy. He said mayhap I'd change my mind if I met someone. I agreed to wait six years, but my decision has not wavered. I will leave after the Highland games."

He couldn't imagine this beautiful, fierce, kind woman in a nun's habit. His heart screamed against her giving up her freedom, her future. Against her being brainwashed. He opened his mouth to ask her why she didn't find someone when quick steps sounded from beyond the door and a figure appeared in the doorway.

"Mistress!" a man cried, panting. "Ah, thank the Lord, here ye are! Come quick!"

Catrìona lowered her hand with the dagger. "What is it?"

"The laird is dead!"

CHAPTER 7

James watched Catrìona's face lose all color. He had delivered the news of death to families several times, and the first reaction was often shock: pale skin, wide eyes, open mouth. She was showing every sign.

He remembered his own shock at hearing of his mother's death from a policeman. The disbelief, the pain, the anger. How could she have died when he'd saved her from the claws of Brody Guthenberg? When he'd fought to free her, to finally give her a chance to live without being controlled or brainwashed or manipulated?

How could she have just died?

Catrìona rose to her feet, letting the wet cloth drop on the ground. Her hand with the dagger hung limply. "Dead? How?"

"I dinna ken, only that he got better after his runs last night. But when he had more of yer tisane, he vomited, had more runs, and screamed his throat out, holding on to his belly. Then, it seemed like his heart gave out... He dropped dead."

Catrìona exhaled. "After my tisane?"

James frowned. That sounded like either poisoning or an acute allergic reaction. Poor Catrìona. If she had poisoned her brother without intending to, she must be distraught.

No, this wasn't real, he reminded himself. Her brother couldn't be dead. It was all part of some reality show. Or a mystery dinner type of situation, maybe?

Despite himself, his mind raced, curious. Like every time he encountered a mystery, a problem to solve, his whole being ached to do so.

"Mistress?" said the servant.

"Go, go, I'm coming." The servant ran out of the room and they were alone again. She turned to her basket, her expression stunned, blank. "Just need to get my things..." she mumbled as she dropped to her knees in front of the basket.

Maybe this was the cue for James to do something in this game. Perhaps, like in an escape room, he needed to act. And with her appearing so shocked, he'd never have a better chance.

The all-familiar need to know the truth, to uncover the mystery, to put chaos into order pulled at him, tugging him to take action, to ask questions, to think.

Catrìona carelessly laid the dagger on the ground as she put the wet cloth and the waterskin back into her basket.

This was it. Now or never.

James grabbed the dagger, wrapped his arms around Catrìona's shoulders, and pressed the blade to her throat. She gasped in indignation.

"I have no intention to hurt you," James whispered in her ear. Her sweet, herbal scent tickled his nostrils and stirred fire in his blood. "But you won't let me out otherwise, will you?"

She jerked in his grasp, trying to free herself.

"All I want is to help. Your brother sounds like he was poisoned. I'm a detective, I solve mysteries for a living. So let me help."

She growled. "Are ye forcing me to let ye help?"

"You forced me to let you treat me. We're even now, don't you think?"

"Dinna dare—"

"Just lead me to your dead brother. I can help, I promise."

In response, she drove her elbow back into his stomach, and he grunted as pain radiated through his body.

"Never."

"As you wish." He pressed the blade tighter against her skin —enough to threaten her but not enough to injure her. "Let's go."

He shoved her a little, but she didn't move. Instead, she stomped on his shoe, pain bursting through his foot.

"Jesus!" He gasped out and held her tighter. "Will you stop? Just go."

He pressed on, and she moved, clearly unwillingly. They made it through the opening in the grating, then into the hall of the dungeon. As they approached the stairs that would lead into the storage room on the ground floor, she tried to free herself and reach out for her knife, but he tightened his grip. Finally, when they'd climbed the stairs and stood by the storage room, he stopped.

"I am not a threat," he breathed out. "Just lead me there and let me ask a few questions. Please."

She didn't reply for a few moments. "Are ye nae going to run away? There's the door, ye could just go."

"No. And if I meant you harm, I would have killed you by now."

She exhaled. "All right. I dinna ken why ye'd want to put yerself under more guards, so I suppose I can assume ye're speaking the truth for now."

"Smart woman. I'm going to let you go now."

She threw a furious glare at him, but underneath that strength, he saw the cracks of her psyche and the beginning of her defeat. "I need to hurry, Sir James. Do give me back my dagger if ye truly mean no harm."

He felt his jaw muscles work. He hated to give back the power he'd gained so unexpectedly.

"No," he said. "Not until I understand what happened."

He put the dagger in his belt, and they made their way up the stairs. People were already eating quietly in the great hall, faces somber. He kept climbing the stairs. The next floor had a large, half-opened door, and the room was empty. There was a big table in the middle, and a fireplace, next to which stood a couple of large, wooden chairs. There was also an ancient loom, and some sort of a cot for a baby.

He kept climbing after Catrìona. On the top floor of the tower, she went through one of the doors, and James followed her. It was a large room, but it looked crowded with five people standing around the canopy bed. Catrìona, her face ashen, rushed to Laomann and pressed her ear to his chest.

Raghnall, his hand on the hilt of his sword, marched up to James. "What is our prisoner doing here, Catrìona?"

But James didn't pay attention to anyone but the golden-haired woman. "Is he really dead?" he asked.

She blinked. "Nae."

Raghnall threw a hard gaze at James, then turned and stared at Laomann, clearly stunned the man was alive. "Catrìona, the prisoner shouldna be here or be concerned with our business."

"I can help," said James. "I'm a policeman...a detective. I know how to investigate crimes."

He looked straight into Catrìona's eyes. "Let me help."

It was important. He couldn't understand why—his logical mind couldn't, at least. But something in him knew that he had to be here and had to do something.

"Let me help," he repeated.

She huffed and nodded, then turned back to Laomann. James went inside the room and took a place in the circle of people surrounding the bed. He knew Catrìona and Raghnall, but the woman holding a cooing baby of ten months or so was new. The other person was Finn, the healer he met yesterday.

"What happened?" said James.

"He was unwell the whole day yesterday," said Catrìona. "I saw him complaining about his stomach."

"Who is this man?" asked the woman with the baby, looking at James.

"An outsider. A Sassenach," said Raghnall, his brows knit together.

"He's looking for Lady Rogene and David," said Catrìona.

"Clan Mackenzie is wary of outsiders." Finn chuckled. His resemblance to a large toad had never been more striking. "Laomann doesna trust even me."

"Ye're nae outsider," said Catrìona.

"And yet, Laomann fell ill after yer potion," said the woman with a grimace.

"Mairead, I gave him the potion," said Catrìona with a quaver in her voice. "If ye want to blame anyone for yer husband being so ill, ye should blame me."

Mairead, who was, apparently, Laomann's wife, shook her head. "I dinna think so, Catrìona. Ye fell prey to this man's plan." She pointed with her finger at Finn. "He gave ye the new herb and the new recipe for the potion. Ye couldna have kent it would harm him. Ye'd never have done anything to harm yer brother."

James frowned. "What were his symptoms?"

Mairead sighed. "He had stomach pain, he said it was as sharp as knives in his bowels." The baby began fussing and she bounced him up and down on her hip. "So then Catrìona gave him this new potion, as Finn Jelly Belly recommended. Laomann didna ken it was from Finn, or he wouldna have taken it." She shook her head, her eyes filling with tears. "He got better at first. But then at night it got worse. He had the runs, he was vomiting. He held his head like it would burst from the inside. At one moment, he couldna breathe nae more."

She whimpered as a tear rolled down her cheek.

"Then he fell and was shaking. Foam came from his mouth and he was jerking. His body was as tense as a tree. And then... he lay still, and I thought he was dead."

James was only trained to give first aid, but he knew enough to realize this all sounded like poison. He made his way to the side of the bed and felt Laomann's pulse on his neck. Weak and low, but it was there.

He lifted one of the man's eyelids. "Has anyone called the ambulance?" he asked.

The pupil was fixed. He moved to let more light from the window fall on Laomann, but the pupil stayed the same size.

"Call who?" asked Raghnall.

"Never mind. What was done to recover him?"

With a chill down his spine, James realized that this wasn't an act. The man was really in a coma. Or unconscious under a strong drug.

Something had happened to him. And if James would accept the impossible explanation of time travel, and he was indeed back in the fourteenth century—or at least in a world reconstructed to resemble the Middle Ages up to the last detail—there was no twenty-first-century medicine available.

"Nothing," said Finn. "He doesna respond. He's probably halfway to the grave, anyway."

Mairead whimpered again and burst into sobs. Catrìona went to her and hugged her by the shoulders. "We dinna ken that, Finn," said Catrìona. "He's still alive. Ye and I will bring him back, nae matter the cost."

"What did he eat and drink yesterday?" James asked Mairead.

"The usual. Everything that the others eat and drink. Chicken. Ale. Bannocks. Parritch. Uisge."

"Did he eat anything else that others didn't?" James asked.

"Only Finn's potion," said Raghnall.

"And what was in that potion?"

"'Tis a regular tisane to treat stomach upsets," said Finn. "But Laomann did have a strange reaction to the simple licorice root so mayhap he did again, to something in that potion."

"He could be allergic to one of the ingredients," said James. "What was in there exactly?"

"Black currant, blackberry thorns, and powder of carob tree," said Catrìona.

"Can any of them do what was done to Laomann?" said James.

Catrìona and Finn exchanged a glance, then looked at Laomann, silent.

"Well?" said Raghnall.

Catrìona shifted. "Black currant and blackberry couldna have. But I dinna ken enough about carob. Can it be a poison, Finn?"

James narrowed his eyes at the man whose dark frog eyes stared at him with no fear. James had been assigned poisoning cases twice in his career. It was a different matter altogether when there was a forensic lab available to analyze the blood samples. One time, a man had been murdered by his wife using rat poisoning—classically, for life insurance money. Interestingly enough, according to the wife, it had been his idea.

The second time, following many popular detective novels, arsenic was used to get rid of an annoying boss. A case of revenge.

James wondered if this may be a case of revenge, also. Finn would certainly have a motive—and the means. He could have easily tricked Catrìona and given her the wrong herb in the mixture.

But that would be too obvious.

Finn stared at James without blinking. "I've never heard of carob bringing harm."

James turned to Catrìona. "I'd like to talk to you in private. After that, I'd like to talk with you, Finn."

Everyone stared at him, their gazes a mixture of confusion and annoyance. But he knew his voice was authoritative enough to gain compliance.

"Aye," said Catrìona. "If this helps to understand what happened to my brother."

She turned to walk out of the room, but Raghnall caught her by the forearm. "Sister, I'll come, also. Ye shouldna be alone with him."

"It's best to talk to people individually," said James.

"'Tis all right," she said. "I can protect myself. Dinna fash about me, brother."

"Can you come with—" Speaking as he turned to the door, James felt his jaw drop.

In the doorway, dressed like a medieval warrior, was David Wakeley.

CHAPTER 8

J ames knew his jaw hung like a bloody donkey's.
Countless photos from social media, from Karin Fischer's wedding—the facial features he'd studied over and
over to make sure he knew them well—clicked into place
in his mind when he saw the boy he'd been looking for.

"David?" he said.

In medieval costume, with several days' stubble that was
almost a short beard, and a modern hairstyle that looked
overdue for a trim, David coughed and looked around the room.
Then his eyes focused on James.

"Yes," said David in Gaelic but with an American accent—
good Lord, that was a crazy combination. He walked cautiously
into the room. "Who're you?"

James looked around at the Mackenzies who were frowning
at him and David. He needed to find out what was really going
on and if David was in danger. The teen may not want to talk
about it with the Mackenzies present, but he might open up if
they were alone. James took David by his elbow and tugged him
out of the room.

"Dinna make a move," growled Raghnall. "David, this
man—"

"I'm Detective James Murray," James said in modern English. "I came here to find you and your sister."

Catrìona frowned at him. "What was that, Sir James?"

David's face went blank. "It's all right," he said in Gaelic to Raghnall. "I know him. He's safe. He's cool."

"Ye really ken him?" asked Catrìona.

"Yeah," said David. "And I need to talk to him alone. I'll explain everything to all of you later. Come, Detective."

Under heavy, astonished gazes, David led James out of the room, down the narrow stairs, and into the great hall. There were men there, but David didn't spare them a second glance. He pulled James into a corner, away from curious ears.

David looked him up and down. "You're the police?"

James nodded. "CID. Investigating your and Rogene's disappearance."

David laughed and clapped James on the shoulder. "Thanks for coming for me, man. I couldn't leave this fucking century, no matter what we tried down by that rock. I'd thought the rock was broken or something. I came here by chance, you know. I should have never been here. But now that you've come for me..." He let out a long sigh and shook his head once. "Maybe it works, after all."

James coughed. "The Pictish rock with the carving?"

"Yeah."

All this sounded like David believed in the nonsense about time travel and portals or streams of time or whatever.

"And where exactly do you think you are?" asked James.

David let him go and stepped back, suddenly serious. "Back in the fourteenth century, of course. Where do you think we are?"

James cleared his throat. "You're not serious."

David stared at him for a long time, as though deciding how to tell a madman he was insane. Then he sighed. "Come with me. You're a cop. You must be even more bullheaded than I am."

David walked down the stairs. "Where are you going?" said James, following him.

"To the rock. Where else?" David's broad back darkened as he descended into the shadows of the narrow stairwell. "If you came for me, here I am. And I'm sure as hell not spending another day here. I got my scholarship, and I need to get back before they revoke it."

"So what happened? Who lured you here?" James asked as he went down the smooth stone steps after David.

"No one." David turned the corner and they were now in the storage room. The flaming torches cast dancing shadows onto the crates, boxes, and sacks. "I mean, time travel is real, man. I know it sounds crazy, and I didn't believe it for a while. But I've been stuck here for about two weeks. So, maybe, you can try the rock again and I can just come along for the ride."

David took a torch from the sconce and opened the door to the underground area. As they descended, James wished distractedly that he had a cig.

"What are you talking about?" James asked, following David's burning torch into the darkness. The already familiar scents of the wet stone and earth reached him. If he could help it, he really didn't want to go back to the place where he'd been held prisoner not a half hour ago. "Are you saying you believe you traveled in time?"

"Yeah. I do," said David as he stepped into the large room. Stony, cold darkness breathed on them from all sides.

"Come on, really?" James said. "I mean, I get that it all looks realistic, and they're all great actors, but you can't seriously believe in magic."

David sighed. The torch crackled softly in his hand. "I don't know what to tell you. It's true. I've searched and searched for the signs of some sort of reenactment but we're really in 1310."

David opened the door to the back room. When they entered, the damned Pictish rock was staring at him, practically mocking him. The carvings jumped and danced as the light of the torch fell on them. Turning away from it, James asked, "Can you tell me everything from the beginning?"

David placed the torch into the sconce on the wall and looked at the Pictish rock longingly. "Can I tell you it in 2021?"

James groaned. "We are in 2021."

"No. We're in 1310."

"All right. Prove it. Tell me."

"And then you'll take me back?"

"Of course I'll take you back. I'm not sure what back is, but that's why I'm here, to investigate where you and Rogene went and to help you return."

David beamed. "Great. It's too bad I won't be able to say goodbye to Rogene, but I'll write her a note."

"Where is she?"

"In Ault a'chruinn, Angus's estate. The three of us left yesterday, but I came back because she forgot her book on herbalism."

James sighed. The cold was creeping around him, tightening its grip. "Tell me from the beginning. What happened to you both?"

David told him the story Rogene had shared with him after she'd returned. She'd fallen in love with Angus Mackenzie, who was supposed to marry Euphemia of Ross. And despite the danger that breaking the marriage agreement would bring, Angus had broken it to be with Rogene. But she didn't want to alter history, so she returned to the twenty-first century. Then she realized she'd made a mistake and given up the love of her life. So she went back in time to 1310, and while David was trying to stop her, he went through the stone, too. And now David couldn't get back into the twenty-first century no matter how many times he tried.

"Maybe it's because I'm not supposed to be here." David walked to the rock and glared at it. "Though I haven't seen Sineag to ask her. But, trust me, I'd beg, I'd bribe, I'd do anything to go back. I've got a life there, man. And here..." He looked around. "It's always cold, it's always damp, and the food...

I mean, just the simple ability to switch on a light or use a toilet is a luxury. You don't appreciate all that when you're in the twenty-first century, but now...I'll never again take for granted being able to open a freezer, pull out a pizza, and put it into an electric oven."

"Sure." James rubbed the scruff on his chin. "And you didn't think this was simply a different castle somewhere in a remote Scottish location where they reconstructed a historically accurate setting and hired actors?"

David picked up a small stone with his pointy shoe and kicked it. It knocked softly against the Pictish rock. "In the beginning, yeah. Something like that. But it's not just this place. It's everything. Ships, horses, the woods are practically untouched. No asphalt roads, no plane trails in the sky, everyone speaks Gaelic... The money—pound Scots they call them. Shillings, pence—metal coins. Silver coins. It's all for real, no matter how much you don't want to believe it."

James shook his head. Perhaps some small part of him could imagine the possibility that it was true. But the boy in him—who had survived a crazy cult, who had hoped every day for his mother to open her eyes and break free from all those who believed in magic and in the supernatural abilities of their leader—refused to. The policeman in him didn't want to allow illusion to enslave him.

And he had to help David see that this was madness.

"You still don't believe me," David said.

James sighed and smiled sadly. "Once I find the bastard who's responsible for brainwashing so many innocent people like yourself, he's going into prison for good."

He stretched out his hand and David grasped it.

"Only to set your mind at ease and to prove that the idea of falling through a rock into another century is foolish," said James. They walked to the rock and James sank to his knees, staring at the rock.

But, strangely, just like with Sìneag, the carving began glowing. James froze and David exclaimed, "It works, see!"

"No, this is just some sort of glowing paint or something." He stretched his hand out to touch the carving and see if there was any paint. But as his hand got closer to the rock, that vibration, that cool sensation of falling, and of his hand being drawn to the rock, began pulling at him. It grew stronger the closer he brought his hand.

David was squeezing James's hand tighter and tighter. "That's it. Just put your hand into the handprint."

James's hand was right over the handprint, and the pull was as strong as ten vacuum cleaners sucking the air in. And then he knew without a doubt that whatever he believed or didn't believe, this was for real. That David was right. That he had traveled in time, and if he just let go and let his hand snap into the handprint, he'd be back home in the twenty-first century. And could bring David home, and this insane adventure would be over.

He'd be back with his sister, whose baby was due any minute. And he had no idea if the baby was even okay. What if she needed an emergency C-section? What if something was wrong with the baby? He couldn't leave his sister to deal with the birth alone.

But if he left now, he wouldn't be able to talk to Rogene Wakeley and ask for her side of the story.

He'd let someone who'd poisoned Laomann Mackenzie roam free.

He'd never see Catrìona again.

He'd return home soon, he thought. He wouldn't need to spend more than a day or so here and could help Catrìona solve this mystery and find out who'd poisoned Laomann. Then she and her family would be safe.

And as much as he wanted it to be different, it was the thought of Catrìona that made him apply all the strength he had and pull his hand away from the rock.

David and he tumbled to the ground, tiny pebbles and rocks

piercing his skull. David jumped up, panting, and covered in dirt. "What the hell did you do?" he demanded, his face red. "We were almost gone from here! I can't believe this!"

James stood up, wiping the dust and dirt off his suit. "I can't believe this, either. But I can't leave yet."

David opened his arms in a wide arc. "What the hell?"

"And didn't you want to write a message to your sister, anyway?"

David rubbed his forehead, staring at the rock helplessly. "Yeah, but... Fuck it! Please, Detective, I felt it, too. It would have worked."

James shook his head, brushing dust and sand from his hair. "Sorry, David. I can't leave just yet. I have to find out what's going on."

"So you believe now that you traveled in time?"

James felt his jaw muscles squeeze tightly together. Did he? He hated to admit it, but if he didn't quite buy into it 100 percent, then he definitely knew something was up. The strength of the force he'd felt from the rock was undeniable. It wasn't really like something was sucking him in. It was more like a magnet, and there had been a vibration through the air... And he had known in that moment that through that rock was something else.

"It appears that I do."

David clenched his fists, marched to the rock, and slammed his hand into the print.

Nothing.

David grunted and jammed his fist into the rock, then howled in pain.

He shook his hand. "Goddamn it!"

James squeezed his shoulder. "Look, I didn't go back now, but I will soon enough. Don't despair. I'll take you back."

"When will that be?"

"As soon as I know that the Mackenzies are safe."

"Safe?"

"Laomann has been poisoned, most likely."

David blinked. "Poisoned? Are you serious?"

"It's not for sure. I don't have a forensic lab here, but the symptoms are right. If he was intentionally poisoned, whoever did it is still out there. So Laomann could still be in danger. If this was a murder attempt, there's a killer in the castle. And they might not stop at one victim."

David's eyes widened. "I have to let Angus know."

"Yeah. You should."

David brushed his hand through his hair. "All right, Detective. Look. If you do this, it's best you blend in. Your suit is nice and all, but people will be more inclined to talk to you if you're dressed like one of them. Plus, your accent... You're English, aren't you?"

"I am."

"You've probably guessed the English aren't exactly loved here."

"Yeah."

"So my advice is, try not to cause more problems than necessary, and don't show any modern stuff that you might have."

"Catrìona already thought I was a sorcerer."

David chuckled. "Catrìona's cool. She wouldn't betray you. But Rogene told me they think there are demons and witches and mages, and those are tried and sometimes even killed. Be careful, Detective."

James threw a last glance at the rock. "Always am."

"I'll go see how Laomann is and ask if they need anything. Then I'm going back to Ault a'chruinn to let Angus and Rogene know what's going on."

James nodded, then took the torch off the wall, the heat of fire radiating against his hand. "Now, let's go."

He turned to walk, but David stopped him by placing his hand on his shoulder. "Swear you won't leave without me."

James patted David's shoulder. "Don't worry, David. I'm a cop even here. I promise not to leave you behind."

CHAPTER 9

"Cat, is that ye?" called Tadhg's voice from behind his partially open door as Catrìona was crossing the landing.

David and Sir James had just returned into Laomann's room, and James had asked her to come with him and let him ask her questions. He was right behind her as she turned towards Tadhg's bedchamber. Tadhg now stood, holding the doorframe, his face flushed, his skin ashen.

She stopped and rushed to him, wrapping her arm around his torso, letting him lean on her.

"What are ye doing standing up, Tadhg?" she chastised him as she guided him back to bed. "Ye should be resting."

As she walked with the injured man, absorbing the full weight of an adult warrior, she felt Sir James watching her.

"Ye barely made it through last night." She let Tadhg slide onto the edge of the bed, and he tried to stifle a groan of pain, scowling at Sir James.

"Who is this, Cat?"

She brushed off his use of the nickname she had specifically asked him not to use, though hearing it on his tongue made her feel like the lass she'd been, the one who'd loved a sweet lad and dreamed of a future as his wife and the mother of his children.

That life wasn't for her anymore, she reminded herself.

She pressed the back of her hand against Tadhg's forehead. Still warm, although not as scorching hot as last night. She'd spent the whole night next to his bed and had fallen asleep in the chair, being awoken by Tadhg's periodic vomiting and groans of pain.

"Sir James of Oxford," she said.

Tadhg was glaring at Sir James like he were a rabid dog.

Climbing back into the bed unwillingly, he asked, "A Sassenach?"

"Aye," she said. "How's yer leg?"

"Who is this man?" Sir James demanded. She looked at him over her shoulder.

"'Tis Tadhg MacCowen," she said and cleared her throat. Who was Tadhg to her now? "An old clansman. Friend of the clan."

"Right," said Sir James, sounding calmer. But there was a steely edge in his voice she didn't understand.

"Sassenach?" repeated Tadhg, looking directly at her.

She lifted the dressing on his head and looked under it. "This wound looks well. Let me see yer other wound. Could ye show me yer leg, please?"

"Aye." He threw the blanket off his legs and pulled the braies up. Feeling her cheeks redden—she was about to inspect a man's bare thigh, after all—she gently lifted the dressing and sniffed. It looked less red. And now she could see the white pus and it didn't smell like anything.

That was good. The pus was healthy; it meant his body was strong enough to fight the disease. She'd need to clean the pus out and change the dressing again. Honey would do its job of fighting the rot in the wound.

"This looks better," she said to Tadhg. "Did ye want something? Water? Food?"

"I wanted to talk to ye."

Sir James, who was standing in the corner, was burning her with his gaze.

"I canna just now, Tadhg, I'm sorry. Something happened to Laomann, and Sir James is helping us to find out what and how to help him get back to health."

Tadhg's face straightened and his eyes shot to meet hers. "What happened to Laomann?"

"He got ill and now he's lying unconscious."

Tadhg's eyes widened. "Will he live?"

"I hope so, and pray to our Lord Jesu Christ." She crossed herself and kissed her cross. Tadhg repeated her gesture and whispered a quick prayer.

Tadhg whitened even further and a grimace of pain flashed through his face. He clutched at his stomach. Poor Tadhg, he was probably about to vomit again. She had thought the vomiting was an odd sign of inflammation, but babies tended to vomit if they had fever, so this wasn't unheard of.

"What happened?" Tadhg said through a groan. "Did someone attack him? Can I help?"

James narrowed his eyes on her, and something within her quivered and fluttered and squeezed deliciously.

"Catrìona, can we please have that talk?" he said in such a husky voice that a wave of hot tingling went through her. What was that?

Tadhg touched her hand. "Is it safe for ye to be with him?" he asked in a low voice.

What was going on? Now that she was about to become a nun, why did she have a feeling two men were tugging at her, fighting for her attention? That couldn't be, could it? Neither of them were interested in her, so why did she have this warmth and this wobbling in her joints at the sight of both of them?

Tadhg was the man who would have been her husband, the only man she'd ever loved.

And Sir James... The way that he made her feel was something she'd never experienced before. Like more was possible, more than she'd ever imagined.

Tadhg interrupted her thoughts by doubling up and wincing in pain. Catrìona frowned. "Are ye all right?"

"Just a wee pain and—"

He didn't even finish the sentence, just turned to his side and vomited right on the floor.

Catrìona felt the blood drain from her face. She rushed to him, put the chamber pot by his bed, and patted his back as he continued retching. She gave him a clean linen cloth to wipe his mouth.

"My head..." He squeezed his head between his palms.

"What did you eat and drink?" asked James.

"Just bread, uisge and water, and..."

"And my tisane?" finished Catrìona.

Tadhg nodded. "Aye."

Catrìona swallowed. "I made it based on Finn's recommendation."

James shook his head. "I must talk to Finn. Catrìona, it would be great if you were present during the talk."

Catrìona's hands shook. "I'm sure if 'tis anyone's fault, 'tis mine. I must have mixed up some herbs or the berries... Finn has never been but a good friend."

"Still. Come. We must find him."

"I canna leave Tadhg, Sir James. If his heart also stops beating..."

James nodded. "Of course. Can I be of help? Bring you something? Or you, Tadhg?"

Catrìona softened. His sudden change of mood was endearing. "Actually, aye. If ye could bring my medicine basket, that would help. And a jug of clean water from the well."

"Of course."

James left the chamber as Tadhg began retching again. Between bouts, he told her he had started having the runs this morning, which he'd been too embarrassed to say in front of

Sir James. This fit the symptoms Laomann had been having too closely to ignore. After a while, Tadhg fell asleep, exhausted.

Sir James returned soon after with her medicine basket. While Tadhg was asleep, she decided to make a fire. The fireplace hadn't been cleaned yet, so she picked up the bowl for ashes and began scraping them into it.

"So," he said. "Who is Tadhg MacCowen and how did he come to be wounded?"

"Tadhg helped Raghnall two days ago when a band of Ross men attacked him on the way to clan Ruaidhrí. Both were hurt and they came back here last night as it was closer than the Isle of Skye where clan Ruaidhrí live."

Sir James stood by her side. "Let me," he said gently. "I can light the fire for you."

She looked up at him. There he stood, all tall and looking mysterious in his gray, silky suit from exotic lands, giving off an air of adventure and life.

"Aye," she said, standing up, suddenly unable to resist him. "Thank ye."

He sank to his knees and took the kindling from the basket next to the fireplace.

He placed three pieces of firewood on the kindling.

"Did Raghnall know Tadhg?"

She noticed the chests standing along the walls were dusty. Rummaging in the secret pockets of her dress she found a clean cloth—she always had one with her. It was handy as a healer. She wetted her cloth in the jug of water and started to wipe the surface of one of the first chests, meticulously rubbing between the carved figures depicting a battle.

Physical activity helped her to feel better, to feel useful. Her mother had said that doing the house chores was like covering the house with God's blessings.

Catrìona had loved that, though she didn't think that always worked, as no matter how much she'd cleaned, swept, or worked on the household, Father had remained the same. Strong, dangerous, and stormy.

"Tadhg was with the clan till he was seventeen." She wiped around the face of a carved warrior with a spear in his hand. "He was my betrothed."

"Your—" Sir James coughed. She didn't look at him, but somehow she knew he had stilled. "Betrothed."

"Aye. We were betrothed secretly."

A silent beat followed. "Secretly?"

"Aye. No one kent. My father was against it." The surface was clean so she moved to another chest. "So we kept it secret."

"But now you want to become a nun," he said. "What happened?"

She took the cloth with both hands and began rubbing against the surface with vigor. The fire started and the room filled with the pleasant scent of woodsmoke. Warm air from the fire kissed her cheek, wafting the loose strands of her hair around her face. An odd image appeared in her head, of James brushing his knuckles over her cheek as gently as the air, and she shuddered as a tingle of warmth went through her.

Good Lord, what was that?

She cleared her throat. "I loved him," she said, the words feeling strange on her tongue. "But the circumstances were against us, and we never marrit. He left the area nine years ago and is with clan Ruaidhrí now."

Fire was crackling pleasantly in the fireplace, and she suddenly felt Sir James standing by her side, towering over her and shielding the light like a mountain.

"Do you regret his leaving?" he asked, his voice husky and low.

She froze, the cloth squeezed between both of her fists, unable to free herself from the captivity of his dark eyes, warm as the shores of distant lands she'd never seen.

Did she regret it? She couldn't think anymore, her mind woozy and blank. "Are ye doing it again?" she whispered.

He took a step closer, and heat rushed through her.

"What?" he asked, covering her hand with his.

"Yer witchcraft?"

He opened his mouth to say something, then changed his mind and took a step closer, his body touching the length of her whole arm.

But before he could do anything and contribute to her ruin even more, he looked away, releasing her from his spell.

"I shouldn't pry," he said. "It's none of my concern. Do you think we can go soon and talk to Finn?"

Finn must be still in Laomann's bedchamber. When she'd left them, Finn had told her he'd start bloodletting, the only thing he thought could help since Laomann was unconscious and couldn't even swallow.

She looked over at Sir James's rich clothes. "Aye. But mayhap 'tis best I fetch ye some of Laomann's clothes as yer rich clothes are now ruined, Sir James."

And as he looked himself over, noting the torn and dirty areas of his suit, she bit her lip and tried in vain to chase away the image of him changing into new clothes.

Maybe he did possess witchcraft, as her mind seemed to go blank every time he was near.

CHAPTER 10

T*he next day...*

CATRÌONA ACCEPTED SIR JAMES'S LARGE HAND TO HELP HER out of the boat. That same jolt of energy ran through her, the small lightning bolt that woke up her very blood.

"Thank ye, Sir James," she murmured.

He let go of her hand, leaving her strangely breathless. How could he have affected her so? Bringing her heart to race like a wild horse in her chest? She stepped onto the jetty, taking long, calming breaths.

When they had arrived at Laomann's chamber yesterday, Finn was already gone. Tadhg had woken up soon after, and Catrìona had spent the day taking care of him. She'd asked Ruth to ask around about Finn, but all her maid had found out was that he must be in Dornie.

By this morning, Tadhg was much better and Catrìona could finally leave him. On top of finding Finn, there were plenty of errands to run in Dornie in preparation for the Highland games.

She needed to ask hunters to hunt deer and tanners to prepare hides for the tents. The blacksmith needed to know how many nails to make for constructing booths. She had to hire men to start felling the trees around the clearing where the games would be held.

Those were all things she needed to do. But there was one thing she *wanted* to do first.

"I have to stop somewhere," she said. "Before we find Finn and run my other errands."

"I don't mind," he said. "I'll wait."

They walked down the jetty and into the village, James staring at everything around him with the eyes of a hawk.

The heavens drizzled rain on the village, and the dirt slurped under Catrìona's feet. As they walked past the thatched-roofed houses, past the small waddle palisades, avoiding chickens and geese running around, Catrìona inhaled the familiar scent of the village: the mud, the woodsmoke, and the blessed scent of cooking food.

Despite the comforting sights and smells, worry for her brother and worry for her clan settled in her heart like a dark cloud. The bleeding hadn't helped and Laomann hadn't gotten any better. Should they even be preparing for the Highland games if the laird was on his deathbed?

Deathbed? Nae! She refused to believe this was it for Laomann.

"Where do you need to stop?" Sir James asked.

"At the church," she said. "I want to pray."

"Oh."

His tone made her feel like she'd said something foul.

"Is there something wrong with praying?" she asked.

His profile was impassive, as it was pretty much every time she looked at him. He'd changed into the dress of the Highlanders. Mairead had been kind enough to lend him Laomann's clothes, though the sleeves were short for James's height and the tunic was too narrow for his shoulders. He wore the sleeves rolled up, and Catrìona's pulse jumped every time she saw his muscular forearms. There was nothing he could do about the shoulders, and the fabric stretched considerably as he moved, the seams constantly threatening to pop.

Her breath caught as she watched him stride beside her with masculine grace and the confidence of a warrior.

What was going on with her?

"No..." he said. "But praying won't help him."

"Sir James!"

She stopped right there, in the drizzle, in the middle of a street. The church was just two dozen steps away.

"What?" he said.

"Ye canna be serious. Ye canna say things like that in front of God's house."

"Look, it's probably not a good idea to argue about religion. I'm sorry I brought it up. Let's go and get it over with."

He resumed walking and she hurried after him.

"What is there to argue about?" she said. "There's our Lord Jesu Christ. What else is there to talk about?"

He kept walking, his jaw working under his stubble. The muscles below his eyes twitched.

"Sir James?"

"Catrìona, let it go."

"Why?"

He stopped abruptly and turned to her, wincing. "Because I do not believe in God."

She gasped at him. "How can ye nae believe in God?"

"Easily."

"Nae, I mean, ye're a Sassenach, but ye have the same church in Oxford, aye? Nae Muslim or Jewish religions."

"I don't believe in any God. I'm an atheist."

It felt like something squeezed her chest, anger rising in her in a hot, bubbling wave. This was preposterous. Everyone was supposed to believe in God, what else was there? "Ye canna say things like that."

"Look, let's agree to disagree, all right? We all have a right to our own beliefs and opinions."

He turned to keep walking and she frowned at him. She'd never heard anyone say anything like that, either. But she liked the idea of respecting different beliefs and opinions.

"But ye can be considered a heretic if ye say openly ye dinna believe in God," she said.

"Then I suppose I better find out what happened to Laomann and get the hell out of here."

"But what made ye like this? What made ye abandon God?"

They were at the doors to the church now and James turned to her. His eyelashes were dark and long and wet, and he blinked so adorably from the accumulated water. She ached to reach out and gently wipe the rain away.

Without saying a word, he opened the door for her, then gestured for her to go inside. "Wouldn't your God disapprove of conversations like this in front of 'His house'?"

"I dinna ken," Catriona said. "I've never talked to Father Nicholas about doubt."

"Well, maybe it's time you start because if you keep talking to me, I might steer you the wrong way."

She raised her chin. "I dinna fash about that. The harder things are and the more challenges and obstacles life presents, the deeper I feel God is with me."

She went in, her heart beating fast. The familiar semidarkness surrounded her, cool and soothing. She walked down the aisle of the church and towards the altar. Like always, she could feel the presence of God lighting her up from within, leaving her awed in the presence of this vast being that was everything good and right in the world.

Feeling Sir James's eyes on her, she looked back at the entrance. He was staring from the shadows, like a dark figure from another world. He could have appeared menacing—tall and muscular, the aura of confidence and a controlled threat emanating from him.

But she wasn't afraid. Instead, she saw a deep concern in his eyes. As if he thought there could be some sort of a threat nearby. As if she could be in danger and he was standing lookout...

What danger could there possibly be in a church? From God? What could have happened to him that disturbed him so much?

And something had disturbed him, she could see it clearly. She'd pray for him, too.

Even if he didn't believe.

~

JAMES WATCHED CATRÌONA'S TOO SLIM FIGURE WALK DEEPER into the church with a sense of unease. Their eyes locked as she looked back, and he could swear his heart gave a lurch. He didn't see judgment in her gaze. Only compassion. Kindness.

Love shone through her eyes—not for him, surely. But love that Catrìona seemed to emanate like an aura...if one believed in things like auras.

She sank to her knees by the simple stone altar at the other end of the room, bowing her head over her hands, which she brought together in prayer. Before her was a large wooden cross on the wall. He watched her, unmoving and solemn, illuminated by the light of two small candles on the sides of the altar. It must be an illusion of the light, but her humble dress seemed to glow in the semidarkness.

With the scent of dust and incense surrounding him, he was amazed at how simple the church interior was. Compared to what he'd seen in cathedrals and abbeys, there was pretty much nothing here. No gold, no benches, no decorations. Small, square windows along the ceiling let in dim gray light that fell on a cleanly swept floor made of stone slabs.

It worried him, to see someone being brainwashed and trained to believe in something that might hurt her like it had hurt his mother, his sister, and him. That blind belief, that manipulation of the masses—he'd never understand or accept that for himself.

He shouldn't even be here, but the need to make sure Catrìona was all right was stronger than any emerging memories or the pain they caused.

He was glad he lived in the twenty-first century, where most people had a choice of what to believe in or not to believe in, and where charlatans could be punished by law.

He remembered the weekly gatherings for prayer and meditation in the sitting room of Brody's old Victorian house. A hundred people had packed into the room, making the air thick with the scent of sweat. Men, women, and children, illuminated by the fireplace and candles, bowed their heads, just like Catrìona, and prayed, listening to Brody reading out the prayers like a priest.

Emily had always done those things, faithfully following her mother's example. Children's days had been spent in a small school, where Brody's second-in-command took the role of a teacher. They were all "homeschooled" as far as the government was concerned, but the beliefs of the cult had been woven through every lesson.

The whole cult had gathered for lunch, and after that, everybody had gone to do their assigned chores. People gardened and cooked. James went hunting with his bow. Emily had helped in the gardens, but sometimes she went along with him.

Emily... The thought of his sister made his gut churn. How had the ultrasound gone? Was everything okay? She must be worried about him since he hadn't returned from Scotland. Guilt burned his insides. He really should go back as soon as possible. Only, his conscience wouldn't allow him to leave the people here in jeopardy, either.

Especially one person.

When Catrìona stood up and turned to him, her face was brighter and calmer. She walked towards him in her feminine, simple gait, her hair so blond it glowed, and yet again, he had the image of an angel coming to him to cast light in the darkness.

He swallowed a hard knot, his pulse accelerating. As she stood in front of him, small and fragile and so beautiful, his heart ached, and he had an almost overwhelming urge to lift her into his arms and carry her away.

"Ready?" he asked, his voice coming out like he'd swallowed a rock.

"Aye," she said and walked past him. "I prayed for ye, too."

He followed her outside, into the village that was, without doubt now, back in the fourteenth century. As he stepped through the doorway, he had to stop for a moment as he had a sense he'd walked into a yet another world. The misty drizzle was gone, and sunshine poured down on the village, bathing the houses, the people, and the wet animals in the golden light.

The mud under his feet glistened, as did the leaves on the nearby trees. The cloud of rain was far away, like a distant worry, and James had a strange thought that it was Catriona's prayer that had done this.

"You prayed for me?" he said as he followed her. "Why?"

"Because ye're a lost soul, Sir James." She looked up at him, and her blue eyes shone with inner light. "And because ye have dark secrets."

A shiver of uneasiness went down his spine. "What?"

"Ye have dark secrets that bother yer soul."

Bugger. She was right, but it could be like one of those horoscope readings that applied to anyone. "Why would you say that?"

"I can see it in yer eyes."

She could see it in his eyes? That was a pile of horseshit that gurus and card readers told people. They didn't see anything in the eyes. At best, they had brilliant skills of reading body language. At worst, they just guessed.

"Well, at least it's not God that whispered it to you," he mumbled.

She opened her mouth to say something, but cries came from behind the next house. Someone yelled in pain.

"'Tis where Finn is staying..." Catrìona whispered.

Exchanging a worried glance, Catrìona and James hurried to turn the corner.

A group of men surrounded Finn Jelly Belly, five of them. Two had pitchforks, one had a dagger, and two had sticks and rocks in their hands. Finn was standing next to a cart that was full of sacks and chests. There was a horse hitched to the cart, looking around as though it was anxious to depart.

Finn was holding his arm, which hung uselessly, his frog-like mouth open and curved downwards in a grimace of pain and fear. He was leaning to his side and forward in a pleading pose.

"Please..." he said. "I'm nae a witcher and I'm nae a demon caster. I'm just a healer."

"I ken what ye did to the laird," said one of the men, jabbing his pitchfork in the air at Finn. Finn took a step back and fell into the mud. "Ye brought a spell on him and now he's dying because of ye. And now ye're trying to escape."

"There will be nae escape, ye demon," said the one who had a dagger in his hand. He spat at Finn, then looked around at his friends. "I say we kill him and rid the laird of the curse."

CHAPTER 11

Catrìona's feet and hands grew as cold as ice. She rushed to them, opening her mouth to yell for them to stop when James's powerful voice rang like a war horn.

"Stop!" he cried, marching towards the group. "Stop right now."

The men turned to him, their brows bunched, eyes deep and dark and glistening with threat. Catrìona hurried over and sank to her knees by Finn's side to help him rise, but he only clung to her with one arm. He smelled like herbs and mud and sweat... and blood. She unclenched his fingers from his arm. A deep gash cut his upper arm, blood flowing freely.

"Come on, I'll help ye," she said.

The man pointed his pitchfork at Catrìona. "Nae so fast, mistress. Ye dinna want to be mixed up with the demon caster."

"He's nae a demon caster," she said. "How dare ye, Ailig? He helped deliver yer son five years ago, and 'tis how ye thank him?"

Ailig looked at the ground. "Doesna change that he hates the laird and cursed him. He wants the laird dead."

James crossed his arms over his chest. "And what's your proof, mate?"

"There's nae need for proof to ken a sorcerer," said Gille-Criosd, the man with the dagger. "People talk."

"That's where you're wrong," said Sir James. "You need to prove someone committed a crime or you could be killing an innocent man. And if he's innocent, then there's the commandment—thou shalt not kill. Which means, on Judgment Day, your God wouldn't let you into heaven, would he, because you committed the sin of murder, right?"

The men scowled at him. "And who would ye be, Sassenach, talking so knowingly about God and Judgment Day and all that? And why do ye protect the witcher at all?"

James smirked.

Smirked!

"A Sassenach, you say?" James said. "A stranger. An outlander. Mate, you have no idea." He laughed, a strange sort of a bitter laughter. "How do you know *I'm* not the witcher?"

Horror dripped down Catriona's spine. What was he doing?

"James..." she said.

"Ye?" said Gille-Criosd, turning to James and slowly advancing on him, the weapon in his hand pointing upwards, at the ready.

"Yeah. Me. You blame the man who delivered your child, who you've probably known for years as he came to help you and your village with your illnesses and aches. And yet, with no proof, you beat the man up and want to kill him because of a rumor? How do you know it's not me that did that to poor Laomann?"

The men looked at one another, confused, then stared at him.

"Dinna listen to him..." said Catriona.

With her arms and legs turning into icicles, Catriona watched all five men turn to James and surround him in a semicircle.

"Who are ye?" said one of them.

"Ah," James said. "You know. Just a friendly time traveler. Came from the future to kill your laird off."

"James!" Catrìona cried in horror.

Finn's eyes narrowed and he frowned, studying James.

"God's arse," said one of the men. "A time traveler..."

"Yeah. I can speak to Highland faeries and was born hundreds of years in the future. What do you say, does it sound like proof to you that demons exist and your laird is being killed off by them?"

"Aye," said one of the men holding the pitchfork. "As a matter of fact, it does."

"Besides, we really dinna like the Sassenachs here," said Gille-Crìosd. "They've been killing our kind for years."

He jabbed the pitchfork at James, who jumped to the side, grabbed the handle, and pulled it towards himself. The man lost his balance, let go of the pitchfork, and fell right into the mud, facedown. One of the men threw a rock at James, who beat it off to the side with the pitchfork. The man with the dagger came towards James, slicing the air in front of his stomach left-right-left-right.

James grabbed the metal tines of the fork and jabbed the man in the stomach with the wooden handle. He fell back into the mud, cursing.

"Stop this nonsense!" cried Catrìona. "He's nae a witcher and he's nae a demon caster." Did she fully believe it herself? She didn't know. What she knew was that she had to protect James. Because he was protecting her friend. "And surely, he's nae a time traveler. He's a guest of the clan and is helping me to find the real murderer."

But no one was listening to her. The men kept fighting, and Gille-Crìosd was scrambling to get up. *God forgive me.* Catrìona took his dagger and pressed it to his throat.

"Tell them to stop, Gille-Crìosd. I am the sister of the laird and of Angus Mackenzie for whom ye fought yer whole life. Ye owe loyalty to my brother, and I'm telling ye, ye need to stop them before they hurt a guest of the clan."

Part of her wondered what was she doing, threatening her

own clansman when she was already doing penance for her previous violence, but she couldn't let him see her doubt.

Gille-Crìosd grunted and shook his head. "Aye. Stop, lads."

The men froze and looked at him.

"Aye, stop. He's a guest of the clan." Catrìona nodded and stretched out her hand to help him get up.

"Since when does the clan invite Sassenachs to be their guests?" mumbled Ailig.

Catrìona helped Gille-Crìosd stand and gave him his dagger back, then wiped her hands that had become muddy from touching him.

"And dinna dare to hurt Finn," she said. "He did nothing to Laomann."

If anyone had done anything, it was her. She'd made and given him that tisane that had almost killed him.

"Aye, mistress," they said, heads bowed but eyes angry and defiant.

"God will show who has cast demons," said Ailig over his shoulder as the five of them walked away. "And that witcher will burn in hell."

If anyone would burn in hell, it would be her. James had said thou shalt not kill. And yet, she had killed all those men in Delny Castle a few sennights ago as she was rescuing Angus. She had put a blade to James's throat and to Gille-Crìosd's. How could she be so quick to embrace violence and yet plan to serve God as a nun? At this rate, she would be doing penance for all eternity.

James came closer and extended a hand to Finn, helping him up. "Are you all right?" he asked Catrìona.

"Aye, of course I am," she said, shrugging off her conflicting emotions. "What came over you, Finn? Are you really trying to leave?"

Finn sighed, his shoulders hunched. He nodded. "I am."

James put his hand on the cart, the strong muscles of his forearm bulging from under the rolled-up sleeve of his tunic. "I have to be honest, that doesn't look great for you, Finn. It makes you look guilty."

But James didn't say it like he blamed Finn. He said it like he felt for the man. James was very kind, she realized. Even if he didn't believe in God, he was still kind. He'd tried not to harm the men, she'd noticed. Only to disarm them. He'd been protecting Finn.

And he'd saved her from that fall down the stairs.

He wanted to find the person who'd poisoned Laomann.

Who was this man? This sharp, kind, nonbelieving man who could make fire from an orange box and who smelled like distant lands and brought small lightning bolts through his touch?

Was he a witcher? Was he a warrior?

One thing was for sure—he was a mystery. A mystery that was flipping her whole world upside down.

She didn't need that. Not when Tadhg had come back, and she'd learned he did love her and had tried to come for her nine years ago.

Not when her brother's life was in danger.

Not when she was preparing to enter the nunnery.

What she needed was to concentrate on finding out what had happened. That was impossible if Finn was gone.

She put a hand on Finn's elbow. "You must stay, Finn. You must clear your name and answer our questions. You must come with us to the castle and canna leave it until we find the truth."

Fear widened Finn's milky gray eyes. "Lass—"

"She's right," James said. "I'd like to arrest you now for your own good, but I can't. So let me strongly suggest you do come with us and you do cooperate."

Arrest? Catrìona frowned, mayhap that was what constables did in Oxford. James had such a peculiar manner of speech.

Finn nodded, but she didn't like the look of complete defeat on his face. And as they walked in the direction of the castle, she wondered if it was possible that her dear friend could be the murderer, after all.

CHAPTER 12

"Catrìona! He woke up!"

Her skirts flapping, Mairead ran towards James, Catrìona, and Finn as they walked through the inner bailey towards the main keep. Catrìona had given orders for the guards to not let Finn out and to see to his safety.

Mairead's face was red and her eyes as wide as an owl's as she stopped before them. "He woke up," she repeated breathlessly.

Catrìona gasped and looked at James. She clutched his arm and beamed at him. Her eyes sparkled with delight, and James's chest squeezed to the degree of a sweet ache. He put his hand over hers before he could stop himself. Something in him became lighter, seeing her smiling like this.

He didn't let a woman in easily, and this gesture felt very intimate—like they were sharing this joy, like they were a team...

He'd never felt like part of a team with a woman. He'd warned the few girlfriends he'd had that he wasn't looking for a long-term relationship. His job as a cop, which always required him to put work first, and his awkward childhood, which he'd never talked about with anyone apart from Emily, were big hurdles to overcome.

He'd always thought once the right woman came along, he'd open up.

But women came and went. They got their hopes up, and he broke their hearts. One ex-girlfriend had said his emotional unavailability was the reason he'd die miserable and alone. Another one had thrown the clichéd "married to your job" accusation.

But he wasn't so emotionally unavailable now, nor had he put his job first. He'd stayed to protect Catriona and to help her.

And to his surprise, Catriona caused a flood of emotions that whirled around like a swarm of bees in his stomach. He'd never felt that with any of the women he'd been with in his own century. Which excited and worried him at the same time.

He fancied her, despite their differences, which were huge no matter the era. Her religiosity and his stubborn atheism. Though she was stubborn, too—she stubbornly believed her friends could do no wrong. And he refused to accept any religious or spiritual beliefs, determined to find logic where Catriona relied on faith.

"Come quick!" Mairead said.

Catriona let go of his hand, leaving him strangely empty. Lifting the skirt of her dress, she ran up the hill towards the tower. James followed her, climbing the stairs as fast as he could after her.

He panted hard when they stood in Laomann's bedroom. The laird was pale and looked dehydrated, his lips cracked and dry. He had dark circles under his eyes and seemed a little woozy.

"Thank God!" Catriona exclaimed, crossed herself, and kissed the wooden cross on her neck. "Lord Almighty, thank ye for bringing him back..." she whispered as her eyes grew damp.

She sat at Laomann's bed and took his hand in hers. Mairead was smiling, clutching both hands to her chest.

"Sister..." said Laomann in a rough voice.

"How are you feeling?" asked James.

Laomann frowned at him.

"Um..." He cleared his throat. "Nae so good."

"Of course," said Catrìona. "Dinna speak just yet, ye need yer strength back. Ye must drink and ye must eat if ye can manage."

"Aye."

"It would be great if I could question you," said James.

"There's some water here," said Mairead as she brought a clay jug and a cup to Catrìona. "If ye want to give it to him. I'll go ask a servant to fetch some bannock."

"Broth would be best," said Catrìona. "He needs something liquid and easy for the body to take in."

"Aye." Mairead kissed Laomann on the forehead. "I'll fetch it."

As she left, Catrìona handed Laomann the cup with water and held his head up as he drank a few sips.

"How much do you remember?" said James.

"Who are ye?" said Laomann, wincing.

"'Tis Sir James of Oxford," said Catrìona. "Do ye remember anything from the day ye got sick? Ye met him already."

Laomann's brow furrowed as he looked into the distance. "I... I dinna ken."

Could he have brain damage? James didn't know enough to determine if he had been in a coma or not.

Catrìona locked her bright-blue eyes on James. "Ye can trust him."

James's heart could burst from those simple words. A shadow of a smile touched her lips, an expression that could crack his chest open and fill it with light. Brody Guthenberg and the cult had taught him not to trust people easily, and her trust was the most precious gift.

"So can you try to remember something?" said James. "Anything from that day. If you were poisoned, the person who did this to you is still out there, which means you may still be in danger, as well as others."

As well as Catrìona... The thought chilled his spine.

Laomann cleared his throat. "I remember the morning. Raghnall and Tadhg came in the morning, wounded. Then Catrìona tended to Tadhg, I remember that."

"Was that in the room where Tadhg is now?" said James.

"Aye," said Catrìona as she brought the cup to Laomann's mouth again.

Was James imagining it, or did she seem to be avoiding looking at him?

"What did you do there, Laomann?" said James.

Laomann cleared his throat and fell back on the pillows. "I dinna ken exactly. I kent I couldna have left Catrìona with him alone. And I turned out to be useful, anyway. I gave Tadhg my waterskin with uisge."

Catrìona was looking pointedly at her clasped hands and kept silent. Laomann was grimacing, looking as though his brain was working hard to remember. Catrìona didn't want to share something.

And in James's experience, when witnesses didn't want to talk about something, that was exactly the thing they should talk about.

James's job was to get them to talk.

Only, he wasn't sure he wanted to know what Catrìona might say.

He came to the bed and sat at the edge facing Catrìona. When she finally met his gaze, he knew for certain she was hiding something.

"Catrìona," James said softly. "I can see you don't want to tell me something... But if you want to help your brother and protect the rest of your clan, you must tell me. Please."

She inhaled sharply. "'Tis nae ye that I'm cautious about telling."

James looked at Laomann, who was frowning at Catrìona. When she said that, Laomann's frown straightened into an expression of realization.

"Ye ken?" he whispered.

Catrìona nodded, her mouth in a straight line.

"What?" said James.

"Oh, Catrìona..." mumbled Laomann as he covered his face with his hands and massaged it. "I'm so sorry."

"What?" repeated James, his heart thumping. This was the clue, he could sense it. Just like when he was fourteen and he recorded Brody say in a sudden onrush of pride how he'd become rich by taking the donations of the cult members and how James would never understand the power of suggestions, the power of charisma.

Because James was no one to him. He'd never considered him his son, just someone he'd fathered.

Like God, Brody had said, *who fathered all humankind. God doesn't know every human he fathers.* And so Brody didn't know every person he'd fathered, either.

James had felt the pain of rejection combined with the excitement that he'd gotten the crucial piece of evidence that would finally end Brody Guthenberg and his cult.

"What happened?"

Catrìona sighed. "Laomann had found out about my engagement to Tadhg."

Laomann nodded slightly, looking even more pained. "I heard them making plans to run away and elope. And I told Father."

The thought of Catrìona with Tadhg still tasted like acid, just as it had the first time she'd told him. But he didn't know what was worse, thinking of her with another man or imagining her becoming a nun. She'd said Laomann had wanted her to wait, hoping she'd change her mind. Could she still change her mind? Should she decide to get married, Tadhg would probably be the best choice.

"Did you love him?" said James, his voice rough and his throat aching.

Knowing the answer to this became suddenly crucial—to something, and he didn't know what. To his survival. To his sanity. To this case.

She looked up at him, her mouth curved in a tight, sad line. The sadness in her eyes broke his heart.

"Aye," she said.

So at one point in her life she'd been in love, engaged, and ready to have a family, lead a normal life.

With Tadhg.

Tadhg, who'd come back and now lay in a room nearby, wolf-eyed and undoubtedly still possessive about her... *Cat*. James hadn't heard anyone else call her that.

Laomann groaned.

"Are ye all right?" said Catrìona.

"My head..." he said. "It still hurts like someone's pounding a hammer against it."

"Didn't Tadhg say the same?" asked James.

"Aye," Catrìona said. "He did complain about terrible headaches. But they're gone now."

"What else did you feel, Laomann?" said James.

"Before I lost consciousness, everything became blurry. My heart beat so fast I thought it would break my rib cage. My mouth was dry and burned, even though I kept drinking, and then...forgive me, sister, it was hard to piss."

Catrìona waved her hand in a "doesn't matter" gesture. "Tadhg also mentioned the burning mouth and the heart beating hard."

James nodded thoughtfully. "Did he complain about difficulty urinating?"

"Aye. But nae about the blurriness."

"But he also didn't go into a coma. If he did ingest the same poison, it was probably a smaller quantity. Anything else, Laomann?"

Laomann sighed and looked somewhere with wide eyes. "I saw demons. Flying demons around me, black clouds, and I knew they wanted to take my life and to bring my soul to hell."

"Hallucinations..." muttered James. "It must be some sort of hallucinogen, too. But Tadhg didn't hallucinate?"

Catrìona shook her head. "He didna say anything about visions."

Laomann kept talking. "There was also this strange numbness and tingling all through my arms and legs, and I couldna lift a finger. I still barely can..."

James looked at Catrìona. "Tadhg was also very weak, wasn't he? We must find out if he felt the numbness, too. But so far, it sounds like it could be the same poison. Do you know what could have caused all those symptoms?"

She slowly shook her head. "Nae, I dinna ken poisons. Mayhap Finn..."

Laomann moaned again, holding his head.

"All right." Catrìona cleared her throat. "I'm going to get my medicine basket and I'll be back. I'll give ye something for the pain."

Laomann widened his eyes at her.

Catrìona stood up. "Brother..." she said. "I wilna hurt ye."

"Aye, of course ye wouldna... It must be Finn."

Her face got an edge of fierceness. She raised her chin stubbornly. "I still ken he didna do it. I ken because I have faith."

The words struck James like lightning.

I know because I have faith. His mother used to say exactly that when he'd question her about why they were in the cult when after so many years of being promised success they still ate roasted squirrels he'd hunted with his bow and arrows and poorly grown turnips. All she could show for herself were daily affirmations, prayers, and group meditations. Her dream to be a movie star meant nothing. She still lived in an ancient house that smelled like mold and had no electricity or central heating. She never even went to auditions.

Faith... The word had been the corrosion of his soul for fourteen years. The word that meant his mother would leave him and his sister locked in the house alone. The word that for James had meant blind trust, manipulation, and, in the end, addiction and even insanity.

That was how it had ended for his mother, anyway.

His sister and he were the by-products of that belief. His pregnant sister, who only had him left and needed him back in the twenty-first century like never before.

"You can't be serious, Catrìona," he said. "You need to see the facts. You can't just blindly believe in anything. Facts and proof are what knowledge is."

She blinked at him, frowning, tears glistening. "Sometimes, Sir James, faith is the only way to really ken. Because sometimes, facts and knowledge are the things that would break ye."

She marched out of the room in a hurried stride. James wondered how it was possible that a woman could be so different from him.

And so intriguing.

CHAPTER 13

T*he next day...*

Catrìona stood up from her embroidery and walked to Mairead, who was bouncing Ualan on her knee. "Let me take him," Catrìona said. "Ye poor thing, ye're exhausted. Every mother needs a wee bit of a rest."

Mairead sighed and smiled at her. Sir James, who was questioning the annoyed Raghnall at the farther corner of the private lord's chamber, looked up at her and stopped talking. She had had this feeling around him, like he was aware of her every move, like he was watching her every breath. But not suspiciously.

On the contrary, it was like he was adoring her, admiring her.

She blushed at the thought that this handsome, mysterious man would think that of her.

Mairead gave a kiss to Ualan, who grinned his most charming five-tooth grin and squealed.

"I do need a wee sleep, sister," said Mairead. "I couldna rest, listening for Laomann's breathing. Didna ken if he'd keep breathing or nae. 'Tis a miracle he's alive and came back to us. God is good."

Catrìona picked up Ualan and gave him a tickle. The lad giggled his sweet baby giggle, delighted. He was an easy baby, and as Catrìona pressed his warm, heavy body against her, her heart ached. As a nun, she'd never hold a bairn of her own. She'd never be able to feel the quickening of life deep in her womb, and feel it grow and flourish within her. She'd never hold her husband's hand and watch their son or daughter sleep in their cot.

Feeling Sir James's eyes again, she looked up at him and stilled as their gazes locked. He stared at her holding the bairn with some sort of intensity that she couldn't decipher. Like a longing, and a loss. Did he have a wife? Or a bairn of his own? Did he want any of that?

Mairead interrupted the silence between them as she walked past by Catrìona. "He wasna outside today. Mayhap ye can take him out into the bailey?"

"I'll take him into the grove by the village. I need to gather some herbs for my basket."

"But how will ye hold him and gather herbs?" said Mairead.

Sir James stood up from the bench across the room, leaving Raghnall glaring at him. "I'll help. I wouldn't let you go by yourself, anyway."

Raghnall shook his head. "If anyone should protect my sister, 'tis me. Nae ye, a Sassenach."

Catrìona raised her brows. "Brother, I dinna need your protection. Sir James, ye're forgetting yerself. No one asked ye to let me do anything."

Raghnall stood up and walked towards the door, but before he walked out, he turned to James. "My sister is right. No one asked ye to do anything. So mayhap 'tis best ye're on yer way."

With that, he left the room.

James let out a long sigh, watching Raghnall leave, then returned his attention to Catrìona. He chuckled, something about his half smile cocky. "I just meant, with a murderer around, I wouldn't want you and the baby to be alone, unprotected."

Mairead's eyes glistened with mischief. "'Tis a good thought, sister. Aye, Sir James, ye thought well about it. Dinna ye think, Catrìona?"

Catrìona couldn't find a single reason to say no to him. He was right, the killer was still around, and she and the bairn would be vulnerable.

"Aye," she said. "Ye may come. Thank ye. But I'll take my dagger just in case. I wilna take any chances with my nephew." She prayed God would forgive her for protecting one so small and innocent if there was a need.

Sir James came towards her and stretched his arms out to take Ualan. "Come here, lad." Ualan eyed him with suspicion, but as Sir James grinned the broadest smile Catrìona had ever seen on him, Ualan, as friendly as he was, grinned in response. Surprisingly, he stretched his wee fat arms out to James. As James took him and bounced him on his hip, he turned to Catrìona.

"'Tis good," she said. To distract herself from the weakness in her knees and the hard beating of her heart from seeing him with the bairn, she turned away and went to one of the beautifully carved chests to look for a sling. "Go lie down, Mairead."

Mairead kissed her son on the cheek and left the room. While James was holding the bairn, who was exploring James's long stubble that, Catrìona thought, suited him very much, Catrìona gathered things: the sling for carrying Ualan, a basket for collecting herbs, food for Ualan, and a waterskin. She made sure her dagger was securely tucked into her belt.

As she helped James put on the sling and safely put Ualan into it, the occasional brushes against the man's arms and chest were like strokes of fire. Jesu, how could he affect her so? For a moment, she had an image of James and her, getting ready for an outing with a bairn of their own. The thought brought deep warmth and a wave of tingling through her, something homey and a sense of love and security. A sense of peace and safety. And that everything was right with the world.

How strange. She couldn't feel anything like that towards a man she'd known for only a few days, could she? There were so many reasons to stay away from him, to be careful. He was a Sassenach, and he did have strange objects in his possession, like that orange box that produced fire, and his rich, impractical clothes. He didn't believe in God, whereas her faith defined who she was.

If she were to decide against becoming a nun, the obvious choice of a husband would be Tadhg. She knew him, she trusted him, and she'd loved him once. He had loved her, too, and he had come for her. He was a Highlander, as she was, and he had been part of her clan until her father had chased him away.

In that respect, he had much in common with Raghnall. Her brother often had that dark, mysterious look that made her wonder what he had lived through during the years away. She didn't really know him anymore.

If she was thinking about bairns and marriage, it should be with Tadhg.

Not James. She shook her head, reminding herself that she shouldn't be thinking of any man that way.

When Ualan was securely attached to James's back, she put a woolen hat on the lad and tied the straps under his chin. Ualan frowned and pulled on one of the straps. Then he found its edge and put it into his mouth with an expression of the highest concentration. She found herself grinning. The bairn melted her heart. James looked at her over his shoulder, and their eyes locked again. His were soft and shiny, and some sort of understanding and connection ran between the two of them, making it impossible to look away.

"Ready?" James asked.

She cleared her throat, trying to break the spell his gaze seemed to have on her. "Aye."

They went to the jetty, and one of the men who'd delivered firewood from Dornie and was on his way back took them in his boat. As they went through Dornie's streets, the village around them was alive with people talking about the Highland games, the rhythmic ringing of the blacksmith's hammer, and the clamor of chickens, geese, and ducks.

By the time they reached the grove, Ualan was asleep, his full pink mouth open and so sweet. Catrìona suppressed an impulse to kiss the bairn all over his cute, chubby face.

Tall trees rose out of the earth and brushed the sky, and pine cones dotted the grassy ground. The grove was quiet, save for birds chirping and wind rustling in the leaves. Branches snapped sharply under Catrìona's and James's feet as they walked deeper into the grove. She welcomed the familiar scent of fresh grass, tree sap, and flowers.

"What are you looking for exactly?" said James.

"Black currants."

"Must be exhausting, to always go searching for things once you run out."

She glanced at him. "Someone has to do it. They canna magically appear in my basket."

The word "magical" weighed heavy in her chest.

James stepped over a thin, fallen tree. "Right. There's not always a traveling herb seller around. Is this how you spent your childhood? Gathering herbs and flowers?"

"Aye, 'tis something my mother and I used to do. Among other things. Weaving, of course. Embroidery. Managing food and servants and making sure the castle is as clean as it can be."

James nodded. "What happened to your mum?"

"She...she became pregnant again. She wasna young nae more. I was fourteen years of age then, and I'm the youngest. She lost the bairn, 'twas very early. But the rot stayed in her womb, and she died a few days later, feverish and pale. She lost much blood."

"I'm so sorry."

She crouched by a black currant bush and began picking the leaves and the berries. "She's with God now. Tadhg helped me so much back then. He prayed with me and talked to me. My brothers grieved in their own ways, and I certainly couldna have turned to my father. Is yer mother alive? Do ye have family in Oxford?"

The scent of black currants filled her nostrils as she broke the stems and leaves.

"My mother also died," he said, suddenly serious. "My father never wanted anything to do with me. I do have a sister who's pregnant. Emily."

She stopped picking the berries for a moment and studied him. "What made ye do this... How did ye call it—detective? 'Tis probably something people in Oxford do?"

Because James was standing still, Ualan wasn't being rocked anymore, and he made a small, sleepy sound. James started bouncing gently in one place.

"Some," he said. "I like being a detective because I like solving mysteries. I like facts, I like numbers, I like information. It was my mother's troubles that made me want to always keep a cool head and think logically. To ask if things are really how they seem, and find order in madness."

She sighed. Facts and numbers...she couldn't even write. She'd always wanted to read the Bible, write down the herbal recipes she'd learned from her mother, from Finn and from Abbess Laurentia in the St. Margaret's nunnery.

"But isna it boring?" she said. "Facts and numbers and nae mystery?"

He chuckled. "I help people. That's what I like about it, also. Those who are in trouble, who've been attacked, or robbed, or need protection."

She met his gaze. "I like helping people, too. 'Tis the main reason why I want to be a nun. To heal people and serve God and take care of those who need help, who have no one else to care for them. I'd like to be that person."

He blinked, his eyes suddenly dark and glossy. "I don't think I've ever met anyone quite like you. There's not a bad bone in your body, Catrìona, is there?"

The words, as sweet and kind as they were, weighed on her heart. She looked away, tears stinging her eyes. Although there was still plenty to pick from the black currant bush, she stood up. If she stayed in one place, she'd fall apart.

"Ye're quite wrong, Sir James." She looked down at her hands, then straightened her shoulders and met his eyes. "I have sinned gravely. I've broken the vow I made to myself."

He walked to her and said nothing for a while, his eyes like warm honey on her. She started breathing easier. "Are you talking about the men you killed?"

"Aye."

"But you did it to—"

"To save my brother. I'm sure there must have been a better way, a more peaceful way to resolve that. I should have looked for it."

"But surely, you don't regret saving your brother, do you? You helped your family. It's not like you craved the blood and the lives of those men."

"Aye, I ken all that, Sir James."

"Come, sit here," he said softly and took her hand in his, pulling her towards a fallen log.

The touch of his big, warm hand sent a tingling sensation up her arm and into her chest. Feeling dazed, she followed him. When they sat on the log, Ualan fussed a little, then sighed and sagged peacefully against James's back.

James held her palm in both of his. Her skin was burning, melting.

He looked deep into her eyes. "I know murderers, Catrìona, people who've killed others for some sort of gain. You're not one of them. You're one of the most beautiful people I've ever met. Inside and out."

Her cheeks were ablaze from his compliment. She took in a

deep breath and asked God for forgiveness for enjoying James's words and for what she would confess next.

"In truth, deep down, I dinna regret it. I liked the feeling of strength and the power to be able to protect my family. So much that part of me wants more. Wants to be that powerful always. Wants to stand on my own feet. Not to listen to an abbess or a priest or a husband. But be my own person and live my life as I wish."

His eyes shone with respect and appreciation. "You're probably the most remarkable woman I've ever met."

No one had ever told her she was remarkable. No one had ever said she was beautiful inside. She liked being remarkable and she liked being beautiful inside. How would it feel to know every day that she was both of those things? How would her life be if she knew she was important and knew she had value whether someone needed her for something or not?

Would she even want to be a nun?

He had complimented her on her strength, on something every man she knew would condemn. A woman should be modest. She should always serve a man. She shouldn't be remarkable or take the role of a warrior protecting her family. Those domains belonged to men.

But she wanted to feel strong, and he appreciated independent women. Her arms itched to wrap around his neck. Her lips ached to kiss him.

But that was temptation. That was lust. And if she gave in to that she'd commit yet another sin.

With great difficulty, she broke the contact, stood up, and marched farther into the grove, not looking back for fear of rushing into his arms. "You're wrong, Sir James. There is nothing remarkable about me. I was born to serve my father and improve his position in the world. Having failed at that, I will serve God and improve the lives of others in whatever small ways I can."

CHAPTER 14

T he next day...

JAMES PULLED BACK THE BOWSTRING, ENJOYING THE BURN OF his muscles from the exercise. The feel of the bow in his hands was strangely invigorating. He hadn't touched a bow and arrow in seventeen years. This bow was big, the weapon of a real man, not the small hunting one he'd had.

He'd always been a natural with archery. It had come easy to him when one of the cult members had made him a bow and taught him how to shoot. As a child and teenager, he'd enjoyed it, finding release in the physical activity and the intense focus required. And it brought him joy and satisfaction to hit his targets almost every time.

After the cult was disbanded, he'd stopped. Archery became one of the memories he'd wanted to forget together with the rest of his experience.

But being surrounded by archers in the castle, he'd asked one of the sentinels if he could hold the weapon for a short while. And now, standing alone in the middle of the curtain wall, he sighted along the arrow in the fading daylight, wishing he could find a target and let the arrow fly. He shook his head, remembering his strange longing for just such a moment when he'd first seen the castle, back in his own time. If he'd only known what awaited him...

Twenty feet to his right was the main keep tower, which connected to the curtain wall, and about thirty feet to his left was a smaller tower on which there were a couple of sentinels. Fifteen or so feet down was nothing but grass and a few bushes. There were no safe targets in sight.

"Who are ye trying to shoot?" said a man's voice behind James's back.

James lowered the bow and turned.

It was Tadhg MacCowen. He was using a stick as a sort of crutch to help him stand. One leg was bandaged and he obviously didn't want to put any weight on it—his toes were barely touching the floor. The bandage that had covered his eye before was gone and there was a sutured cut over his eyebrow.

James leaned the bow and arrow against the parapet. "Just feeling the bow. What are you doing here, anyway? Are you even well enough to stand and walk to the wall?"

"I'm all right," growled Tadhg. "Looking for Catrìona."

Bugger. James had spent the day with her yesterday, but hadn't seen much of her today. Every time he'd seen her passing by, his heart had careened like a bloody ship in a storm. And she'd barely cast him a glance and even seemed to avoid his eyes. No doubt the result of their conversation yesterday.

"Right," said James, trying his best to appear nonchalant. "Anything I can do for you?"

Tadhg threw him a doubtful glance. "Nae. Just wanted to ask if she's all right. She's been running around all day."

"The day when you arrived, did you notice anything strange?"

"Nae. I was taken to that bedchamber right away. Catrìona stitched me up and cleaned my wounds, then I was drunk and asleep. I could barely move."

"Did anyone else come with you and Raghnall?"

"Nae."

"So that day, when Laomann's symptoms began, the new people in the castle were you and Raghnall."

"And Finn," added Tadhg. "And ye."

Yes, of course Finn, and him. They had all appeared on the same day, four days ago.

Four days... Guilt stabbed him in the gut at the thought of Emily. How was she? He had promised to be there for the birth, so there was still time. But he wouldn't forgive himself if she was in trouble and he wasn't there for her.

Still. People here needed him, too. Lives were at risk and the murderer was still on the loose. Finn was a known suspect. But James didn't know much about Raghnall at all.

"You were a clansman before," said James. "So you must have seen how Raghnall and Laomann were together. Do you know if Raghnall has anything against Laomann?"

Tadhg raised his brows. "Of course he does. Raghnall was chased away from the clan and Laomann is still nae taking him back, even though their da is dead. If Angus were laird, I'm sure it would be different. Those two have always been as thick as thieves."

James could see better now why Raghnall and Laomann were at such odds.

"So that day when you arrived, Laomann was in the room when Catrìona treated you, right?"

"Aye."

"How did he seem to you?"

Tadhg shrugged. "Dinna ken. I havena seen him for nine years."

"Laomann said he gave you his waterskin of uisge, which is

something no one else touched apart from you two. Did the uisge taste different to you?"

Tadhg blinked. "Ye think the poison was in the uisge?"

"It might have been. You also had Catrìona's tisane, didn't you? But probably not the same one she'd made for Laomann as you had different symptoms initially."

Tadhg looked into the darkness and shrugged. "The uisge tasted the same as always."

"I heard you met with Raghnall while he was being ambushed and helped him?"

"Aye."

"Can you talk me through that day? Where was this? What happened exactly? I'd like to confirm a few details."

Raghnall had already briefly told him what had happened then, but his mistrust had led to a reluctance to tell James all the details, and he'd seemed to want to get out of the conversation quickly.

Tadhg held his eyes for a time, then nodded. He turned away from James and looked at the dying sunset. Twilight was getting thicker by the moment.

"I was on my way from the Isle of Skye, where my clan is."

"That's Ruaidhrí, right?"

"Aye."

"Weren't you in clan Mackenzie before?" He cleared his throat. "When you were engaged to Catrìona?"

Tadhg looked at him with a masculine arrogance. "Aye, 'tis right."

"Was your engagement connected to why you left the clan?"

Tadhg sighed deeply and ran his fingers over the rough stone of the parapet. "Aye, 'twas. To tell it quickly, her father found out and chased me away from the clan. Her father, Laird Kenneth Og, was a...a bad man," he finished.

"Right..." said James with a frown. He knew all about bad fathers.

"He wanted to marry her off to a rich, noble man. Never treated her right. She'd always been a possession to him, a bonnie wee thing to use to expand his position in Scotland."

James swallowed a hard knot that felt like a rock.

"What did he do to her?" he growled.

Among Brody's nineteen children, he'd had twelve girls and seven boys. Every year, on Brody's birthday, all his children were supposed to gather and show off to him how they used his methods of belief and meditation to advance in life. Though how exactly children, from toddlers to teenagers, were supposed to advance in life through meditation and the power of belief was hard to imagine. They were all supposed to wow the man who'd contributed to their conception. It was a sort of a talent show. Girls and boys sang and danced and showed him their watercolors. And based on whatever criteria Brody saw fit, he chose one of them to come and sit on his lap and talk to him all evening long.

James had recognized the sick need to impress the man who meant absolutely nothing to him, despite the unfair competition, despite the unreasonable requests for perfection.

His sister had been even more drawn in. She was younger and she didn't have the same cold mind as James. She'd wanted to impress her father so much, she'd cried every year, every time he'd skipped her. He'd never even acknowledged her. And yet, she'd kept repeating those affirmations with her mother every night.

If Kenneth Og had been anything like Brody—and from what Catrìona had said, James knew he was worse, violent— James was glad Tadhg had been there to save Catrìona from him.

"Everything ye may imagine, Sir James," said Tadhg darkly. "He beat her mother and her brothers. Her, too. I saw bruises, though I ken her brother Angus took most of it for all of them. Then her mother died. I prayed with her. Prayed and prayed. 'Tis the only thing that got her through it. 'Tis how we fell in love."

Love... The word slashed across James's chest like a razor blade. They had been in love.

And even more than that.

They had the same spiritual beliefs. They connected deeply on that level.

The deepest level possible. Intimate. Vulnerable.

Religion was a big part of her life, whereas James rejected it completely. And he was a rational man. He knew people who didn't share the same religious beliefs were doomed.

He also knew that part of his rejection of spirituality and anything supernatural was emotional. It was about his upbringing, about the way he and his mother and his sister had been manipulated.

Only, realizing it and doing something about it were two different things.

And yet, look at that, he had traveled in time with the help of a Highland faerie. His father would have rejoiced.

"When you were chased away, you went to the Isle of Skye?"

Tadhg picked up a small stone from the parapet and threw it beyond the castle walls. He had dark-blond hair and a pleasant, handsome face that had probably won him plenty of women. Certainly Catrìona.

"Why there?" asked James.

"I have distant family there."

"And did they take you in?"

"Aye. I swore allegiance to the clan. Told the laird the whole story. Then served on their trading ships. Ruaidhrí are traders. Come from Viking roots. Strong ships, they control the Irish sea. I served on those ships for years."

"And how did you come to encounter Raghnall on that day?"

Tadhg picked up another small rock and threw it into the grayish abyss. He kept silent, only crickets chirped distantly, and the stone swished as it landed somewhere in the leaves on the ground below.

"I was on my way to trade in Evanton."

"By horse? Isn't it easier to reach the land by boat?"

Tadhg shook his head, clearly losing his patience. "Look, man, I dinna ken what ye're looking for. Mayhap 'tis me who needs to be asking questions to ye."

"Me?"

"Aye. Ye appear out of nowhere, with strange clothes and manner of speech. No one kens ye. And the same day, Laomann falls ill and almost dies. At least I used to be a clansman. Besides, I wouldna ever do anything to harm Catriona or her family. But ye... Ye may be a Sassenach spy. Ye may be an assassin that Euphemia of Ross sent to kill the laird of clan Mackenzie in the worst possible moment. Who kens ye, really?"

James cleared his throat at the outburst, momentarily speechless.

"The more information I have, the better the chances are to discover the real murderer."

Tadhg stared at him. "Aye. The real murderer."

Men appeared from the main keep and walked down the wall towards the other tower. This was, perhaps, the change of sentinels. He hadn't had dinner, and the aroma of cooked food was coming from the kitchen just below the wall, in the inner bailey. Warriors passed by, brushing rudely against James's shoulder.

"All right?" he said to their backs, but they ignored him. Did they think he was the murderer? James wondered.

"Thanks for your help," said James. "Do you need help getting back?"

"Nae. I can manage."

James picked up the bow and arrow and walked down the wall to the main keep tower, wondering how much of what Tadhg had told him was true. He wished he were from this century—there was so much he didn't know about how things worked here. Before he entered the tower, he threw a last glance back at Tadhg. His silhouette was dark against the dusk sky, staring into the distance.

As James began descending, he noticed a tall figure move away from the tower on the opposite side of the wall. Must be one of the guards.

CHAPTER 15

A man's scream pierced the air from somewhere outside the slit window of the great hall.

Catrìona raised her head from her tray containing a single bannock, the only dinner she'd get tonight in her penance. Men looked around, bringing their hands to the hilts of their swords. Their faces were somber in the orange light of the fire from the fireplace and braziers standing between the tables.

Catrìona dropped the bannock on the table. "Oh dear God, Laomann..."

She jumped to her feet from the bench and, picking up her skirts, ran towards the exit of the hall.

"Mistress, wait..." Men followed her, heavy steps pounding against the floor.

As Catrìona ran into the dark landing, the scream repeated, quieter. Mairead looked from the corner of the upper landing, her head illuminated by the torch she was holding.

"What happened?" Mairead asked.

"'Tis nae Laomann?" Catrìona asked.

"Nae. He's sleeping."

Good Lord, was it James? Catrìona's heart pounded so hard, it felt painful.

"Someone fell from the wall!" came a cry from the outside.

A chill ran through her. *Oh, please let it nae be James!*

"Go!" she said to the men behind her. "I'll just get my medicine basket."

"Go, lads," one of them said. "I'll wait for ye, mistress. I canna let ye walk alone in the darkness."

When she had her basket, they hurried down the stairs and through the bailey, sprinting towards a gathering of torches where the guards must have found the victim. Her stomach squeezed from worry, and she prayed that she wouldn't find James there.

But as they joined the circle of the men, she saw that Tadhg lay, holding his side, wincing in pain. A wave of shame rolled over her that she hadn't considered him and that she was so relieved not to see James lying there, wounded or dead. She quickly examined Tadhg, but there were no open wounds and no broken limbs as far as she could see.

"Take him back to the castle," she said. "Carefully! And someone go find Finn."

Once they were back in Tadhg's bedchamber, Catrìona could examine him properly.

"Broken ribs..." Catrìona muttered.

Flickering candlelight danced on the hard muscles of Tadhg's torso and stomach, battle scars silvery against his mostly pale skin. A purple bruise the size of a hand was right under his right pectoral muscle. She pressed gently on the area, and Tadhg sucked in air. At least it wasn't hard, which meant the rib hadn't punctured any organs and there was no internal bleeding.

As Catrìona felt Tadhg's bruise, he gave a long, suppressed groan of pain. His handsome face paled.

"Aye," she muttered, standing up. "Mayhap cracked. Yer wound had opened up, so I'll need to stitch ye again. At least ye didna break yer arm or leg. Does yer head hurt?"

He shook his head, looking at her with some sort of intense

emotion—sweet and lovely, and so apparent, it made her want to turn away.

"Is everything all right?" said a male voice.

She turned to the open door. James stood there. The light of the torch in the landing behind him cast shadows on his handsome face. God, how could he be so tall and so...imposing. Like he took all the space, sucked in all the air, muffled all the sounds around her but his voice. Was it his demonic magic, or was it just her stupid heart?

"Tadhg had an accident," she said.

"What happened?" James asked, walking into the room.

Catrìona turned to Tadhg; at least looking at him and tending at his wounds would distract her from James.

She rummaged in her medicine basket for linen. She'd need to bandage his torso to make sure the ribs were in place.

"Someone pushed me off the wall," Tadhg said.

James and Catrìona both looked at him.

"Pushed you off the wall?" repeated James. "When?"

"Just now," said Tadhg.

James paled. "Who were you with?"

Tadhg gave him a long, hard glare. "No one but ye."

Catrìona stared at James. "Ye?"

"Tadhg and I had a little chat on top of the wall," said James, still staring at Tadhg, as though trying to convey some sort of message with his eyes.

Tadhg didn't reply for a few moments, looking at James heavily. Catrìona's heart thumped hard against her rib cage. James couldn't... No, he couldn't have done it, please God.

Tadhg leaned back against the pillows, watching James from under his eyelashes. "It wasna Sir James."

"Then who?" said Catrìona.

"I dinna ken," said Tadhg. "Someone passed by me, a wee bit after Sir James left and the guards passed to change the watch. I stood with my back to the passage and didna notice them until they were lifting my leg and pushing me off."

James held his gaze for a long time, estimating. "I think I did see someone move in his direction, though I don't know who it was." He blinked. "How do you feel? That's a fifteen-foot fall. You could have died."

"That may have been their plan all along," said Tadhg.

James looked him over. "You broke something?"

"Aye, his ribs," said Catrìona. "He may have hit his head hard, too. Other than that, just bruises and scratches."

"That's very lucky," said James. "Did you notice anything at all about the person who pushed you? Must be a strong man if he could lift you... You weigh, what, a hundred and eighty pounds, or thirteen stones, something like that?"

Catrìona and Tadhg stared at him. "How would ye weigh a person...and why?" she asked.

Sir James's eyes widened and an expression of panic flashed across his face for just a moment. "Ah." He waved his hand. "Just a habit we have in Oxford. We like to imagine how many stones a person might weigh. It's like a game. My point is, it's only a strong man or an equally strong woman who would be able to lift him up. Not just anyone."

"Aye," said Tadhg thoughtfully. "Ye mean someone yer size and build?"

Catrìona blinked, not willing to believe Sir James was in any way involved in this.

"Yeah," said James darkly. "Someone my size and build."

Silence hung in the room. "Where did ye go, Sir James?" said Catrìona. "After ye left the wall?"

Sir James tightened his jaw muscles. "I went to return Iòna's bow. He was in the barracks."

"Did anyone see ye?" she said.

"Iòna did. Tadhg, you're not seriously thinking I pushed you off, are you?"

Tadhg looked at him for a long time, and Catrìona's pulse pumped erratically. Then he finally shook his head once. "Nae. I dinna think 'twas him."

Catrìona released a long breath and began rolling out a fresh linen bandage. "I dinna think Sir James could do something like that."

Catrìona put the first layer of linen over Tadhg's ribs.

"Can ye lift just a wee bit?" she said to him as she put her arm around his torso to run the linen under his back. As a result, she was almost lying on his chest. She heard Tadhg chuckle, then he lifted his body, and Catrìona passed the bandage beneath him. "Thanks."

She ran the bandage under Tadhg's back again and checked that it was tight enough to hold his torso in place, but loose enough to let him breathe comfortably.

Catrìona ran the final layer under his back. "This should do." She tightened the layers up again, checking that he had enough breathing space. She met his eyes and pointed her finger, assuming a strict face. "This time around, dinna dare to stand up. I dinna ken what possessed ye to go to that wall in the first place."

"I was looking for ye," said Tadhg. "Wanted to make sure ye ate. Ye're so thin. So pale."

"Oh." She pulled the edge of his tunic down to cover his stomach. He said it so gently, with so much care, that it surprised her and made her feel embarrassed. Like in the old days...

She stood up. "Ye shouldna worry about me, Tadhg. I'm fasting. 'Tis all right."

"Fasting?" he said, wincing. "Why?"

"Penance," she said. "But why, 'tis between me and God."

She was a sinner, and she didn't want Tadhg to know how far she'd fallen from the woman he'd thought worthy of his love so many years ago.

Tadhg didn't say anything, but his frown deepened. He caught her hand for a moment and tugged her closer. "I want to talk to ye, Cat," he whispered. "Please, stay with me tonight.

Stay, and pray. I've missed praying with ye. I'll pray for ye, for whatever ye did that brought this penance on ye."

His care, the worry in his voice warmed her heart. Someone understood her, knew what was important. Shared this sacred connection to God. She realized she had missed praying with him, too.

"Aye," she said. "Let me finish tending to ye first."

With embarrassment, because he was more than a patient, because he could have been so, so much more, she asked him to pull his breeches down so that she could examine the wound on his thigh. He did, and if she was not mistaken, a gleeful expression crossed his features. The stitches had broken, and the wound had opened.

Loud voices came from somewhere behind the door, sounds of several men yelling and struggling. Catrìona stood up, alarmed.

In a moment, Finn Jelly Belly fell into the room, panting and holding his chest. Two guards came in after him, one with a spear and the other with his sword atilt.

Finn gasped for air, his large frog-like lips open, showing his sparse teeth. His eyes widened and flicked quickly between Catrìona and Tadhg.

"I didna do it, I swear, mistress!"

Catrìona stepped forward, shielding Finn from the two men. "What's going on?"

"I saw him, mistress," said the man with the spear. "I saw the demon caster on the wall, right after Tadhg MacCowen fell. I was sentinel on the southern tower and I saw him."

"What?" Catrìona cried.

"I did see a tall figure, too," said James. "But it was already quite dark... How can you be sure it was Finn?"

"'Twas a large shadow with a huge belly like a sack."

"'Tis a lie!" shouted Finn. "I was in the underground area, cutting the herbs—"

"Did anyone see you?" said James. "Can anyone confirm that?"

Finn bowed his head and shook it, his shoulders jumping up and down as he sobbed. "I was alone."

"I caught him as he headed from the main keep to somewhere in the bailey," the guard said.

"I wanted to go to the kitchen."

Catrìona exchanged a long glance with James. She saw it in his eyes—the doubt.

"We have a witness," said James.

The guards came and grabbed Finn by the arms and dragged him towards the door. "Lock him up, mistress," said one of them. "He's the sorcerer who's always wanted to avenge the laird. Mayhap ye'll be next."

"'Twas his tisane that did it to the laird!" cried the other guard.

But why would Finn want to hurt Tadhg? She opened her mouth, but another guard interrupted her. "The laird must torture the truth out of him, as he would any criminal! Flog him!"

Finn was struggling, beating his arms, trying to free himself. His large belly was jiggling like meat jelly.

They dragged him out of the room, and Catrìona watched them, helpless, biting her fist.

And then an idea struck her. Abbess Laurentia of the St. Margaret's convent was very knowledgeable about plants and was an even more experienced healer than Finn. She should go and ask her about what could have been used to poison Laomann...and probably Tadhg, too. Why hadn't she thought of it before?

"I'll go to the convent tomorrow," she said.

"Tomorrow?" said James and Tadhg at the same time.

"I mean nae to become a nun." She chuckled. "To ask the abbess if she may have an idea about the poison."

"Oh," said James. "I'll go with you."

She glanced at him. "There's nae need, Sir James. I'm sure Raghnall can—"

"I'd like to hear what she has to say about that plant Finn mentioned," James said. "Besides, you need someone to make sure you're safe."

Tadhg gnashed his teeth, practically glaring at Sir James. Was it possible he was jealous, that he still had feelings for her? The thought brought a sweet warmth to her chest, and memories of how close they'd been when she was a lass.

But she was a different person now. A woman who no longer believed love could solve her problems.

"Thanks," she said. "I've made the journey plenty of times. It'll be quick..."

"Great," said James.

As she pierced Tadhg's leg with the needle and catgut, closing his wound again, she wondered if a day-long trip with Sir James was a good idea. Because spending time alone with this man sent tingles down her spine and a warm and pleasant fire through her veins.

And she already had enough to do penance for.

CHAPTER 16

James eyed Catrìona as she led the horse towards a stream meandering through the trees. Stones and branches peeked out from the carpet of fallen leaves and green grass. Birds called and squirrels chattered through the creaks and rustles of the trees swaying in the wind. The earthy smell of decomposing leaves and sun-warmed soil filled his nostrils. His lungs were full of sweet, fresh air.

They'd been on the road for half a day, and James thanked God he didn't have to ride. He'd probably have raised further questions in Catrìona if he'd shown he had no idea how to ride a horse.

The horse pulled them in a simple wooden cart. Apparently it was more economical to take one horse for two people. Tadhg would be displeased to see how close they'd been sitting in the cart. He had watched James like a dog that saw a threat to his mistress.

Even a blind person could see the man still fancied her. Or maybe something more. Loved her.

The thought set a deep, heavy uneasiness in the pit of his gut. Did she still love Tadhg, too?

Something within James hoped she didn't. Even though she could never love him.

As Catrìona let the horse drink, she turned to him, and their eyes locked. The woods surrounding them seemed to shrink closer. Like never before, he became aware that they were alone.

Minus the horse.

He cleared his throat. "Want me to start a fire?" he said.

"Are ye cold?" she asked, rubbing the palms of her hands on her dress.

"No."

"Then we can just eat and wait for the horse to take a rest."

She went to the cart and retrieved a pouch of food she'd packed for the road. "Isna it interesting that this is called Snake Mountain?" she said as she sat down on a fallen tree.

"Are there many snakes here?" he asked, taking a place next to her.

She looked around. "I've never seen any. Must be a local myth. The Highlands are filled with stories."

James swallowed, thinking of the real Highland myth that had come alive and sent him here. Sìneag.

"You don't believe in them?" he asked.

She shrugged. "Nae, the only true wonders come from God."

He wondered what she would think if he said a faerie had sent him through time.

It was probably best not to speak of that.

James looked around, wondering what sort of myth could have caused the name of the mountain. It felt right to be in the woods again. Back in the compound, James had been exposed to nature daily. They'd grown their own vegetables, wheat, and rye and had their own poultry, cows, and goats. His chores had included caring for the animals and weeding the vegetables. It was interesting how quickly a human being got used to new things and forgot others. When the cult had been busted, he'd started living with his grandparents and buying food in the supermarkets. At first it had felt strange, but within weeks it had started to feel like normal life.

"Ale?" she said, holding out a waterskin to him. "The alewife delivered this fresh brew this morn'."

"Thanks." He took the waterskin and drank from it.

Medieval ale wasn't as strong as that from the twenty-first century. It was a weaker, more sour version of modern beer. He liked it.

"Why didn't you bring water?" he said. "Aren't you supposed to not drink alcohol or something?"

She took out a loaf of bread and broke it, then handed the largest piece to him. "Water?" She chuckled. "Most people think ale is healthier. Water makes ye sick sometimes, aye?"

Right. Because of the hygiene. At least with beer the water had been cooked in the brewing process.

"You know, you could just boil water and all the bacteria would be killed?"

She sank her teeth in her piece of bread but froze, the bread in her mouth, her eyes wide. "Kill who?"

He chuckled. "The wee demons that live in water and make people sick. Heat kills all that is bad for you."

She blinked and removed the bread from her mouth. "Sir James, please dinna talk like that if ye dinna want me to think ye a sorcerer."

Her eyes were huge in her pale, thin face. He drank more ale, then shrugged. "Try. You'll see. Water is better for you than ale, once it's clean. Otherwise, you're either constantly drunk or at risk of catching dysentery."

He handed her the ale. Maybe that was why monks brewed beer. It had probably been considered a good and healthy source of hydration.

James bit into the bread and chewed. Catrìona had such perfect, rosy lips. Her face was innocent, but her lips moved seductively, and he had an urge to bite them.

Bloody hell, what was wrong with him?

A crumb stuck to the edge of her mouth, and, before he could stop himself, he reached out and gently wiped it away with his thumb. The effect was magnetic, as though his thumb was glued to her skin. Everything around them faded, quieted, and floated away. He felt only her—his heart beat for her—and he had the strangest feeling from somewhere outside himself that he had been born for this moment.

Her lips parted, her eyelashes trembled, and color flowed to her cheeks.

"You're not yet a nun, right?" he breathed out.

"Nae."

"Good. Because I don't think I can take another breath if I don't kiss you."

Her eyes became the color of the ocean under the sun, so blue and bottomless, he was drowning in them.

No protest came from her, thank God, but she stared at his mouth as if it were the source of all pain and pleasure in the world.

Setting the bread aside, he took her face in his hands, leaned towards her lips, and...

Wide eyed, she leaned back. Two fists pushed against his chest. He released her instantly, and she stood, then backed away from him. Touching her lips, she panted, alarm in her eyes.

She shook her head, blinking, and James hung his head between his shoulders, cursing. Great.

He stood up and took a step towards her.

AS JAMES APPROACHED, SHE TOOK ANOTHER STEP BACK. SHE wasn't afraid of him.

She was afraid of herself.

To allow him to kiss her.

"Fuck. Sorry..." he said. "I...I don't usually do stuff like this."

"Like what?"

"Try to kiss women out of the blue. Usually, I'm on a date. A kiss is expected."

A *date*?

"Expected?" she muttered. "I dinna ken what ye mean by that. Even Tadhg, who was my betrothed, only ever kissed me on the cheek."

"Goddamn it..." he spat under his breath. Her chest was contracting. She knew exactly why. She'd known for nine years. You didn't decide to commit your life to God without knowing the reason. "I'd thought you wanted me to kiss you. I'm sorry."

"I...I think I did."

"Why do you want to be a nun? You're so real, and lively, and a beautiful woman. Do you really want to lock yourself away?"

She'd told herself it was because that was how she could be useful. How she could do something good in this world.

But the true reason was different.

The true reason was something she wasn't prepared to say out loud. Something so deep that even saying it to someone would make her sound childish, make her sound like a wee lass who always ran after her father, trying to make him love her.

It was because deep down she knew she was unlovable. Her only value in this world was as possession. Nobody would want her as she truly was. And with God, she had a deep sense of peace, that everything was all right within her.

She didn't say anything, and he stepped closer. "Did you feel the call?"

"The call?"

"You know, what I hear priests or pastors—"

"Aye, I ken what ye're talking about. Father Nicholas, the priest in Dornie, he had the call from God."

"What about you?"

She swallowed as she met his eyes. In the sunlight, they were so warm, so...sweet. The eyes of the man who'd wanted to kiss her. Who made her feel like a woman. Made her feel like there was so much more than she'd ever experienced, ever felt, ever even imagined was possible.

He watched her calmly, so big and tall and gorgeous, so breathtaking. Asking all these questions she didn't even want to ask herself.

"Me... Nae, I canna say I had the same experience as Father Nicholas. But it doesna mean that it wilna come. Or that my path is the wrong one."

"No, of course not. As long as you're sure. And I'm not trying to persuade you to change your mind or anything like that."

"Ye wilna change my mind," she said with a sudden fierceness that surprised even herself. "No one can ever change my mind, Sir James. I spent nine years waiting for this. Ready as a wee lass of fifteen. Waiting simply for the sake of my brother."

"Right. I'm just curious."

"Ye're nae just curious, are ye, Sir James?" she said. "Ye dinna believe in God. Are ye trying to make me doubt Him?"

He shook his head and laughed. "I'm not."

"Can ye tell me, then, what made ye so?"

"So...how?"

"So cold."

"Cold?"

"Aye, cold. And distant. Do ye think I dinna see it? Ye watch everything as though ye're nae even here. Like ye wish ye were up in a tower. A mere observer, afraid to allow yerself to live. And feel. And accept that there's something there that ye canna understand."

His brown gaze turned dark, and a thrill went through her. "Cold?" he repeated, taking a step forward. She stepped back. "I burn for you." With each word, he was advancing and she was backing up, suddenly weak-legged. She didn't feel where she was stepping, didn't see anything but him and that burning gaze. Was he about to kiss her?

"I'll show you cold," he growled, and something sweet and warm within her clenched.

The next step she took, a branch snapped under her foot and an angry hissing sounded from below.

"Don't move!" he said. "Whatever you do, do not move."

She looked down.

By the roots of a large tree was a hole that looked like a tiny cave. There, right under Catrìona's feet, among fallen leaves, grass, and twigs, slithered long gray and reddish-brown bodies with black patterns. Adders. Two of them were long and thick, the others—it was hard to say how many—smaller.

A snake's nest.

Although adders were usually timid creatures, they would bite when threatened.

One of them started to slowly move its tail into a tighter position. There was a fallen, rotting branch, and it propped its tail against it.

Those were the signs it was ready to attack.

Shock hit Catrìona, and without thinking, she took another step back...onto something springy and hard.

A dark shape flashed by and sharp pain pierced her ankle. She cried out as fire shot through her leg. She jumped away. Big mistake. The other snake struck with the speed of lightning, biting into her foot.

She cried out again as pain tore her leg apart.

"Easy now." Strong arms caught her by the elbows. "Slowly, come to me."

Suddenly, the ground disappeared as James picked her up and carried her towards the tree trunk.

"So, there's something about that name after all," muttered James as he put her down on the trunk. "Snake Mountain. Maybe it's a snake nesting area."

"Ye have to suck it out..." she said.

"Sucking the venom out isn't effective. What you need is a doctor. And a good antivenom medication."

There he went again, with his strange words. Her head was woozy. Something was wrong. The bite was beginning to burn more and more. It was as though liquid fire was spreading through her leg.

But that wasn't the worst of it—she was having difficulty breathing, and her wheezing breaths rushed in and out.

She felt dizzy.

"Catrìona..." James's voice was worried, and he was all blurry.

"'Tis all right. Adder venom is only dangerous for the old and the bairns..."

"But you're weak from your fasting..."

As he was saying that, the world tilted and the ground shifted under her feet. Her lungs were burning. Her chest hurt.

"Catrìona!"

She sank into inky blackness.

CHAPTER 17

J ames watched with horror as Catrìona's eyes rolled back in her head and she slid down from the tree trunk.

He caught her before her head reached the ground.

"Catrìona!" He laid her on the ground and listened to her chest. She was still breathing, but the wheezing sounds didn't stop. Was she going into anaphylactic shock?

With his heart drumming hard, his fingers as cold as ice, he lifted her skirt up to her knee. The bites didn't look inflamed or red, just two dark red dots at the side of her ankle and another set on her foot.

He listened to her breathing again. Still slow, shallow wheezing. Her pulse was fast and weak.

Cold sweat broke through his skin. Please, please let her live... Whoever was listening... Even God.

He picked her up and carried her to the cart, placing her gently inside. Then he went up to the horse and looked it in the eye. "Listen, mate, you and I, we have to save her. I have no bloody clue how to drive this cart, so please, cooperate. Yeah?"

The horse looked at him with its wet, chocolate eyes. He had no idea if the talk worked, but he felt better for it. He clapped the horse on the neck and climbed into the driver's seat.

He looked back at the pale Catrìona, slapped the reins, and the horse went.

"Go on! Go on!" he called. "To the nunnery! Go on, mate!"

The horse walked slowly down the path. Then, probably urged on by James's voice, went faster. Somehow, James got it to run and then gallop. He didn't know how much time passed—too long. It felt like a year. Trees and bushes flashed by, the cart rattling violently against the uneven, rocky path. Wind was blowing into his face, occasional flies thumping gently against his nose and cheeks.

"Good mate! Go on, you!"

Finally, at the top of the hill, there was a building. It did look like an abbey, or a nunnery, and the closer he got, the more sure he was that this was it. There was a small chapel made of rough granite rock, and a building with two floors that looked like a big square. The chapel had a cross on top of the small tower, and there was an arched entrance with a cross on top of it and some sort of carved words that he didn't even have time to read.

But as they climbed the hill, the cart slowed down. And before they reached the top, the horse began stumbling, moving its head up and down and snorting. Finally, it stopped and drooped its head and stood, breathing heavily.

The poor thing wouldn't make it.

James stood up in the cart and yelled as loud as he could, "Heeeeeelp! Heeeeeelp!"

He climbed into the back of the cart and picked up Catrìona. She was so thin, so light. Carefully, he jumped down and ran up the hill, his pulse pounding hard in his temples.

"Help!" he kept yelling as he sprinted through the grass and rocks and moss. "Someone help!"

The nunnery was slowly getting closer. So slowly! His chest burning, he kept running, his feet pounding against the ground. Finally, centuries later, the arched door opened and a nun in a habit looked out, wide-eyed.

"I need the abbess! Catrìona Mackenzie has been bitten by a snake and she's dying!"

~

CATRÌONA WAS VERY WARM. TOO WARM. FIRE WAS CONSUMING her. Distant pain was cracking her skull open. Her chest ached, too, and she had some trouble breathing.

She was probably alive. She opened her eyes, her lids heavy and hot.

She had a fever, she realized.

The room was almost dark, the only source of light a single candle flickering somewhere by her side. She was...she didn't know where. A simple room, rough stone walls, the shape of a cross above a plain door... She looked to her right and something released in her heart, letting in a small burst of happiness.

Sir James was sitting in a chair by her side, next to the chest on top of which was a tallow candle and a clay bowl of water, and clean linen cloths. He was asleep, his chin lying on his chest, his eyes closed. Everything was blurry, but she could very well distinguish his handsome features: the straight nose, the square jaw under what already was a short beard, high cheekbones. She remembered the almost-kiss... Then the snake... Then his worried *"Catrìona!"*

Jesu, he'd saved her again. The first time, she'd almost fallen down the stairs after seeing the fire he cast from the orange box. And now the second time, he'd saved her from the snakebites. He'd found the monastery—how, she'd never understand.

Sir James being inside the nunnery was forbidden. A man could only be allowed in if he was wounded or sick... She supposed the abbess had made an exception for him.

Not that he'd do anything bad.

A shiver ran through her, and she knew her fever was rising. She turned to her side to better watch him, and the wooden bed gave out a small screech. James opened his eyes and raised his head and looked straight at her.

"Catrìona." He dropped to his knees by her bed and took her hands in his. He kissed her knuckles, and even though her muscles were aching, the sensation was soothing, his lips cool against her hot hand. "I'm so sorry I scared you, made you back away. I promise I will never do anything against your will. How are you feeling?"

"Dinna fash, I'm all right."

"Should I call the abbess?"

"Nae. Nae yet. Stay."

She looked at him, so handsome in the yellow light of the candle. His lips were so close, his dark eyes so intense.

"Can you breathe all right?" he said.

She sucked in the air. "Aye."

"Does it hurt?"

"Nae more."

"Good."

She remembered his eyes as he'd leaned over her... *I don't think I can take another breath if I don't kiss you.* His eyes had been hot and glistening with intensity that made her bones melt.

She looked at his lips. Those full, beautiful, masculine lips...

Snake Mountain, with its serpents that bit her... This was the opposite of the serpent that had tempted Eve with knowledge. The snakes on that mountain had actually prevented her from kissing James.

Because of them, if she died now, she'd die never having experienced James's lips on hers. Perhaps it was her woozy mind, but a deep regret pinched her at the thought.

And while she was thinking with such difficulty, she could allow her body to take over.

She pulled his hands, bringing him closer, until she could smell his mysterious, masculine scent.

He stared at her with the intensity of a thirsty man staring at a cup of water. "I can't... You're unwell..."

"Mayhap yer kiss is the only thing that can save me..." she whispered. Cupping his jaw, she leaned forward and pressed her lips to his.

They were cool compared to her hot ones, and unexpectedly soft. She was falling into a cloud. The urge to dissolve in him, to become one, grew and she pressed her lips to his. His short beard scratched her skin, heightening all her feverish sensations.

Adder-like demons must have injected warm honey wine into her blood, making her all hot and pliable like molten wax, and wanting to do things to him...like touch him with no clothes, rub herself against him like a cat.

James stopped and leaned back.

That was it. Her first kiss. Now she could die. She'd think later about the fact that she'd sinned with a man in the nunnery. That she'd desecrated a holy place of God.

But that would be later.

Now she was still burning.

"Catrìona, love, you're burning up. You really have a fever."

"I ken..." she said through parched lips.

He reached to the cup of water sitting on the chest. "Here, drink."

While she drank, thanking God for the mercy of water, he wetted one of the cloths in the bowl and put it on her forehead. The shock of cold against her heated skin hurt.

But it also brought relief.

For now, she let the first man she'd ever kissed care for her, change the wet cloths, and give her water.

And as she sank into another burning, bothered oblivion, she prayed that she hadn't dreamed the kiss.

But if it was real, how could she ever stop wanting for more?

CHAPTER 18

After two days of fever, Catrìona enjoyed walking down the semidark walkway of the cloister, the walls golden from the rays of the late-afternoon sun. Catrìona watched the nuns care for the small garden in the middle of the cloister, and her heart filled with calmness.

It was so peaceful here, but she was ready to return to Eilean Donan. James had been allowed to stay with Catrìona through her fever, but now that they were about to depart, he waited for her in the cart beyond the walls of the St. Margaret's nunnery.

The walls of the cloister surrounding the square courtyard were soothing, protective. Once she came to live here, she wouldn't need to worry about any man, about whether she'd be loved or not, whether another man would define her future, her well-being, or her thoughts of herself.

She'd be God's wife.

Would God forgive her for kissing a man in His house? The thought weighed around her neck like a rock.

But she needed to accomplish what she'd come here for. Farther down the walkway, she saw Abbess Laurentia's tall figure and hurried after her.

"Abbess Laurentia," Catrìona said. "I need a word."

The abbess had the grace of a highly educated noblewoman. She was in her fifties, with a long, pleasant face and translucent skin, and kind brown eyes with almost no eyelashes. It seemed they could see right into Catrìona's soul.

Abbess Laurentia said something quietly to a nun who walked by her side, who then kept going down the walkway. She turned to Catrìona.

"God bless ye, child. Are ye feeling well enough?"

Catrìona nodded. "Aye. Much better, thank ye. If it wasna for ye, I may have been with God now."

"That man, Sir James, he brought ye here quickly. 'Twas important."

Catrìona looked down at her feet. If only the abbess knew what Catrìona had done...

"The whole reason I wanted to see ye was about my brother Laomann. We think he was poisoned, as well as one other man in the castle."

The abbess frowned. "Poisoned? 'Tis a serious accusation against someone."

"Aye. Everything points at Finn Jelly Belly, but we still dinna ken what the poison was and if he had it with him."

"Oh." She put her hand on Catrìona's shoulder and guided her down the walkway. Catrìona knew this was the way to the sacristy, where the most precious altar vessels as well as manuscripts were stored. "Tell me everything."

Catrìona always had such a feeling of peace around the abbess, and now it felt like even the abbess's touch covered her with a veil of relief and completeness. Whatever Sir James's kiss had done to her, she'd been right to come here. Any doubt that she'd had evaporated. The protection of the walls and the abbess's kind touch, and just the scent of this air—full of incense and herbs and stone dust—were like a protective charm against a temporary illusion.

An illusion that becoming a nun might be the wrong choice.

As they walked, Catrìona told her everything she knew about

Laomann's illness. She told her the events as they'd unfolded, without missing any detail, especially the symptoms: the pain, the runs, the vomiting, the unconsciousness, and what Laomann had eaten and drunk.

They passed by the refectory, which was, as always, clean and orderly and smelled like polished wood. Through there, they walked into the west range, to the abbess's office.

The light was poor here, with only one slit window. The abbess lit a tallow candle and the room filled with the acrid stench of burning animal fat.

Approaching the bookcase behind her desk, Abbess Laurentia said, "I have the medical manuscript right here."

There were only a dozen books on the shelf, and Catrìona knew how precious they were. Valuable knowledge of medicine, of herbs, as well as the Bible itself, and other important works. Catrìona was an exception among noble ladies, not being able to read and write, thanks to her father's desire to keep her and her siblings ignorant and dependent. She was looking forward to learning how to do both, and perhaps even being able to read those precious books herself.

Several of them were dozens, or perhaps even hundreds, of years old. The book that the abbess picked up was thick and heavy, and as she laid it on the desk before her and opened it, Catrìona saw it was already yellowed. There were paintings of plants and below them, text. She swallowed, nervous. She ached to know the secrets of all those plants and herbs and couldn't wait until she was as knowledgeable a healer as the abbess.

"Let me see..." Abbess Laurentia said as she scanned through the pages and quickly turned them. "The diarrhea, the vomiting, and the pain in the abdomen are common," she muttered. "So based on what ye told me, tingling in the limbs, burning and dryness in the mouth, weakness in the limbs, means there was damage of the nerves. Which suggests it was some sort of painkilling plant. That could be a variety of plants." She turned the pages quickly. "Baneberries...monkshood..."

"Finn did sell me dried black currants. Could they have actually been baneberries?"

"Mayhap, but there were other symptoms ye told me about. Hallucinations, his heart beating rapidly, and, most interesting, difficulty pissing..."

Then suddenly, she stopped and leaned over the book, her finger tracing the text under a painting of a plant. "Aye..." She looked up at Catrìona. "I think I ken what it is."

She tapped against the image with one of her long fingers. "Mandrake."

Catrìona frowned. "Mandrake? But mandrake isna typically used for poisoning."

"Exactly. 'Tis an analgetic. A very, very rare plant. So rare, some think 'tis a mysterious plant that witches grow. Pure nonsense, of course. I dinna see a whole lot of it in my experience, but 'tis a most excellent painkiller. In the right amounts, child, it'll kill."

Catrìona frowned. She hadn't known that. If only a precious, rare medical book contained that knowledge, and even the abbess had to look it up, then who in the castle would have known to use mandrake? Who would know that this amount of mandrake was needed to kill?

The most obvious answer was...

Her face sagged. Someone who knew plants and had access to the rarest herbs. Someone who did have reason to wish Laomann harm.

Someone who could hide under the pretense of being a friend of the clan.

"Finn..." she muttered and met the abbess's wise, concerned eyes.

"Ye think he poisoned yer brother?"

Catrìona wanted to shake her head, desperately. She wanted to, yet again, assure herself—and the abbess—that Finn couldn't have done that. Finn had no reason that she knew of to harm Tadhg. But there were many things she didn't know.

She shook her head thoughtfully. "I dinna think so. Nae. He wouldna do that."

"Aye, child, ye need to be sure before ye make any accusations."

Catrìona nodded.

"Sir James would find this new information very interesting."

It felt wrong to talk about James in the abbess's chamber. Like that sweet demon of lust and sin and everything that felt good to her would appear right here and bring Catrìona to doubt all over again. "He is good at solving mysteries."

"Good. Well. I will pray that this will help ye both. And whoever is responsible for Laomann's poisoning, I hope ye find them. I'll pray for their soul."

Catrìona stood up. "Thank ye, Abbess."

"Will we see ye here?"

Catrìona looked at her, a painful lump in her throat. "Why, do ye doubt me?"

The abbess smiled sadly. "I dinna doubt ye, sweet child. But... there's something different about ye."

"Oh?"

The abbess sighed. "Ye're thoughtful, and that shine in yer eyes, that eagerness that I've seen in ye every time ye came here, 'tis nae there. I saw it, though, as ye mentioned Sir James."

Catrìona found her mouth opening and closing. "Sir James?"

Abbess smiled. "There's nothing wrong with falling in love. I was in love with my husband when we wed."

Catrìona blinked. "And ye still became a nun? Why?"

"He died. I was childless. His brother, who became the next laird, told me he wouldna care for me. 'Tis often the only choice that women in my position have."

Catrìona nodded but said nothing.

"Unlike those women, ye do have a choice," said the abbess. "Ye are allowed to change yer mind."

Catrìona shook her head fiercely. "I wilna. I gave ye my word."

"Ye didna give me yer word." The abbess smiled. "And I'd rather have a nun here who kens she wants to do this. Have ye ever wanted to lead a secular life?"

Catrìona nodded. "Aye. I was betrothed once. I wanted children and a husband...all that."

"Do ye still want those things?"

Catrìona opened her mouth to say no. Not anymore.

But the words didn't come. And she didn't want to lie to the abbess. She took in a sharp breath.

"Pray for me, Abbess Laurentia. Please, pray for me, for Laomann, and for my clan. I need to make sure my brother and the clan are safe, but I'll be back after the Highland games."

But as she said that, she knew she had committed another sin.

She'd lied.

CHAPTER 19

James stood in the inner bailey, watching Catrìona's thin figure in her baggy brown dress as she walked to the main keep to check on Laomann and Tadhg.

The last three days spent with her had been the biggest adventure of his life. Exciting. Unforgettable. Somehow, he knew he'd never be the same.

The kiss... He still didn't know what had possessed him to break all chains of caution and let her kiss him.

Other than that he'd wanted to—so much he didn't think there could be a power strong enough to keep him from her.

But the trip back had been quiet at first. Then, in their usual manner, they'd started chatting. Conversation had flowed easily. He'd asked her about her life, about Rogene and David and what had happened since May. About Euphemia of Ross, too, and the events that had led to Euphemia pretty much declaring a war on clan Mackenzie.

And she told him about the herb that the abbess had told her about—mandrake. That it was usually given as a painkiller, not to poison people. That it was a rare herb, very hard to find, which was why Catrìona had never used it and had never even known it could kill when used in large amounts.

The most obvious suspect was Finn.

And to confirm that, James would have to search through Finn's things and have Catrìona verify if he had mandrake among his herbs

He saw the doubt in Catrìona's eyes, and when he'd asked her about it, she'd said she still believed him innocent. But she was lying. He heard that in her cracked voice, saw it in the frown as she vigorously shook her head.

When Catrìona reached the entrance to the main keep, she turned to him and their eyes met. Standing there, ten feet away from her, he felt his heart skip a beat. She was sweet and almost eerie in the twilight of the late evening—not an angel anymore, but a vision from another world. So distant and so beautiful, she didn't seem real. Sìneag's words came to him again—*Catrìona, a sweet lass, and the love of yer life.*

The bloody love of his life...

With a dull ache in his chest, he turned away from her. He didn't want to. He wanted to cross the distance between them, kiss her, bury his face in her hair and inhale the scent of clean linen, grass, and wildflowers. Wanted to take her into his arms and carry her away from here to somewhere where they could be alone—and happy.

But he didn't. What good would that do? She wanted to be a nun. He had to go back to the twenty-first century. Emily and her baby had been on his mind every day, but less and less so the more time he spent here. The thought stabbed him in the gut. What was wrong with him that he'd forget his only family, when he'd promised Em to help her and be there for her?

He should run into the dungeon right now, slam his palm into the rock, and go back. How could he play romantic games with a medieval woman? How could he kiss her and think of her and imagine what it would be like to be with her?

But he couldn't leave her in danger. He still had to solve this mystery. They were close. If they found mandrake in Finn's things, he'd be a clear suspect. Then it would be a matter of getting him to confess, and James knew how to do that. He'd be home soon, he promised himself. *Em, just hold on for a bit longer.*

Forcing his heavy feet to move, James walked along the wall, inhaling the lakey scent of the Highlands mixed with the pleasant odors of greenery and woodsmoke. Passing by the kitchen, he realized he was able to smell more scents than before. Now he could clearly distinguish bread and parsnips and cooked meat, and even boiled onion and garlic. Usually, his sense of smell was overwhelmed by nicotine and the acrid scent of cigarette smoke. He coughed a little, the clean air tickling his lungs.

After he'd been released from the dungeon, he'd been given a mattress in the barracks together with the warriors. As he approached the building, a tall, muscular figure appeared from behind the barracks, whistling a tune James didn't know. As the man walked towards the gates, James recognized Raghnall's swagger. He was rotating something in his hand—a knife?

James watched him thoughtfully for a while, wondering why Raghnall had come back to the clan after years away. Making a mental note to question him about it, he resumed walking towards the barracks. About ten feet from the entrance door, he heard a strange sound, like a moan. He stopped, unsure if it was an owl hooting or someone from the top of the walls.

Then he heard it again.

A groan.

"Hello?" James looked around frantically. "Who's there?"

Nothing.

But as his gaze scanned by the corner of the timber barracks building, he saw the edge of a pointy foot protruding through a small patch of grass.

"Bloody hell," James muttered as he rushed to the fallen man.

What he saw made him freeze.

In the ashen-gray twilight, laid Laomann, a large, almost

black spot on his side, dark blood flowing down onto the green grass.

Laomann was clutching at his wound, his mouth opening and closing, emitting the weak groans that James had heard.

"Bugger..." James said as he sank to his knees to examine the wound. He needed light—he couldn't see a thing. Where was his lighter when he needed one?

"Guards!" he yelled as loud as he could.

"Who's calling?" a voice asked from the wall.

"Your laird has been stabbed, call Catrìona!" yelled James. "Now!"

Muffled voices came from above, and the sound of hurried footsteps told James the men were coming. James pulled his tunic over his head. It wasn't clean, but it was the best thing he had nearby. He pressed it tightly to the wound.

"Hold on, Laomann," James said, ignoring the chill from the evening wind against his sweat-damp bare back.

"Sir James?" Her voice made his stomach squeeze in anticipation even if he couldn't see her yet.

The light of torches came closer. He looked up at the figures that approached. Catrìona, her eyes wide on James and Laomann. He hated seeing her like this. Worried. Afraid.

Two men stood behind her, torches in their hands. She sank to her knees. "Oh, Laomann."

"He's alive," said James.

"Oh, God in heaven," she murmured as she laid her hand on his and gently pulled it up to look at the wound. "Oh, no, Laomann! Who did this?"

The image of Raghnall walking away with a knife in his hand came to mind. But James wouldn't accuse anyone without solid proof, especially given medieval punishments and mob justice.

"I don't know."

"I have to stitch him up..."

"I'll help," said James, ignoring the burning heaviness in his limbs from the exhaustion of the day.

"We must carry him inside," she said to the guards. "One of ye, bring the stretcher. We canna let him lose any more blood."

A man ran off and soon came back with a simple stretcher. They lifted Laomann onto it, and the guards carried him into the main keep and up the stairs to the lord's hall. It was empty, but the fire was still alive, flames playing brightly. This was probably the most light Catrìona would get in the whole castle.

The men brought him to the fireplace and Catrìona asked them to move the big table closer and call as many men as they could and bring as many torches as could be spared. She sent another man to fetch her medicine basket from the great hall where she'd left it.

"We'll also need plenty of water," said James. "Boiled water."

She frowned. "*Boiled* water?"

"Yes, it's best to use it to clean the wound," said James. "He'll have less chance of an infection...or rot, as you say."

She shook her head in confusion. "How would boiled water—"

But James interrupted. "Please, trust me on this." He looked at the guard. "Boiled water. Maybe there's some in the kitchen. Also, bring another cauldron or a pot with water here—we need to boil the linen as well as the needles and threads to use in the surgery."

The guard frowned at Catrìona, but when she nodded to him, he hurried out of the hall. "Do ye nae use vinegar in Oxford?"

"Vinegar?"

Yes, vinegar was probably as close to an antibacterial liquid as there could be in the Middle Ages.

"Whisky would be better," he said to her.

"Uisge?"

"Yes. Uisge. And boiling your cloth and the surgical instruments in water. These are some of the latest developments in the medical field." He was improvising, hating that he had to lie to her at the same time. "Maybe you haven't heard about it yet here in the Highlands, but if you want your brother to live, you have to trust me."

Still pressing on the stab wound, she shook her head and looked at the immobile Laomann, and blinked. "I'll do what I can. The rest is in God's hands."

Then all hell broke loose. Mairead ran into the room, wailing and crying. The men came back with torches, and the room filled with a bright-orange glow that danced and cast shadows around. Their feet pounding up the stairs, more men came, carrying two cauldrons—one they put on a spit in the fireplace, the other they put in front of Catrìona and James. The scents of blood and food, combined with the torch smoke and the body odor of too many unwashed men in one room, made his gut churn.

Catrìona started commanding. The men stood murmuring quietly in a circle around Laomann, holding the torches. James told one of them to boil Catrìona's tools in the cauldron in the fireplace, and, though frowning, she nodded. She sent another man to fetch Angus's uisge from the underground storerooms. Then she was throwing commands at James.

She told him to hold the wound's edges tightly together as she washed and cleaned the area with the freshly boiled water. James saw that there were pieces of onions and parsnips floating around, and he guessed this was the cauldron where the cooks boiled food, but the water was steaming and as close to sterilized as it could get.

As Catrìona began wiping the wound with vinegar that someone had brought, James glanced at Laomann. Good thing the man was unconscious, the pain of vinegar on his open wound must be terrible. When the uisge arrived, her instruments were ready in the cauldron of boiling water, and James helped the man to retrieve them and lay them on the table on the clean, dry cloth. When the needle was cold enough, Catrìona began making sutures. The wound was deep, and it was impossible to know if it pierced the kidney or the bowels. If it did, James doubted Laomann would live.

As she worked, James was checking Laomann's pulse. It was weak and slow, but it was there. She looked surprised every time he checked it, but she didn't say anything. When Catrìona was done, she put her regular honey and bear fat dressing on the wound. Mairead clung to her, wrapping her arms around her neck, and sobbed.

Catrìona, standing straight, her face stern, hugged her back and patted her on the shoulder. But behind her eyes was fear and sadness, and James realized the stern face was probably nothing more than strength and willpower to keep herself from falling apart like her sister-in-law.

"'Tis all right," Catrìona kept whispering. "Dinna fash. We did all we could. 'Tis in God's hands now, sister."

"Oh, Catrìona..." wept Mairead.

"I'll stay with him," Catrìona said. "Go rest. Ye will need yer strength for Ualan."

"Nae, ye must be exhausted..."

"I'll be fine. Go."

"I'll stay with her," said James.

He craved bed himself; the exhaustion of the journey and the last few days were sucking on his limbs, making his eyelids heavy and his body tingle with tiredness.

"Aye, someone should," said Mairead. "Thank ye, sister."

Catrìona squeezed her hand and smiled at her weakly. Catrìona let the men go, and when she and James were alone— except for the unconscious Laomann—James could see for the first time how truly exhausted she was. Her eyes were red and dull, her lips were dry and pale, and her eyelids were heavy. With a sigh, she sat on the bench by Laomann's side.

James didn't think he'd ever had more respect and admiration for anyone in his life.

"Go and sleep, Catrìona," he said. "I'll stay with him. I'll call you if there's a change."

She shook her head. "I canna."

"Then sleep here," he said. "I'll keep watch."

She frowned at him. He smiled and nodded at the fox and wolfskins that covered the benches. He walked to her, picked up a wolfskin, and laid it on the bench, then sat by her side and clapped his thigh.

"Put your head here," he said. "I'll keep watch over you."

Something flashed in her eyes, and for a moment she looked like a scared little girl. Then, with a sigh, she nodded and lay on her side, resting her head on his thigh. James put another wolf-skin over her and leaned back against the side of the table. Not knowing where to put his arm, he finally rested it on Catriona's side.

To his surprise, she didn't tell him off but sighed peacefully and sank into him. Her golden hair was spilled over his thigh, and he itched to run his hand over it and feel if it was as silky as it looked.

She was soon breathing rhythmically, and James sat for a while, staring at the side of her peaceful face. Once, as a boy, he had managed to get a sparrow to sit on his open palm and peck at breadcrumbs.

That was how he felt now. He could barely breathe, afraid to spook this rare and wonderful creature that had put her trust in him.

Because he wasn't Sir James of Oxford from the fourteenth century. He was a cop from the twenty-first. Hundreds of years separated them, more unforgiving than hundreds or thousands of miles.

And if he told her the truth, he'd spook the sparrow and it would never return to him again.

He had to leave. Tomorrow, right after he dealt with Finn.

CHAPTER 20

"What, God's bones, is this?"

The voice boomed and Catrìona jerked up, leaving the soft, warm sense of security she had been wrapped in. The wolfskin she'd been covered with slipped down to the floor. She blinked through the heavy veil of slumber and rubbed her eyes. Sir James was sitting by her side —shirtless...

She stilled, blinded by the sight of a mighty chest covered with soft light-brown hairs, and the sight of a hard stomach and broad, muscular shoulders. He was staring at the entrance into the lord's hall. Laomann lay on the table, covered with blankets, as immobile as a corpse.

The fire was out. Gray light seeped through the slit windows.

Did she sleep through the night?

Tadhg stood in the doorway, leaning against his crutch, one leg bent.

Memories of the day before flowed into her memory like a waterfall. Laomann... Sir James finding him... Them working together to close the wound and save his life.

Oh God! Her, laying her head on Sir James's lap...

Feeling like she'd never been safer or more at peace in her whole life...

Heat slapped her cheeks, and she slammed her feet down from the bench onto the floor. She pivoted to Tadhg and stood up. Good God, why did she feel like he'd caught them in a sin?

"Tadhg, what are ye doing here?" Catrìona said, rubbing her hands down her dress to smooth the creases. "Ye need to be in bed. Ye have broken ribs, for heaven's sake!"

Tadhg glared at Sir James like he was his blood enemy.

"I'm fine," Tadhg spat through gritted teeth. "What is going on here? Did this man do anything to ye, Cat? Why were ye alone with him?"

Catrìona sighed and walked around the table to examine Laomann. She pressed her ear to his chest to listen to his heart.

"Nothing happened." The heartbeat was weak, but stronger than last night. "Sir James helped me to save my brother."

Sir James stood, still bare-chested and so gorgeous she stopped thinking for a moment.

"Someone attacked Laomann," he said to Tadhg. "Have you heard anything? Noticed anything?"

Tadhg proceeded inside the room, the crutch knocking against the wooden floor.

"When was this?"

"I found him at twilight," said Sir James.

Catrìona lifted the dressing a bit to examine the wound. It was swollen and red, but she didn't see any signs of rot—not yet.

"*Ye* found him?" said Tadhg.

"Yes."

"How?"

Sir James walked closer to Tadhg. Catrìona laid the back of her hand against Laomann's forehead. He was a little warm, but that was to be expected after the surgery.

"I heard him moan, and I found him behind the barracks."

"Mistress Catrìona!" came a call from somewhere behind Tadhg. "Where's the mistress?"

Tadhg turned to the door. "Mistress Catrìona's in here!"

Six men entered through the arched door, looking wildly around. They were all guards in the castle, including Gille-Crìosd and Ailig, who lived in Dornie and had attacked Finn.

Gille-Crìosd pointed his finger at James. "'Tis him, isna it?"

Ailig stretched out his arm with an open palm, on which laid a knife, brown from dry blood. The rest of them rushed towards James and grasped him by the shoulders and arms.

"Look what I found in his things, mistress," said Ailig. "The bloody knife. He tried to kill our laird!"

Shock hit Catrìona like a hard slap. She straightened and looked at James, his elegant eyebrows knit together in one straight line, his brown eyes blazing.

Ailig came to Catrìona and showed her the knife.

"Look, 'tis English." He showed her the three lions, the symbol of the English Crown, on the hilt. "It all started when he arrived, didna it? The very same day."

"Aye, the very same!" jeered Gille-Crìosd. "And then he protected Finn Jelly Belly, talking shite about time traveling and casting demons!"

"Do not let him get into your head, Catrìona," said Sir James. "The knife is not mine. And we still need to check Finn's things for mandrake. And find out where he was last night."

They did need to question Finn about the mandrake, and she wanted to believe Sir James. But it was an English knife, and who else would have one? Plus, it had been found in his things...

"The Sassenach's the one that poisoned our laird," said Ailig. "And stabbed him."

"And he could have thrown me off the wall..." mused Tadhg.

"And then stabbed the laird!" yelled Gille-Crìosd. "Kill him! Kill him, I say!"

Catrìona's hands shook. "Ye're mistaken! Sir James was helping me this whole time. He helped me save Laomann's life last night."

"Well, he may pretend he is doing that," said Tadhg, adding

to the furious bloodthirst of the six guards. "'Tis the perfect cover, isna it?"

It was. She glanced at Sir James. What did she really know about him? She had no idea what his family was like, who his parents were, if he was a landowner or not. And all those strange things about casting fire and demons and using uisge instead of vinegar and boiling instruments... All that did sound very strange. What if, instead of cleaning them, he'd convinced her to make it worse and Laomann was now dying?

But that feeling of safety...and his knowledge of medicine... the right questions he had been asking...

Still, how did she really know it wasn't James behind all the attempted murders? One thing she knew, no one had made her feel the way he did. And she still wasn't sure if it was some sort of witchcraft or simply him. Could Tadhg be right that Sir James was tricking her?

James jerked his arms, trying to free himself from the grasp of the guards. "Let me go, you fools!"

He raised his foot and stomped on one man's shoe hard. The man yelled and let him go. Using their momentary bewilderment, James managed to rotate his torso, brought his head back, and drove his forehead into the nose of another guard. He let go, too, grunting and holding his bleeding nose.

But Gille-Crìosd brought his arm back and let his fist fly into James's stomach. "Fools? I'll show ye fools, ye Sassenach pig!" he roared, watching James gasp and double up. The rest of the men took advantage of the moment to get hold of James again. "Ye killed my clansmen for years in the war, and now ye come to kill my laird? I'll show ye! Let's go, lads! He wilna kill our kin nae more!"

With roars, they dragged the bucking, kicking Sir James down towards the arched entrance. This was getting serious, and Catrìona was helpless.

All the blood drained from her face as she ran after the angry mob. "Stop! Ye canna just kill him! Stop!"

"Stay out of this, mistress," barked Ailig as they dragged James down the stairs. "Ye have too kind a heart. We will deal with this. We'll protect the clan."

James's furious white face was flashing between the guards' shoulders and heads as he pushed, kicked, and tried to fight his way out of their grasp.

"Nae! He couldna have! Stop!"

Mairead called from somewhere up in the tower, "What's wrong?" Ualan was wailing.

"Stop!" Catrìona yelled again and again.

The inner bailey met them with cool gray air, the curtain walls looming high and menacing around them. Warriors stopped what they were doing and watched them, wide-eyed. Somehow, among the scent of manure, hay, and earth, she could smell blood. Even the squawking and the bleating silenced, and only the grunts of James trying to free himself and the angry, vicious jeers of the guards filled the space.

The men headed towards a large stump used for cutting firewood, an ax stuck in the middle of the flat surface.

The ground under Catrìona's feet was slipping as she realized what they were about to do.

She grasped Ailig's tunic and pulled. "He saved me! Twice! Stop, he's nae the murderer!"

But Ailig only brushed her off and together with the rest of the men kept yelling about killing the Sassenach and protecting the clan. Tadhg was wobbling behind her, calling her name, but she didn't care.

The stump was getting closer, and before she could do anything, Ailig and Gille-Crìosd pressed James down onto his knees. One of the men held James's hands behind his back, while Gille-Crìosd and Ailig held him by the shoulders.

James was yelling and trying to free himself. Another guard pulled out the ax. Catrìona ran to him and grasped the handle, trying in vain to fight it out of the large man's hands.

He just pushed her away and she landed into someone's arms. When she looked up, it was Tadhg who stared at the mob.

With horror, Catrìona saw the ax rise high above the guard's head.

She prayed.

God in heaven, please let James live. God in heaven, I'll do anything. Please, save him...

She wanted to close her eyes, to shut her ears, to look away. But she couldn't. She'd give Sir James the honor of being with him in the moment of his death.

She saw the ax fall.

But it never reached James's neck.

A big male body rammed into the guard from the side, and he fell, the ax flying from his hands.

"What is this?" roared Angus, standing over James and looking with fury at the guards.

The men, who'd always had as much respect for Angus as if he were their laird, shrank under the fury in his face.

"He's the murderer, Lord Angus," said Gille-Crìosd. "He stabbed our laird last night and Ailig found the bloody knife in his things this morning."

Rogene came to stand by Angus's side. "Laomann was stabbed?"

David pushed the men away from James. "Let him go!" He helped James stand.

Catrìona, who found the strength back in her legs, ran to James and hung on his neck. He wrapped one arm around her, and his scent filled her nostrils.

Angus looked at the men. "How dare ye do this carnage without yer laird saying so? Even if someone is guilty, ye leave it to the laird to rule justice. 'Tis mob law, what ye're doing."

The men scowled at him. Angus looked heavily at Tadhg, who was watching them with a thoughtful frown.

Angus turned to James and led him away from the men to

stand by the round stone well, where they couldn't be overheard. Rogene, David, and Catrìona followed them.

"How's Laomann?" Angus asked.

Now, away from the angry mob and closer to her family, Catrìona could breathe easier. The onlookers resumed their activities and movement, and sounds filled the bailey again.

"The worst is over," said Catrìona. "Sir James found him, and he helped me to stitch him up last night. And where were ye? Why havena ye come right after David brought ye the news?"

"Euphemia's men were assaulting my villages. I had to deal with them first."

Euphemia... The murderer in the castle... James almost being beheaded... Would the danger ever be over? Would she feel at peace in the nunnery with such things happening to her clan?

Catrìona leaned over the well and looked down. The reflection of the gray sky glistened like liquid onyx from below, and the scent of earthy water filled her nostrils. She took a deep breath in, letting cool air calm her heated face.

"Ye found him, James?" said Angus. "And they found the knife in yer things? Did anyone see ye discover Laomann?"

Catrìona straightened up, worrying that Sir James was still in danger after all.

"Angus, do you seriously think James is trying to kill Laomann?" said Rogene as she turned to him. "But you know he's from—" She threw a quick glance at Catrìona and stopped herself. "You know where he's from, Angus. David told you. Why would someone like him want to kill Laomann?"

Catrìona frowned. Rogene sounded like she was hiding something.

Angus took the bucket from the edge of the well and threw it into the depths. It gave an echoey splash. "I dinna ken. I only look at the evidence."

"Yeah, he's a cop," said David. "He came here to find us, met...you know who...placed his hand...you know where...and *poof*..."

While waiting for the bucket to fill, Angus shook his head, eyeing James.

"What is the *poof*?" said Catrìona. "Why are ye talking in riddles, David?"

Rogene and Angus exchanged a long look, and Rogene gave her a kind, sweet smile. "He's not a murderer, Catrìona. He's just lost, like I was and like David is. The real murderer is still out there."

"And ye came here despite me forbidding ye to," growled Angus to his wife as he pulled the rope back up. "Ye're putting yerself and the bairn in danger."

"Well, someone has to make sure Detective James isn't falsely accused and thrown into prison...or worse. You remember, perhaps, that the same thing did happen to me, and right in this prison?"

Angus put the bucket on the wall of the well. He picked up a ladle and filled it with water, then held it out to James. "Ye look like ye need this, man." James took the ladle and drank thirstily.

Angus studied Sir James as he drank. "What are we going to do with ye?"

"Release him," said Rogene. "And help him solve this. I'm sure you have some ideas, James?"

James nodded. "I do."

Catrìona shook her head. "Rogene, ye're like my sister, but I feel like ye all ken something I dinna. What is it?"

"I can't tell you."

"Why nae?"

Rogene was opening and closing her mouth. David looked as unsure as she was. Angus cleared his throat and shifted his weight.

James put the ladle in the bucket and stared at Rogene and David Wakeley wearing medieval clothes. He himself was dressed like a medieval man, wearing a long tunic, a belt, and weird breeches instead of trousers. Finally, he'd met Angus Mackenzie, the man he'd been trying to imagine, wondering what role he'd played in Rogene's disappearance.

And now they were all here. Three time travelers and two Highlanders—only one of them had no idea.

How long were they going to hide the truth from Catrìona? Their whole lives? James was tired of tiptoeing around what he knew was the truth. It had taken him a while to accept it, and he still didn't believe in God or magic or anything supernatural.

And yet, here he was.

Maybe learning the truth about him would help Catrìona see he wasn't involved in the attempted murder. "I'm a time traveler," said James.

"James..." said Rogene, but he raised his hand to stop her.

"Please, Rogene, let me."

Catrìona stepped closer to him. "Sir James, why are ye telling stories about time travel again?"

He nodded. "Because they're true. I am from the twenty-first century, like Rogene and David."

She looked back at Rogene and David, both of whom were silently waiting for her reaction. Catrìona glanced at Angus, who stared at her without movement. Goats bleated in the distance. A horse neighed. Male laughter came from somewhere above on the wall.

Catrìona chuckled. Then gave another chuckle. Then she burst out laughing, a full, throaty, slightly manic laughter. She tilted her head back, her mouth open as she laughed. Rogene smiled politely, and James moved closer to Catrìona and touched her shoulder.

A sweet buzzing went through him at the touch, like the wings of a hummingbird brushing him. What was this woman doing to him?

She stopped, eyeing him, though a few last bursts of laughter sputtered from her lips.

She wiped her eyes with the back of her hand. "Sir James, 'tis an amusing jest, I admit."

"I know it sounds strange, but I want you to know the whole truth. I have no interest in killing your brother, or anyone. I appeared here by mistake because a deranged faerie, or whoever Sìneag is, decided to open a tunnel through the river of time and send me here. Angus, you believe me, right?"

Angus let out a long sigh and looked at Rogene. "I believe my wife. Therefore, I believe ye."

Catrìona looked back at Rogene with a frown. "Sister?"

Rogene nodded. "He's telling the truth, Catrìona. David and I are from the twenty-first century, and just like James, landed here by the will of Sìneag."

Catrìona stared at James with wide eyes and shook her head. "But...but isna it the work of demons, then?" she said. "Nae our Lord Jesu Christ..."

Before James could say anything, feet pounded from the direction of the gate, and a panting Ìona appeared by Angus's side.

"Laird... Sorry, I mean, Lord Angus, there's news from the north of Kintail."

Angus clasped Ìona by the shoulder. "What is it, Ìona?"

"Euphemia...she started a massive attack in the north."

CHAPTER 21

Catrìona's head spun as they rushed to meet the warriors gathering by the keep.

Sir James walked behind her, and she felt his presence because her whole body was charged with something like excitement and anticipation and...

Life.

A time traveler, she kept thinking. But how was that possible? Never in her life had she heard such a notion. There was nothing in the Bible. Mayhap there was something in the old Celtic stories, but she'd never paid them much attention.

This did explain everything that was strange and different about him. The fire from the orange container, the odd manner of speaking...talking about dates and expecting kisses.

But she wasn't a naive lass. No. She was a grown woman. She needed to talk to Sir James before she could decide if she believed him or not.

Men crowded in front of the main keep, most of them with swords and shields already at hand. They all looked expectantly at Angus as he walked up. "There ye are," said one of them. "Lord, what do we do? Do we march?"

Angus looked around at his men. "Aye, we march. Of course

we march. We dinna let no one take our lands and abuse our clansmen."

He took out his own sword and beat it against his shield. The men beat their own swords against their shields and roared.

Angus hugged Rogene by the waist and kissed her. "Dinna fash, my love, I will come back to ye and my son."

She nodded, her eyes watery, and smiled through her tears. Catrìona's heart always ached when she saw the two of them, so in love, so happy. Rogene was a good woman and deserved Angus's love. Catrìona had always wondered about the strangeness of her sister-in-law's speech, her accent and mannerisms, as well as David's. If they were from the future, that would explain it.

And if Rogene was indeed from the future, she had made a great sacrifice to be with Angus. But she looked incredibly happy. Something in Catrìona wished she could one day be happy with a man, too.

Without wanting to, she glanced at Sir James. He was watching her with longing, and her stomach flipped, her breath leaving her body.

Tadhg shouldered his way through the circle of men and stood next to her, his eyes glistening, his shoulders straight, his expression determined. Without wanting to, she compared James and Tadhg. Of a similar height and build, James was dark-haired and -eyed, watching everything from under his brows. He always looked like he was an observer, a mystery.

Tadhg was golden-haired and green-eyed, a man born and raised in her clan. Someone she could rely on, someone who knew her and understood her. He didn't hold back. He belonged here—he had nothing to hide and no secrets to protect. Even though he'd hurt her in the past, she now knew it was her father's fault. She felt safe and secure with him.

"I'll go, too," Tadhg's voice pulled her out of her thoughts. "I'll fight for you."

"Tadhg..." said Catrìona, walking to him and laying a hand on his shoulder. "Ye're nae well. Ye still have broken ribs and a bad wound on yer thigh…"

His eyes fell on her hand and then moved to her face, and if she was right, they watered. She stepped back, suddenly uncomfortable. He blinked, and his face became fierce. "Cat, ye were once my clan," he said. "I will fight for ye, and when I'm back, mayhap we can—"

He didn't finish the thought because the sound of two quarreling voices interrupted him.

"Don't you dare, David!" cried Rogene. "I forbid you!"

David was shaking his head and hastily pulling on a *leine croich*, his eyebrows drawn together. "You can't forbid me anything. I'm going."

"Yer what?" said Angus.

"You're what?" said James at the same time.

Fastening the *leine croich* on his chest, David looked up at Angus. "I'm going with you. Time for me to fight."

"No!" said Rogene firmly. "You didn't even train for a month!"

Angus sighed and shook his head. "Ye can go."

Rogene gasped. "Angus!"

"One day he must, love. And I'll be by his side…"

"So will I," said Raghnall, who was walking up the hill from the gates, playfully rotating his sword in a circle. "Time for my new, wee brother to become a man," he said, looking up at the broad-shouldered young man who didn't look like he was a "wee" anything. "We'll make sure he's all right."

Rogene was shaking her head, tears streaming down her face. Angus turned her to him and looked her in the eyes. "Listen to me, lass. I wilna let a thing happen to him. He's a man now and 'tis what men do. He canna hold on to yer skirt forever. Better now when we're all prepared than if the enemy knocks at our doors and he doesna ken which end of the sword to hold. Aye?"

She nodded through her tears, and Angus pulled her into a bear hug. He kissed her head and kept whispering something into her hair. Catrìona mentally made a cross over them, whispering a prayer to bless him and ask God to protect them.

Then Sir James came to her. "Where can I find a bow?" he asked.

She stared at him. "A bow? Do ye ken how to shoot?"

"Yes, though I'm very rusty. And I can't just sit here and do nothing. I'm a police detective, it's my job to protect people."

The thought of him wounded or dead burst her heart into a thousand shards.

"Ye're nae going anywhere," said Angus, who appeared suddenly by Sir James's side. "With everyone gone from the castle, and only women and a few guards left, I need a man I can trust to keep an eye here. I want ye to stay and make sure my family is all right." He put his big arm around James's shoulders.

"No," said James. "I can't stay behind when you're all going to fight. I'm a decent archer. I'm coming with you."

His warm brown eyes were on her again. Something cold and dark squeezed in her stomach. And she knew it was the fear of losing James.

"Aye, my thanks, Sir James." He turned to the rest of his men. "And now, let's go and show those treacherous bastarts that they canna come and take our lands!"

The men erupted in cheers.

~

"Is this mandrake?" James asked.

The dried brown root in his hand looked like an interlacement of hairy, old carrots. It was twisted, knobbed, and hard, so it was easy to imagine this plant could be the source of evil itself.

The torch's flame jumped as Catrìona came to stand by his side.

While the troops were gathering weapons and food for the journey, James could finally search Finn's things and talk to him.

The dungeon was menacing and dark. Scowling at them from

behind the grating, Finn looked like a sad, angry toad. The guard sat on a bench eating a strong-smelling boiled fish from the trencher Catrìona had brought him. His chewing and Finn's puffing were the only sounds in the dark cell.

"I havena seen one," she said, taking the root and turning it in her hand so that light fell on it from different sides. She looked up. "Finn, is it mandrake?"

Finn's mouth curved downwards as he glared at her. His puffy fingers tightened as they curled around the grating.

Closing his eyes briefly, he sighed. "Aye."

Ah, mate... That he admitted it was good, but a small part of James had hoped Finn was innocent. He crouched down at Finn's basket, which was filled with herbs, pouches, clay jars and boxes, and picked up the linen pouch with four more mandrake roots.

"You had this with you when Laomann was poisoned?" said James.

Finn nodded. His shoulders were slumped, his head bowed. He certainly looked guilty.

"And ye ken 'tis poisonous?" said Catrìona, her voice trembling.

"Aye."

"Then why didna ye say anything?" Catrìona shoved the mandrake into James's hand and marched to stand by the grating. "Did ye ken Laomann's symptoms were from mandrake poisoning?"

Finn's face crumpled like a napkin as he gave out a single sob. "I suspected it. I didna say anything because mandrake is so rare. 'Tis very hard to find it in nature and very hard to grow one, so very few people have them. And since I have them, who else would ye think guilty than me?"

James nodded. "Yeah, mate, it doesn't look good. You seem to be digging your own grave." He put the pouch of mandrake roots back into the basket. "So, now that we know you have mandrake, you can confess. Did you do it?"

Finn glared at James fiercely, his eyes two dark, glistening coals. "I didna! I would never! I'm a healer, nae a murderer!"

He sounded truthful, but he could be a great actor.

James walked to the grating and leaned against it with his shoulder. "All right." He eyed the guard who had finished eating and was now sucking at his fingers. "Mate, were you here with him last night by any chance?"

The guard looked up. "Aye."

"Was he here the whole evening? At dusk?"

"Nae. He was begging to use the outhouse in the bailey and Lady Mairead said he could."

"I had an upset stomach," said Finn. "Nerves give me the runs and I didna want to sit here smelling my own shite for days."

The guard shrugged. "Neither did I."

James blinked. So it could have been Finn who stabbed Laomann. But where would he have gotten an English dagger from while under guard? He could have hidden it somewhere in the bailey and picked it up on his way to the outhouse. That would have required some planning on his behalf. And then, how would he have put it in James's things afterwards?

Unless...the stabber was someone else. Could it be that two people wanted Laomann and Tadhg dead? Was Finn working with someone?

"And he was under your watchful eyes the whole time while outside?" James asked the guard.

"Nae while he was inside the outhouse."

"Could he have escaped and then returned?"

The guard winced thoughtfully. "I dinna think so."

"I didna escape and stab Laomann if 'tis what ye're asking."

Catrìona shook her head. "I dinna believe he did, James."

James didn't think it was possible, either. He had seen someone around that time, though, walking away from the barracks—Raghnall.

Should he tell Catrìona? How could he break her heart by implying her brother could have stabbed Laomann?

The truth was, James simply didn't know. He should ask Raghnall for an explanation before upsetting Catrìona further.

Footsteps sounded from the doorway. A man poked his head through the open door. "Lord Angus asked me to fetch ye, Sir James. They're departing."

CHAPTER 22

T*he next day...*

THE SIMPLE, WOODEN ARROW JAMES SIGHTED DOWN WAS slightly crooked—just like those he'd had in the cult.

So different from mass-produced stuff that flooded modern life in the twenty-first century. This bow and these arrows were handcrafted. Imperfect. Beautiful.

He'd learned as a boy that each bow was different. If you wanted a precise shot, you needed to spend time getting to know your bow.

Time James wouldn't have in the battle.

But time he had now, while the Mackenzie warriors took a field break. He sighted the tree along the edge of the arrow. There was a charcoal circle drawn on the trunk, in the middle of which was a fat dot—his target.

Men were eating and drinking all around him. Horses snorted peacefully, grazing on the grass of the mountain grove.

They hadn't made fires as they were taking only a short break before going north again.

James felt the hemp string scratching his skin. For seventeen years he hadn't used a bow, seventeen years with no practice. And now his own life and the lives of other men lay in his hands. He'd always been a natural with archery, instinctively understanding how the weapon worked. Would he be able to jump back into it?

He took into account the gusts of wind, the distance, the imperfection of the arrow and the bow. He loosed the arrow.

The string gave an audible *swoosh*, stinging his face slightly as it sprang back into position. The arrow flew, rotating in the air in a crooked arch, and softly *thunked* into the ground behind the tree.

James cursed under his breath and stretched his arm back to the quiver to get another arrow.

Raghnall came to stand next to James, chewing on a bannock. "Did ye say ye were a good archer?" he asked through a mouthful.

James cocked his head slightly to the side and placed the new arrow against the bow. "I am. Or I was many years ago."

"Let's see it."

Mentally shielding his confidence from Raghnall's judgment, James nocked the new arrow, then pulled the string back.

"Ye dinna have a bad technique..." said Raghnall.

James sighed out and kept his body completely still. He aimed at the black dot in the middle of the tree. He only needed to get used to this bow and these arrows. The last arrow had flown crookedly, so maybe he should aim a little more to the left.

He did so, and once he thought his aim was right, he let go.

The arrow grazed the trunk as it *thunked* into the ground.

"Bloody hell," James spat, reaching for a third arrow.

"And nae bother that my life depends on an archer like ye."

James threw a glare at Raghnall. "My life depends on you, too, mate. And those are not straight arrows."

Raghnall swallowed the bannock. "Well, excuse ye. Where do ye come from, the kingdom where every arrow is straight and every shot hits the target?"

James breathed out. Having never done archery as an adult, the feel of a sixty-pound draw weight bow was new to him. The smooth finish of well-worn wood in his hands was invigorating. Someone had made it with their bare hands, with zero technology, just their experience and instinct, based on knowledge passed from generation to generation.

And he was now part of it. He aimed at the target and released.

The arrow flew imperfectly, rotating in the strange dance of aerodynamics that happens with an uneven object.

And struck right in the middle of the black dot.

Raghnall laughed and clapped James on the shoulder. "Ah, now I feel better. Ye ken, 'tis nae the English warbow or anything like that. Just a simple bow that we Highlanders use for hunting and skirmishes. Mayhap 'tis what didna agree with ye?"

James nocked the next arrow. "Yeah. That must be it."

He pulled the string back, feeling the pleasant burn of his back muscles and his biceps. He pointed with his finger, which held the arrow at the junction with the bow, at the black dot on the tree, and let go.

The arrow hit the space next to the black dot.

Raghnall grunted. "Look at this. We mayhap have a chance, after all."

"Loved archery as a boy," James said. "Good to see I've still got it."

Archery had always been a way for him to unwind, to do something that he was good at and that made him feel good about himself. In the world of the cult where everything had felt wrong, and where he'd been constantly told he was not doing well enough, the simple act of shooting an arrow had been cathartic.

As his next arrow hit the edge of the black dot, he wondered if archery would still feel good when his arrows hit a human body and not a tree.

"So," James said as he pushed this troubling thought aside. "What made you come back?"

Raghnall snorted. "What do ye care?"

Whether Raghnall wished Laomann harm or not, for now, they had to set their differences aside, fight together for one common purpose, and protect each other.

James took another arrow from his quiver and looked him straight in the eye. "I know what it's like when your father doesn't give a shit if you exist."

Raghnall narrowed his eyes at James. "Do ye?"

James nodded. "My father had nineteen children. All he cared about was being adored and admired. All he wanted was to have people worship him."

Raghnall's furrowed eyebrows crawled up, giving James a glimpse of how he may have looked as a boy. "Did he?"

"Yeah. So I'm just curious." James nocked the arrow. "Why suddenly come back?"

"'Tis enough to say I got tired of years sleeping on the cold ground."

James met Raghnall's piercing gaze. The man looked like Catrìona—a dark-haired, dark-eyed, tall male version. But James could see the high cheekbones, the same perfect nose, the slanted Celtic eyes.

"Yeah."

Raghnall took one step towards James and pointed his hunting knife at him. "My father owes me an estate. And I'll be damned if I dinna take it."

"Because?"

Raghnall breathed heavily, and if James was right, color flushed his cheeks. "Because, my friend," Raghnall said slowly, "had I had it before, like I should have, many things would have been different."

There was something dark at the edge of that voice, something James knew he shouldn't push. He shouldn't force.

"Did you mention you lived in England while you were away from the clan?"

Raghnall stopped breathing. "I did."

"Do you own an English dagger?"

"What are ye implying?"

"I saw you. The night when Laomann was stabbed. I saw you walk away from the barracks."

"I was in the kitchens!" Raghnall roared. "Ye think I'd try to kill my brother?"

They glared at each other for a few moments. James wasn't sure if he believed Raghnall. What he knew was that Raghnall had things he didn't want to share about his past.

But so did James.

He pulled and shot his arrow, hitting the target in the space between the inner dot and the outline of the circle.

"Whatever it is, Raghnall," he said, "you found your way back to your sister and your brothers. Whatever your father did to you—to all of you—clearly, they want you here. Even if Laomann hasn't given you your land back yet."

Raghnall blinked several times, as though touched but fighting the new feeling of liking James.

"Catrìona...she is so happy you returned."

His throat clenched as he thought of his own sister. Yet another day had passed, and he was farther away from returning than ever. She was probably worried sick by now. It must be about ten days since he had disappeared, and the more time passed, the closer his sister would be to labor.

Stressed. Nervous. Worried about him.

He was fighting someone else's war, solving the problems of another family while his own family needed him.

He felt like shit. But he couldn't turn back now.

"I have a sister, too," he said. "And she's waiting for me in Oxford." He had to get back to Emily, to help her with his future nephew or niece. But he hated the idea of leaving Catrìona.

And first, he had to stay alive.

Raghnall fingered the handle of his knife. "Oh, aye?"

"Family is everything," said James, and he knew Raghnall understood him deeper than he'd showed. "It's everything that can destroy you and yet everything that makes you who you are. Isn't it?"

Raghnall gave a barely perceptible nod and clapped James on his shoulder. "Ye're all right. But if ye touch a hair on my sister's head, I'll kill ye."

"Men, to the horses!" called Angus from somewhere down in the grove. "Time to move!"

As Raghnall gave James a last hard-and-yet-approving chuckle, James thought he'd gladly risk being killed by Raghnall if only the Ross men didn't kill him first.

~

AN ARROW FLEW PAST JAMES'S HEAD AND *THUNKED* SOMEWHERE behind him.

His heart drumming hard in his rib cage, he ducked, hid behind a tree, and peered around the trunk. His blood was burning in his veins, his back sweaty and prickly. He didn't think he'd ever been so terrified for his life and for the lives of the men who fought by his side.

Even as a cop, he'd faced real bullets only once and fought men armed with knives four times. He'd been in a few fistfights.

But nothing compared with the bloody, messy violence that unraveled before him. He'd seen stuff like this in movies. *Braveheart* had nothing on the acrid reek of spilled guts and blood as people got wounded and died.

From the slight cover of the tree, he watched men fight, claymores, axes, spears clashing.

They'd attacked the two-hundred-man band like true High-landers, as Raghnall had told him they would. Quietly. Efficiently. With no warning.

They'd crept like cats, their flat shoes making no sound against the forest floor. They were like the children of nature itself.

James had learned about the infamous guerilla warfare of the Highlanders from historical documentaries he'd watched, but it was altogether different to witness it in real life, to be among them.

It had started so quickly, he couldn't believe it. They slit throats and pierced chests with no shame, but with a savage effi-ciency, like butchers. With a cold streak of horror sliding down his spine, James had raised his bow and, pushing down the voice asking him if he was really about to take a human life for the first time, he let the arrow fly. When the first man had fallen from the force of James's arrow going straight through his shoul-der, a small explosion of shock had shot through his system.

But he'd pushed it down. There was no time to dwell on the fact that the arrows he'd only ever imagined piercing through wood and hay had actually hurt a person.

This was war.

And if he didn't hurt them, they'd hurt him. They'd hurt Raghnall and David and Angus and then they could get to Catrìona.

He saw David, the boy he'd come here to save, swing his sword, crashing it over and over into his enemy. Only, he wasn't a boy anymore, James realized. David was a man. He was tall, broad-shouldered, and fierce, and his face was distorted in a mask of both rage and fear, and James wondered if every soldier since the dawn of time had worn a face like that in their first battle.

This was his first battle, too.

That last thought was what gave him the strength and the determination to keep going. Slowing his heart rate down with some deep, steady breaths, he kept shooting. One after another, his arrows wounded, grazed, and killed.

And then he saw Raghnall.

Catrìona's brother was swinging his sword against a man almost twice his size in proper iron armor, like a knight. The man wielded a giant mace with sharp, angular flanges that were probably able to pierce iron armor, not to mention the simple, heavily quilted coat Raghnall had on.

That thing would crush his bones like a meat grinder.

The giant had raised the mace above his head with both hands. Raghnall leaned down to swing his sword back at the man, but he wasn't in a good position to dart away or deflect the strike.

James stepped out from behind the tree and aimed. And just as the mace began its deadly descent, he let his arrow fly. It hit the man right in the neck, in the small slit between his heavy armor and his helmet.

He let go of the mace, clutched at the arrow, and fell backwards.

Raghnall straightened and looked back, his eyes wild. They locked eyes for a moment, but James didn't see gratitude there. Nor the relief of someone who'd just escaped certain death.

He saw surprise—probably because it was James who had saved him—and an expression that said, *Well look at that, death, I played you yet again. I'll see you soon, for another match.*

Then Raghnall wiped his face, leaving smears of dirt and blood, and ran forward, searching for his next victim.

James stared at him for a moment, wondering if he'd imagined the look, if he'd read too much into it.

He probably had.

Though, he didn't know what Raghnall had lived through. What he did know was that Raghnall was a man capable of stabbing someone behind the corner of a building.

But whether he had or not was still in question.

As he aimed his next arrow, James knew that whatever the

outcome of the battle was, he wouldn't come out of it the same person. And he understood Catriona's struggle with taking lives much better than he had before.

Life in the Middle Ages was intense, life and death playing together like unruly children. What more could anyone hope for here than finding happiness in the small things and precious moments with those they loved?

CHAPTER 23

Catriona slid her knife along the white willow branch in the darkness of the campfire. She watched the thin line of willow bark curl from her knife. The cauldron was already boiling in the darkness of the inner bailey.

The troops had left this morning, and when they returned, there would be wounded. There would be dead, too, but she wouldn't be able to help them anymore. Therefore, she'd need a lot of pain remedy, which she didn't have.

As she kept stripping the white willow branches of their bark, she sighed. Please, God, let her brothers and James be not among those wounded. Please...

She sent up a prayer and wondered if God heard her.

"Can I help ye, Cat?"

She looked up at the voice that spoke behind her.

Tadhg, of course. Who else would call her Cat? She was grateful he, at least, had been persuaded not to go to war. He looked better and stronger. His face, illuminated by the dancing orange and red flames, looked almost devilishly handsome, his green eyes amber now. His golden hair was clean and curly locks fell on his forehead. Without the bandage over his eye, he looked like the old Tadhg she'd known as a lass of fifteen, and her heart squeezed as she remembered that girl and her dreams and the love she'd felt for her golden wolf.

"Well," she said. "I'd like ye to return to bed and rest, but... are ye well enough?"

"What are ye doing?"

"Making willow bark tea for the wounded. I will run out of tincture soon enough, and it takes six to eight sennights until a fresh tincture would be ready, anyway. So tea, even if 'tis a weaker solution, will have to suffice for now."

"Ah. I can strip the bark, if ye like."

A warm wave of gratefulness washed over her. This was the Tadhg that she'd known, the good, kind man, the servant of God.

"Thank ye," she said and moved over on the tree trunk that served as her bench.

He sat down slowly and carefully, with a grimace of pain as he stretched his leg out. "I like to be useful. Hate lying about like a bloody log, doing nothing. Did Finn nae have tincture ready?" He retrieved a small knife, flat and in the form of an almost perfect triangle. The leather sheath glistened in the firelight, and Catrìona saw it bore a beautiful Celtic cross.

"I dinna want to take Finn's things," she said. "Finn is still the most likely suspect and is under guard in the dungeon. Sir James said we need to keep everything like it was because 'tis evidence and we'll need it for the laird's court later."

"Why?"

She swallowed a painful knot. "He has mandrake. What has likely poisoned Laomann and ye."

She handed him one of the branches and their fingers touched briefly. He froze for a moment as they did, his Adam's apple bobbing under his short, blond beard. His eyes burned, fire dancing in them as he looked at her.

"Ye're so bonnie, Cat," he said, his voice rasping. "Jesu, as a lass ye were bonnie and sweet. But now, as a woman, ye're breathtaking."

She couldn't move, not even to breathe. What wouldn't she have given to hear that from him nine years ago...

"Tadhg..."

He looked down at the branch and quickly and efficiently slid the blade down the wood, stripping the bark. "I ken. Ye made up yer mind. The nunnery." The next strip of bark slid into the large bowl. He looked up and met her eyes. "Didn't ye?"

Catrìona let out a shaky breath and focused on her own bark, stripping the next side. "Aye. 'Tis where I belong."

"But do ye? Tell me ye're sure."

Why was he insisting on this now? "I'm sure."

"Tell me there's nae one single part of ye that doesna imagine a family. A husband. A bairn."

She stabbed her blade under the bark and slid it so strongly, a splinter pierced her finger, and she put it into her mouth. Tadhg's questions felt like pressure, like he was pushing her towards a certain conclusion.

With James...no matter how different he was, no matter that he did not believe in God and did not even belong to this century, which she had finally accepted as truth after talking to Rogene today, the feeling that she had around him was...

Freedom.

She watched the efficient movements of Tadhg's hand, going up and down with the knife, the strips of bark falling into the sack faster and faster. He seemed to be very experienced, as though he'd done this countless times. He probably had—he'd probably made kindling, arrows, and prepared wood for carpenters.

"There's part of me that wants a husband and a bairn. The part of me that had wanted all that with ye."

He stopped midbranch and met her eyes. "If ye'd truly wanted that then, canna ye want it again?" He swallowed. "With me?"

She licked her lips. There he was, exactly where she'd wanted him nine years ago.

Back. Wanting her again.

Her heart drummed in her chest so fast, she put her hand on her rib cage in a futile attempt to slow it. Something in her stomach was fluttering, like a swarm of dandelion fluff blown by a young lass.

She could say yes. What had started her wish to be a nun, if she was honest with herself, was that their marriage had never happened. But what if it could happen now?

The fifteen-year-old lass in her rejoiced. She was bouncing up and down on her heels, clapping her hands.

But the grown-up her, the twenty-three-year-old her, was stunned. She imagined a life with Tadhg, just like she used to. Going to bed with him every night, snuggling into his strong arms, the scent of him, musky and manly. His skin, smooth and warm under her palm.

Only, the twenty-three-year-old her didn't see his face. The face she saw in that image was James's.

Someone she'd never be able to marry, anyway.

And here was the man she used to love, who wouldn't disappear through time. Who wanted her...

Could this be the happy ending for that fifteen-year-old lass standing in a dark and stormy night on the jetty staring into freezing rain and waiting for a boat that would rescue her?

She felt her face burn. "Tadhg... I..."

His eyes softened, and a smile touched his lips. "Ye're even bonnier when ye flush. Jesu, how I love yer blushes."

He put down the branch and his knife and took the branch from her hand, setting it aside. His eyes burning with an intense resolve, he took her hands in his and squeezed them. His skin was callused and his hands big, manly. The hands of a weathered warrior.

"Cat, if ye let me, I wilna leave yer side for a moment. We can marry tonight if ye like, go to Dornie and wake Father Nicholas up. Let me correct the mistake of the past. Please."

Her mouth went dry. What was she waiting for? Why was

she hesitating? Why was the "aye" stuck in her throat like a rock?

Seeing her hesitation, he pressed, "'Tis the place of a woman, to be by her husband's side, caring for her bairns. Nae in a nunnery, reading and writing, and boiling concoctions."

She frowned. "What?"

"I just mean, ye wilna have to do this nae more. Ye can take the place any woman should. By her husband's side. Nae riding around and trying to heal everyone who might have an ailment."

She slid her hands out of his. Anger hit her like a slap. "A woman's place?"

"Aye. Of course. I will provide for ye—"

"I dinna want to just take a place by a man's side," she said, feeling her eyes burning with tears of rage. "I want to heal. I want to help."

"I thought ye were doing it to be useful to yer brother—"

"Nae! I like it. I want to be useful and to provide people with help and assistance. Do ye understand?"

Tadhg was frowning at her as though she'd just spoke Galician. "Aye. 'Tis a wee bit unusual, Cat. 'Tis what unmarrit women do. Midwives. Conjure women."

"Aye, well..." She turned to the cauldron, which was starting to boil now, picked up her branch and began stripping more bark. "I suppose I'm nae like most women, then."

"But, Cat," Tadhg said as he leaned closer to her. "I dinna think ye can do both even if ye want to. If ye want to marry me, the household, the harvest, the cooking, the bairns, they'll take all yer time. Who would sit and harvest willow bark for ye if ye have yer hands full?"

With annoyance, she looked at him and realized he was right. If she wanted to be a mother, she couldn't be a healer. When would she have time to gather herbs and prepare tinctures when there'd be so much cooking and cleaning and laundry? Mayhap when the children were older. But by then, she might forget many things. Without being able to read and write, she wouldn't be able to write down all the knowledge she'd gathered over the years.

If she were Tadhg's wife, Laomann would, perhaps, give her a good dowry—mayhap a farm or a small estate with tenants that would keep the family fed and taken care of. Only, being a wife and a mother would definitely inhibit her passion for healing. If not completely end it.

He was right. It was not just Tadhg. It was this life.

Her shoulders slumped as she thought of the sacrifices she'd have to make.

Strangely, she didn't have that feeling with James.

But she had a better chance of marrying a king than a man from another time who planned to leave as soon as possible.

She stood up, lifted the sack, and poured willow bark strips into the boiling water.

"I thank ye for yer offer, Tadhg," she said, watching as the bark whirled and turned in the bubbling water. "But I dinna ken if marrying is something I want."

What she meant was *marrying ye*.

Because if James had asked her to marry him, she didn't think she'd say no so easily.

CHAPTER 24

They arrived in the late afternoon of the next day.

Watching the warriors pour through the gates, Catrìona thanked God for protecting them all. Standing in the outer bailey, she searched the faces of those who were riding in, sitting on their horses and in the wagons, looking for her brothers and James. She called upon the Holy Virgin to help her calm the cold chills of worry. Part of her had wished she could be there, by her brothers' side, protecting them. Part of her was thankful she hadn't needed to take more lives.

She was clutching the hand of Rogene, who was standing next to her and watching the warriors with similarly wide eyes.

Given they had many wounded and horses, they'd crossed the loch from Dornie on a barge. Angus rode in on his horse, Raghnall and David by his side. The three of them looked well enough, save scratches and bruises, and relief flooded Catrìona. Angus saw them and jumped off his horse, hurried to Rogene, and took her into a hug so strong, Catrìona thought he wanted to swallow her whole. David came to hug Rogene after him. He looked older. Somber. Battle-clad.

Raghnall saw Catrìona and winked to her. She beamed at him and made the sign of the cross over him.

Then he looked back over his shoulder and pointed.

She followed the direction he indicated and saw him...James.

He was sitting among other warriors on one of the carts and was leaning over something—or someone.

He looked up and their gazes met.

Centuries seemed to pass during that moment as she was sinking into the warm, chocolate depths of his eyes. He held her in his gaze as though no one and nothing else existed, as though *she* was his religion.

Tingles flushed over her in a prickly, warm wave. But she didn't have time to dwell on it or enjoy James's full attention because the cart turned towards her, and once it stood before her, she saw why he was leaning—he held a cloth, pressing it over a man's wound.

After that, everything was a blur. She treated the wounds which had been hastily patched up in the manner of battlefield medicine. She gave tisane and potions, cleaned and sutured. She stopped bleeding and cut out barbed arrowheads. There were dislocated shoulders and broken arms, but mostly scratches and bruises. Most of those with worse injuries had not made it home.

Later, without even talking to James—who'd been helping her every step of the way—she fell into an exhausted sleep, feeling satisfied with how many people she'd helped today.

EARLY THE NEXT DAY, CATRÌONA CHECKED ON ALL HER patients. She re-dressed the wounds, made sure the sutures held, and gave the wounded more medicine. Her willow bark tisane came in handy. Then she asked Ruth to ensure everyone had food and drink.

Once she was satisfied that all the wounded had been tended, she decided to help prepare for the Highland games, which were in three days. She could start baking bannock, which wouldn't go bad before then. They'd sell bannock and other food at the games fair to help pay the rest of their tribute—though she had to wonder if Euphemia would stop her assault even if they did pay what they owed.

In the kitchen, the cook, a man in his forties, was finishing cleaning. Judging by the aromatic steam coming out of the cauldron and the low, gurgling sound, the midday meal was underway.

"Mistress," said the cook. "I just wanted to go for a wee rest before getting ready for the midday meal. Can I do something for ye?"

She shook her head. "Nae need to fash, Sgàire. Go take a rest, I came to start on the bannocks for the Highland games."

He made a last, broad swipe of the large table standing in the middle of the kitchen. "Aye, thank ye, mistress. I wanted to start them today, as well. Any help is appreciated."

The cook gave a respectful nod and left the kitchen, going into a small chamber at the back where he usually slept. Catrìona went into the pantry and found a clay pot of fresh butter and a pot of precious honey. She opened the wooden box where freshly ground flour was usually kept, but it was empty. She picked up a small sack of oats and returned to the kitchen.

She placed the butter and the honey on the table and walked to the quern-stone, which stood on a small table in the corner.

When she turned her head, James appeared at the entrance to the kitchen, stealing her breath. The dark room suddenly lit up. He was so tall and handsome, with shadows under his eyes she hadn't noticed before. What had he gone through in that battle? Her heart ached for him, and she had to suppress the sudden urge to run to him and wrap her arms around his neck.

"There isna any flour left," she said to James, realizing this sounded like an odd thing to say, and her face heated. "I'm going to make bannocks for the Highland games. So I have to grind some flour first."

"With that?" He frowned at the two rounded stones fit close

together with a hole in the middle and a wee handle on top of the upper stone.

"Why nae? Do ye nae grind yer flour in the future?"

"No."

"Do ye nae eat bread, then?"

"We buy it. Bread or flour."

She shook her head once and poured the oats into the hole in the center, took the handle and rotated it quickly. The mill began making a satisfying grinding sound, and slowly, rough flour started to spill out from between the stones.

"Hold on," James said, and she stopped. "That must be hard work. Let me do it. You do something...less labor-intensive."

"Ah, there's nae need. I've done this many times..."

"No, please. I'd like to be useful. I'm sure there are dozens of things you can do that I'm not able to."

She appreciated him trying to be helpful. "Aye, well, ye're right, someone has to start the oven for the bannocks."

"You do that and I'll do the grinding." He came to stand close to her, and she swallowed as his masculine scent reached her.

For the first time, she realized she was alone with him, and her heart drummed hard against her rib cage.

"Aye." She let go of the handle and stepped away as if the ground around him was on fire. "My thanks."

He took the handle and began rotating the stone. She stood speechless, staring at the hard biceps bulging under his tunic as he moved. An image in her head of those arms bulging as he loomed over her, bare-chested and naked, made her stop breathing.

Good Lord, what was she doing? She turned away so fast, her braid slapped her on the cheek. She walked to the big oven on the opposite wall and opened it. As she expected, it was cold. She went to the pile of firewood and began placing the wood in the crook of her arm.

"Were you worried about them?" James asked over the satisfying grinding of the stones.

She had been. Just as she'd been worried about her brothers every day when they were fighting for Robert the Bruce. "God was with them and with you, Sir James," she said as she laid the last piece of firewood in her arm.

"Please, stop calling me sir. I'm not a sir. I'm no one. Just a cop."

She walked to the oven and started placing the firewood into its mouth. "I dinna ken if I can believe that. 'Tis all so..."

For a moment, the kitchen was silent except for the whirling of the stones against each other, then it faded away. Catriona turned to James over her shoulder. He watched her so intently, his eyes were black. Something in her squeezed to the point of ache. They were so different, he and she. He was from the future and lived by the strangest rules and values. How could one not believe in God? And yet, she'd never felt so at ease and so alive near anyone.

She had to know why.

"Is that why ye dinna believe in God?" she said. "Because ye're from the twenty-first century?"

He looked at her lips like they were ripe berries and he wanted to taste them.

"No," he said, resuming the grinding. "That is not why."

"Why, then?"

"It's not a pretty story."

The story of why she believed in God so fiercely wasn't a pretty one, either. Catriona turned away from him and placed the final piece of firewood into the oven. She blinked as the memories of her, huddling against her mother, terrified, praying to God that her father would calm down, flooded into her. "I'm nae stranger to those."

The grinding stopped. "The oats are gone. Do I make more flour?" said James.

She looked up at him. "Let me see."

As though being drawn to him by a rope, she slowly came to stand next to him. Crudely ground flour lay on the table around the mill. "It needs to be ground once more."

She took a clean bowl, bent over the table, and began sweeping the rough flour into the bowl with her hands. James rolled up the sleeves of his tunic and she froze, mesmerized as the strong, beautiful forearms covered with soft brown hair moved to her hands. One of his hands brushed against hers as he took the bowl, making her bones melt. She let go of the bowl as though it were made of molten iron and stepped back.

"Careful," he said, a soft chuckle urging her to come closer and brush his lips with her own. "You don't want to spill all that precious flour, do you?"

Heat flushed her cheeks. He'd caught her reacting to him like this... She shouldn't. She straightened her shoulders and marched towards the lit fireplace.

"I wilna," she said as she sank to her knees, picked up a long piece of kindling, and poked its end into the fire.

As the grinding sound resumed, she walked back to the oven and placed the long, burning stick into the small pile of kindling under her strategically constructed pile of firewood. She blew gently, watching the fire grow and consume the tiny pieces of wood. As the flames began licking the firewood, she wondered if James's hands would feel like that on her body. Hot...molten...

Consuming her whole.

With a force that surprised her, she slammed the cover of the oven shut.

James looked up at her with interest but didn't stop rotating the stone. As she walked around the table, picked up a cast-iron grill pan, then placed it on the table, she felt his eyes on her, heavy and sizzling.

"Did he ever do anything to you?" he said, searching her eyes.

"Who?"

"Tadhg. You two were engaged. Did he ever hurt you?"

"Why would ye think that?"

He sighed and slowed the grinding. "Because I still can't get my head around why a beautiful, loving woman like you would want to rob herself of the possibility of happiness with a man. And you're so jumpy around me..."

Blood scalded her face. She undid the string that tied a cloth on top of the jar of butter. "Nae, Sir James..."

She wanted to distract him, start talking of something else, but the concern in his face was real. And she wanted to tell him.

"Nae physically. We'd...we'd agreed on a time when he'd come to pick me up and we'd run away together to elope. Everything was ready, and I risked everything for him. I went and waited by the jetty. And when he never came, I was hurt."

His eyes became as dark as a storm at night. "Because you loved him?"

She chuckled as she scooped a handful of butter. Loved Tadhg...what a strange notion that seemed to her now. Now that every time she closed her eyes she saw the warm gaze and chiseled features of the man from another time.

"Aye, I did," she said as she began spreading the butter on the surface of the pan.

He stopped grinding. "Do you still love him?" His voice rasped like he'd swallowed a toad.

She wasn't sure what she felt for Tadhg now. She cared for him, but was it a different kind of love or just an echo from the past? From the hope for the future that she had had as a lass of fifteen? Whatever it was, it was surely much different from the intense longing she felt for James. But she could never tell him that.

"It doesna matter." She took another pan. "I am going to serve God for the rest of my life."

He nodded and pursed his lips. He swiped the flour from the surface of the table into the bowl. "It's your choice, of course. But tell me one thing, are you going to become a nun because he broke your heart?" Swipe, swipe, swipe. A small white cloud formed around the bowl. "Because if you are, there are better men for you than Tadhg. He's not worth ruining your whole life over."

"Ruining my life?" She began rubbing the pan with butter like she was trying to rub a hole through it. "What are ye talking about? I'm going to be free. Free of men and their opinions of what I should do. Free to make a difference in other people's lives. Free to read, and write, and learn. Do ye ken that my father is the reason I canna read and write? Do ye realize that if I dinna go to the convent, my other choice is to be marrit to a man who will make all the decisions for me? The only place where women have power is in the monastery."

James studied her with a frown. "But you will never have children. Never know what it is like to spend a life with someone. Never kiss... Never make love..."

She blinked, the memory of their kiss invading her psyche like a crashing wave. The warmth of his lips, the wicked things he did with his tongue, the feeling of floating and swimming in some sort of delicious potion of pleasure swarmed through her veins. Make love... If one kiss made her feel like that, how would it be to lie with him, naked, skin to skin, to be entangled in his big, hard body.

As a healer, she knew what went on between a man and a woman in theory, and she'd seen enough animals coupling to realize something like this must happen between humans, also.

But how would it actually feel?

She stared into his eyes, unable to move or look away. "Make love, ye say?" she whispered, not knowing where the words were coming from. "Who'd love me? The real me, not a bonnie doll to make bonnie babies and clean the house?"

There it was, the truth, spilled out for the first time in her life. Something she could barely even admit to herself. James blinked and her own pain seemed to be reflected in his eyes.

"My whole life," she said in a voice that didn't sound like herself, "my father made sure I kent I was just a means to an end for him, a possession to make him more important. Every day he told me that, and my mother encouraged me to become a nun and escape the life where I'd become another man's property as she was."

She let out a sharp breath. "My mother died, and Tadhg came along. He listened to me, prayed with me, talked to me. He made me smile. For the first time in my life, I felt appreciated and valued and...aye, loved."

"You should have felt that every day of your life."

She felt a tear fall down her cheek. His words seeped inside her chest and warmed her heart, sealing the thin cracks in it. For a brief moment, she imagined how it would feel to know that she was lovable. Would she have even fallen in love with Tadhg? Would she have even considered becoming a nun?

"Mayhap," she said. "But he was the first person who made me feel like I was. And then, when we'd agreed to get marrit, he broke my heart when he disappeared. Just like my mother said, dinna wait for someone to love ye. When I decided my way would be the way of God, 'twas because if I couldna be loved for who I was, I wouldna be marrit. I wouldna be in the hands of another tyrant, like my father. I'd be strong and independent and educated in a community of women whose whole lives were dedicated to helping others."

"But what if someone loved you?" James walked to her and placed the bowl full of flour on the table in front of her. "Really loved you as you are and gave you all the freedom you want. Would you still wish to be nun?"

She paused. The idea was wild, but so seductive.

"I do want children," she whispered. "A husband."

"Then don't go to the monastery," he said.

"Why? Who would love me, James? Who wouldn't treat me as their possession?"

He took her hand in his, sending a frenzy of starlight through her. Their hands connected—his covered with flour, hers with butter. She was sinking in the warm darkness of his eyes.

"For such a strong believer you have surprisingly little faith."

Her heart slammed against her chest so hard, she thought he might hear it. What was he saying? This man who was so handsome she couldn't fathom how he could even exist. Who woke her whole body and made her feel alive, as no one had ever done before. Who was kind and unnervingly perceptive.

"In what?" she said, the butter on her skin melting from the heat of his fingers.

"In yourself."

CHAPTER 25

Her eyes were so huge and so blue it was like a piece of sky shone through them at him. Her lips parted, pink and lush, and he ached to claim them. She stared at him with a mixture of vulnerability and light that brightened his world.

"Whoever made you believe you're unlovable deserves to burn in hell," he croaked. "You're so lovable for exactly who you are, I can't help but—"

His throat closed with a mixture of emotion. Anger at her father for making her believe she was unworthy...

Fear of hurting her and saying out loud that one word that was so true he thought he could see everything clearly for the first time in his life.

Love.

She was so lovable, he couldn't help but start to fall in love with her. That was what he'd wanted to say.

So lovable, he wished for a moment they weren't from different centuries.

So lovable, he wanted to drop to his knees and give his allegiance to her like a bloody knight in shining armor.

Only, he wasn't.

And soon, he'd be gone from her life forever. He couldn't be the third man to hurt her. She didn't deserve it.

"Ye canna help but what?" Catrìona said.

He exhaled and stepped back, breaking contact with her.

"Sorry... Um..." He dragged his fingers through his hair, and as Catrìona's eyes widened, he remembered his hands were covered with flour—and now butter, too.

She giggled, making him grin in response. "I can't help but wonder how your life would change if you realized it yourself," he said as he walked back to his grinding stones. "You need more, don't you?"

She blinked, still chuckling. She was so gorgeous, lit up with inner light and confidence, a bright smile on her face, little dimples in her cheeks and sparkles in her eyes.

She dumped the flour on the table and took a handful of butter. "Aye, would ye, please?"

"Of course." Standing at his workstation again, he poured in more oats till the hole in the middle of the grindstone was full of them. He didn't mind the work. He realized where the term "grinder" must have come from. This was tedious, hard work. If only all these people knew that hundreds of years after them, humanity would achieve progress they all would probably consider magic.

But as he took the handle and started rotating it, he realized there was something so satisfying in this simple work with his hands. Connection with the body, connection to the earth. He remembered, in the cult, gardening was always assigned to the corporate types, those who were too much in their heads, and, surprisingly, it had always balanced them out.

Catrìona began mixing the dough, her hands working in the fast, economical motions of someone who'd done this hundreds of times. How would it feel to have those hands on his back, massaging him?

How would it feel if those hands slid down his stomach, one of them wrapping around his cock... Instantly hardening, he cleared his throat, guilt weighing on his shoulders. Best concentrate on the work before him.

"Ye ken, Sir James, for someone who doesna believe in God, ye sound like a priest."

He chuckled. "What?"

"Aye, ye sound like Father Nicholas, the priest in our church in Dornie."

He shook his head, laughing. "Never thought I'd ever be accused of that."

She pressed the dough into the table and eyed him thoughtfully. "What made ye what ye are, Sir James?"

The only place he wanted her to call him sir was if she were squirming in ecstasy under him, and if the "sir" would be followed by "please."

"What am I, Catrìona?" he said, deciding to let the issue go in the hopes the image of her naked beneath him would disappear.

"A man standing at the end of a rainbow with a pot of gold under your feet, claiming there's nothing but moss."

James stopped grinding, staring at the pair of brilliant blue eyes that looked straight into his soul. His jaw worked as the painful truth of her words sank in.

"A rainbow is just drops of water in the air," he said through gritted teeth. "An illusion made by sunlight."

She raised her eyebrows victoriously, in a "you're proving my point" expression, then got back to kneading.

"Do you think I don't want to believe?" he said, making a wide gesture that left a trace of flour in the air. "I wish I were as naive and as innocent as most people. But I'm not. Too early I realized my existence was a mistake. The result of brainwashing, and a means to an end."

Catrìona stilled. "Brain...what?"

He sighed and leaned on the grindstone with both his arms, his head hanging between his shoulders. Then he looked straight up at her. "I was born in a cult. I suppose you don't know what that is. It's worshiping of a single person who makes the members believe he can cure them or make miracles for them, and they have to pay a lot of money for that."

She frowned. "So 'tis like paganism?"

"Well...no. Kind of. Let's say, yes, only instead of gods like Thor and Odin and Zeus, people believe in one concrete person. He is being praised and pretty much considered a deity. And instead of donations that people give to churches and monasteries and such, they give money to him directly for the privilege of being members of the cult and for him to improve their lives in some way."

"Oh. That doesna sound like a right thing to do."

He nodded. "It's not. It's illegal in my time."

He'd never talked about it to anyone apart from Emily and the policemen who had busted the cult. The moment they'd left the compound, he had resolved to bury the memories deep down and forget the first few years of his life had ever happened. On first glance, he and Catrìona couldn't be any more different. They'd been born and raised hundreds of years apart from each other. But there was this likeness between them, something he couldn't put into words. Like everything was electrified when she was around. Like life made sense, and he could be himself.

He wanted to tell her about his childhood. She wouldn't understand the details. But she'd understand his experience.

"My mother got involved in Unseen Wonders, a cult led by Brody Guthenberg. It was all about believing in the power of thought, positive intentions, and success. All sounds great, right? Only, he was the source of that success. He told everyone he was like a tuning fork that could align to the frequency of marvels. He was the only man in the world that could do that, and then channel that magic into people and change their lives. Surprisingly, it worked for some, at least in part. They call it a self-fulfilling prophecy in psychology. It worked just enough for my mother to believe she could achieve more the more she paid and the higher she moved up the ladder of membership."

"What does that mean?"

"She had to pay money to get closer to Brody. The closer you got, the more he'd pray and sing and read with you. Fewer members were in each circle. The fewer members, the more individual attention. The more individual attention, the more success and happiness you had in life."

"Success and happiness? Are those the most important things in yer time?"

"A couple of, yes. My mum—I think she always had an addictive personality, and he was like a drug to her. Bringing her the high, the thrill she needed in her life. She had me—I'm Brody's son—in the hopes of tying him to her with a child. That didn't work. The bastard already had like a dozen other babies in the compound. Then she had my sister, Emily."

His grinding was slowing down as he sank deeper into his memories.

"I had to pray and meditate with Mum ever since I can remember. I was growing up believing those things, Catrìona. Believing Brody was God. And seeing that blind faith was the destruction of my mother."

Catrìona's eyes watered, and she blinked. Her hand, fingers covered in dough, clutched at the base of her neck, where, James knew, her cross hung. It was an instinctive, automatic gesture she'd probably done her whole life, meant to give her strength, he guessed. But it was also meant to call on God.

And he'd just said faith was the destruction of his mother.

He saw the realization straighten her face. She blinked, then wiped her fingers against a cloth and slowly walked to him, as if he were a wild animal she was afraid to spook.

"What happened then?" she said as she stood right before him.

He saw no judgment, no desire to convert him to the real God, Jesus Christ, and that alone made him breathe easier. She was standing next to him, and her presence warmed him and calmed down the turmoil of emotions in his chest.

"She started drinking," said James. "He started using her, manipulating her to give him every cent she made.

"I started to realize something was terribly wrong one day when I saw Brody hit my sister behind our house so that no one would see. I ran to him to try to stop him, but he only brushed me off and threatened me. He said if I told anyone, he'd hurt my mum, too.

"Then my mum sent me on an errand to the city, and a police officer talked to me outside the compound, asking what was going on. We were instructed not to tell anyone about our lives there. But somehow, the officer got to me, and at least I listened to her. When she asked if my mum was okay, I knew she wasn't. My sister wasn't. All those men and women who were under Brody's spell weren't. That was the moment I knew I was an idiot. I had believed. I'd had faith. I'd failed to see the facts.

"My sister would be in more danger from Brody the older she got. Brody was a rotten man. And my mum would never be enlightened.

"I swore never to let Brody hurt my family again. I helped the police gather evidence and shut down the cult. Brody went to prison for life. The police detectives found my grandparents, and we moved in with them. My mum started drinking heavily and died two years after."

"I'm so sorry, James," Catrìona whispered, tears glistening in her eyes. "I dinna understand everything. But I ken one thing. Ye ken what 'tis like to live under the spell of a tyrant and watch yer mother die in his shadow."

"Only you found salvation in religion," James said. "And I found it by destroying my religion. That's why I don't want you to make a mistake you'll regret your whole life."

Catrìona blinked and a single tear rolled down her cheek.

"What if I reconsider becoming a nun, James?" she said. "What if you make me change my mind? What then?"

Then I'm never going to leave your side, home be damned. The words urged to spill out, hot and seductive and so freeing.

But the door to the cook's private chamber opened and he entered, scratching at his round belly and yawning. Catrìona jumped away from James as though she'd touched a hot stove.

"Mistress..." the cook said, eyeing her with a frown. "Let me knead that dough. Ye need to eat. Ye fasted enough. Here, take some—"

But Catrìona only squeezed his shoulder with a weak smile, gave a nod to James, and fled away. James stared at the door where she'd disappeared.

What would she have said had he managed to tell her how he really felt?

James resumed grinding with force, the stone rubbing the oats into flour.

Perhaps this was for the best. Staying here was a silly fantasy. Emily and her baby needed him in the twenty-first century. No matter what he felt for Catrìona, he had to put it out of his mind.

CHAPTER 26

C atriona was dreaming she was running. Warm wind tickled her skin as she moved, light and free. Black branches of trees flashed by. There was no moon in the inky sky, but she didn't need light to know where she was going. She had no clothes on but that felt right...

Interesting.

Exciting.

Her own breath was loud in her ears, and her heart battered her rib cage in anticipation. Her body felt different. She wasn't the scarecrow she'd become recently. No, she was lush—hips round, breasts heavy, belly round, legs big and strong.

And she liked it.

There was no sense of shame or guilt or a trace of unworthiness. She was whole, she felt beautiful. She was part of this world, and this world was hers.

Somewhere ahead of her, between the trees, fires flickered—her destination. He was calling her, the big man with eyes like dark chestnuts, with rolling muscles and more mysteries than she could uncover. She arrived at a tall house made of polished stone, carvings of rivers and hands on its surface. A large door opened, and he stood there, as naked as she, and stretched out his hand to her.

Why wasn't she ashamed, covering herself, or running away? She wanted it. She wanted him, in that dream. Behind him, golden light shone as though a sun was rising somewhere in that house, and she knew it was warm and beautiful and good.

As she walked closer to him, the same sunlight was born somewhere in the middle of her chest, and as she took his hand, the sunlight in her chest spread through her like fire consuming a thin wood shaving. The man was filling with the same sunlight, the closer she came to him. Then he took her in his arms and kissed her.

Kissed her...soft lips brushing, tongue stroking, gliding against hers, sending a fiery current of pleasure through her veins. His arms went up and down her back, then down to take two handfuls of her arse. A sound broke from her as a wonderful onslaught of desire assaulted her insides. An animalistic growl escaped his mouth as he picked her up. She wrapped her legs around his narrow waist and something hard and hot pressed against her swollen sex, rubbing, making her burn and ache deliciously. He walked with her into the house of light, and the friction sent bursts of pleasure through her that made her move her hips to rub herself against him, wanting more, more, more...

She sat up with a jerk and the warm sunlight was swallowed by the darkness of her bedchamber. Breathing hard, she stared at the same stone wall she'd seen every day of her life. No sunlight. No James. Her body was still hot, the flesh between her thighs aching for him, for him to touch her there, to do...something...

Oh God! What was happening to her? How could she dream such an indecent, sinful dream? Clearly, being anywhere near him was bad for her psyche. He was a temptation, a sweet, irresistible temptation. The apple of sin that made God chase Eve and Adam away from paradise.

Only, Catrìona's dream had nothing to do with the true God or Adam and Eve. In fact, there was something pagan about it, something that she'd always been taught was wrong. Sinful. Had some demon led her astray?

Everything around James was so confusing. She hadn't just desired James in that dream, but had felt complete and at peace and whole. For the first time in her memory, she'd felt free, loving herself and her body. Unashamed. Worthy.

Was it wrong to feel all those things?

For someone who believes so fiercely, you have surprisingly little faith in yourself, he had said.

Truer words had never been spoken to her.

And in that dream, with him, she'd had faith in herself. And it had felt wonderful.

Wiping her palm against her face, she lay back in bed and looked at the narrow sliver of silver moonlight on the floor.

Too bad she couldn't stay in that dream forever. There'd be no convents she needed to go to. No sins she had committed. No pain and heartache.

Just love and sunlight and James.

She covered herself with the blanket. Silly dreams.

But were they that silly? She'd told him she did want children and did want a husband. She hadn't taken the vow yet. She could still change her mind. She could still allow herself to live a simple, secular life.

Only, the most logical husband to have that life with would be Tadhg. She could still tell him she'd changed her mind.

But the man she *wanted* was James.

She had to know if these were nothing but silly dreams.

Wrapping her blanket around herself, she put on her shoes and walked out of her room. She hurried down the stairs, through the quiet, chilly bailey and into the barracks building. There were just two other men sleeping in the room, and she moved without a sound towards the mattress on the floor where James's long figure slept.

She marveled for a moment at his peaceful profile, but before she could wake him up, he turned and looked straight at her.

"Catrìona?"

She pressed her finger to her mouth. "Shh," she whispered. "Come, please."

He nodded and sat up. His powerful chest whitened in the semidarkness of the room, the strong muscles of his shoulders and arms rolling as he put on his tunic and stood up.

"Everything all right?" he whispered.

"Aye," she said. "Come."

She took his hand, and it was warm and big and rough. Sunlight didn't burst through her chest, but the already familiar feeling of calmness and wholeness spread through her. She tugged him after her and led him back to her room. As she went in, he stopped and frowned.

"Aren't you supposed to avoid being alone with a man?" he said.

"Aye," she said. "'Tis fine, come in. I must talk to ye."

He glanced back at the landing, then entered, closing the door behind him. She lit the tallow candle that stood on the chest by her bed and looked at him.

"What is it?" asked James.

"I just had a dream about ye," she said.

His face straightened and something like shock crossed his features. "Did you?"

"Ye... Um... Ye were in a house full of sunlight, and ye took my hand, and I...I never felt as good."

James paced and ran his fingers through his short hair. "Fuck."

"What?"

"I can't believe I'm going to say this. Were there carvings of rivers—"

"—and hands," they finished together.

A shiver ran through her. Their eyes locked, his completely black and shining with intensity.

"You're turning my whole world upside down, Catrìona," he whispered. "I...I've never felt anything like that for anyone.

Never had these spiritual, out-of-this-world experiences. Never traveled in time, for God's sake. What are you doing to me?"

His words were hot and heavy, his voice raspy and full of need.

She crossed the distance between them and hooked her arms around his neck. "What are *ye* doing to me?"

He wrapped his arms around her, pressing her to him, melting her muscles into warm honey.

"Don't you have a monastery to go to?" he said, eyeing her with an expression resembling pain.

"I dinna ken if I want to... I...I canna stay away, James."

"You know I will leave, don't you?"

She swallowed hard and nodded. "Aye. But do ye really have to?"

"I have a life there. My sister is pregnant and her fiancé died. She only has me to help her. I can't leave her to be a single mum. Besides, I can't stay in the Middle Ages..."

Silence hung between them. "Even for me?"

He swallowed. "That is not how I meant it, Catrìona. I..."

She shook her head and smiled. "Dinna explain it. I ken yer meaning."

She was unlovable. Or at least not lovable enough for him to abandon his life and stay here for her.

But she couldn't think about that now.

"Then 'tis what we will have," she whispered. "Till ye leave. Till I have to go to the convent. 'Tis what we'll have. Take me to the house of sunlight, James. Make me yers."

Only, deep down, she knew she was about to ruin herself and was heading to a heartbreak that would never heal.

She'd go to the convent and spend the rest of her life doing penance for the sin of lust. She'd never be a wife or mother, but she'd have this memory. This must be enough.

Memories of James and dreams of the life she'd never have would need to be enough for her to live by for the rest of her life.

CHAPTER 27

J ames crushed his mouth to Catrìona's. She pulled him to
her like a gravitational force. Her soft lips parted,
welcoming him, responding to his kiss with a desire that
echoed his own. She was so small and felt fragile in his
arms, and, oh God, he wanted her.

That dream...her, naked, all glowing and breathtaking. Him,
hard and burning for her...

As in his dream, he picked her up, letting her legs wrap
around his waist. He carried her to the bed and sat down with
her on the edge of it. He moaned from the sweet friction as his
erection pressed into the hot, soft crease between her thighs.

Just like in the dream, the sound she made in her throat set
his blood to seethe and boil.

Bloody hell, he was ready to take her.

Make me yers, she'd said.

He stopped the kiss and leaned back, searching her eyes.

"What did you mean, make you mine?"

She exhaled. "This...and more... How does a man make a
woman his?"

"But you're a virgin..."

"Aye."

He cursed under his breath. He'd never been with a virgin and never wanted to. His idea of a relationship was two consenting adults enjoying each other with no expectations and no labels. Deflowering a medieval virgin who was planning to become a nun wasn't a responsibility he wanted to take on.

"Is it not a sin or something?" he said, still breathing hard.

"Aye, 'tis..." she whispered. "And I'll have my whole life to pray for expiation."

She sealed her lips with his, the kiss both gentle and burning with need. Her scent was all over him, herbs and her own sweet, feminine aroma, and he wanted to plunge into that scent like it was a soft cloud. She tasted divine, delicious, and pure.

She wanted him. She wanted to sin with him. Who the hell was he to deny her that pleasure when he was burning for her like a torch?

Only that small, bloody voice of reason nagged him that it wasn't so simple.

When she gave out a throaty moan of pleasure, his burning blood turned into a brush fire and roared, shutting up any voices inside his head but those that echoed her moans. He left her mouth and began making his way down her jaw, down her silky neck, inhaling her scent like it was oxygen. She tilted her head back, exposing her neck to him. The pulse in her throat beat under his lips in a ragged, rapid rhythm that echoed his own.

The hem of her night gown was coarse against his lips—rough linen, he realized. God, her skin was so soft, he wondered how these clothes didn't irritate her. She deserved to wear the silkiest, most flattering clothes. How would she look in a pale-blue dress that would brighten her eyes and highlight the pale gold of her hair? He undid the strings that tied her gown and pulled it down, but it didn't go lower than her shoulders. He kissed a trail down to her breasts, and she shattered when he cupped her soft breast through the fabric. He circled her nipple and it hardened into a small bud.

Getting so hard he thought he would burst, he lowered his

head and took her breast into his mouth through the material of her dress, sucking on her nipple. She gasped, arching into his mouth, her fingers clutching at his hair, digging into his scalp.

"Oh, Lord!" she moaned out. "Oh, forgive me, God..."

With that, the voice of reason in his head came back. She was still not entirely okay with this, despite all that she had said. She still thought this was wrong. She was just feeling weak and confused, and he'd be taking advantage of her.

James sat back and looked at her. She gazed at him, her mouth half open as she panted, her eyes two dark pools of lust. The sunrise was breaking through the slit window, pale-peach and blue light shining on her.

"Whatever's the matter?" she said.

He closed his eyes briefly. Stopping now felt physically painful.

"I'm sorry." He met her beautiful eyes. "I can't."

He saw that this rejection stung. She cringed slightly, and a crease formed between her arched brows. "Why?"

"Because I can't do that to you. You want me now, but one day, you'll regret this. And once done, this cannot be undone. I won't stand between you and your immortal soul."

She stood up, still panting, only now her eyes flashed with anger. "But ye dinna believe in God or souls. How can ye lecture me on my immortal soul?"

He sighed. "A long time ago, I believed in both." Their eyes were locked, the air between them crackling with electricity, with heavy, unspoken pain and desire. "And I'm not lecturing you," he said softly. "I'm just trying to look out for you."

She straightened her shoulders. She started tying the ties of her gown. "I dinna need you to look out for me. 'Tis my soul, and my body, and my life. I made my own decision, why canna ye respect that?"

He hated hurting her, especially given that she already felt rejected.

"Would ye have stopped if we were marrit?" she said.

"Married?" He winced, not sure if he heard her right. "But—"

"I ken ye have to leave soon," she interrupted him, a note of steel in her voice. "But if ye werena leaving. If ye could...wanted to...stay. And if we were to be marrit. Would ye have stopped?"

No. He'd never stop. He'd never let her go. He'd make sure not a single tear ever rolled down her cheek again, unless it was a tear of happiness.

He opened his mouth to say something... Something that wouldn't hurt her, but wouldn't betray how much he enjoyed the idea of her being his forever.

But he couldn't. There was a man who'd suit her much better than him. And if she was thinking about marriage, Tadhg would be the one who'd trump James.

James shouldn't keep Catriona from Tadhg—her best chance of happiness.

Because Tadhg would be staying, and James would leave as soon as he was sure they'd caught the right assailant. His sister needed him, and he didn't belong here.

"I can't tell you that," said James, and before she could do something to tempt him beyond his already fragile resolve, he stood up and left.

CHAPTER 28

The next two days passed in a frenzy of activity in preparation for the Highland games. While the whole castle seemed to have been running around getting things ready, James found himself helping, too. He had several more talks with Finn, and with the guards who claimed to have seen him up on the wall, but found out nothing new.

Despite Raghnall's claim to have been in the kitchens, no one could confirm his whereabouts during the night of the stabbing.

There were all these loose threads, but he was missing something. Something important to create a complete picture.

Although Catrìona seemed to be avoiding him and was spending more time with Tadhg, James couldn't get her out of his mind.

Every second that passed by, she was in his thoughts, no matter what he did. And even though he'd thought Tadhg must be a better match for her, he hated seeing him near her. And Tadhg never seemed to be far from her. He was helping her cook, and was even stitching up cloth and canvas for the booths and tents that would be set up for the games.

James had spent a lot of time in the big field where the games would be held, a thirty-minute walk or so outside of Dornie. Together with David, Raghnall, and several other Mackenzie men, he'd built wooden booths for trades and sales, raised tents, helped prepare the field for different sorts of games, made targets for the ax-throwing competition, collected rocks for stone putting, and created a separate, safe space for children. They'd cut some nearby trees for firewood, filling the clearing with the pungent scent of fresh wood and pine resin, and prepared places for bonfires for cooking and for warmth. Soon, the clearing looked like a proper medieval fair. The day before, visitors had started to arrive, filling the surroundings with relaxed laughter, songs, and chitchat.

During the past two days, James had found himself spending a lot of time with David, whom he really liked. There was this seriousness and kindness about him, along with the desperate determination to accomplish his goals.

David had come back from the battle with scratches and bruises, but was otherwise unharmed. Though, something had changed in him. Like a man stranded on an uninhabitable island, there was a haunted loneliness in his eyes, despite the fact that he'd spent little time alone in the Middle Ages. It seemed everyone was in everyone's business, and the sense of community was very strong.

But he understood David. This wasn't his world. Nor was this the future he'd dreamed of. James knew David was eager to go back to the twenty-first century with him as soon as possible.

James had talked to Rogene, who'd told him everything that had happened and explained a lot of things about the Middle Ages.

Finally, the first day of the Highland games came, and the whole castle, save Laomann and a couple of servants and guards, went to the clearing. The procession was long ahead of James, people carrying bulging sacks of freshly woven linen and sewn clothes and shoes, as well as casks of Angus's uisge and wooden crates with pastries, bread, and bannocks to sell. The castle blacksmith had made new axes, swords, shields, and horseshoes, and several people were carrying those to sell, as well.

It was probably because the procession was so long that James had to stop right after they went out of the castle gates and stand in a long queue waiting to be boarded into the boats. He stood, enjoying the clean air, and looked around. He remembered the day he'd come here with Leonie and how they'd walked down the long, stone bridge that didn't exist yet in this time.

Uncharacteristically, the weather was warm and dry, and perfect for the Highland games. James looked at the wall and wondered if this was where he and Tadhg had been talking the night someone had pushed Tadhg off the wall.

He tried to imagine how it had been for Tadhg, to fall, helpless, trying to grab on to something, and how lucky he had been, having only a few injuries, and not losing his life.

Though he was lucky to be alive, overall Tadhg seemed to have had a run of bad luck recently. The man had been wounded, then, likely poisoned, and then pushed off the fifteen-foot-tall wall. Who would try to kill Tadhg, and why? What was the connection between him and Laomann?

The most obvious reason to kill Laomann was because he was the laird of the clan. But Tadhg...he wasn't even a clansman anymore, hadn't been for many years. Could he know something? Something important that he might not even realize was dangerous?

James's gaze landed along the base of the wall, where something brown caught his attention.

He put the crate with bannocks that he was carrying on the ground and told David he'd be right back. He jogged to the wall, not letting the light-brown shape out of his sight. As he drew closer, he first thought he was looking at a snake hiding in the grass. Then he realized it was a thick rope.

What was it doing here? He picked it up and studied it. About ten feet long, he reckoned. He looked up at the looming, rough stone wall. One of the guards must have dropped it and forgotten about it. It might be useful for the games.

After they arrived at the meadow, time passed quickly. The first day was the day of the market. Red, green, and blue booths lined the square meadow. The space was filled with the lively shouts of the traders calling for customers, passionate negotiations, and playful banter, which resulted in bursts of laughter. The booths were full of weapons, food and drinks, clothes, and shoes, as well as leather belts, armor, and tapestries. There was even a booth for books, and James saw Catrìona lean over a book of French poetry longingly. He wished he could buy it for her and teach her to read—he knew how badly she wanted to learn, and she was so bright she'd be reading thick volumes in no time. Though, he'd first need to learn French himself.

Hundreds of people gathered around the large meadow, and there was a lot of trading, drinking and eating, and singing. It looked like the event was a success, and he hoped it would bring in as much money as the Mackenzies needed.

The second day was the day of the games.

The sun shone cheerfully on the green grass of the meadow that had been cleared for the games. Tents had been erected at the farther side of the field, where most people were gathered. Booths sold pastries, bannocks, ale, a medieval version of haggis, and meat pies.

A band of five people played bagpipes and drums, the medieval melody unfamiliar but beautiful to James.

Boars were being grilled over several campfires, and more bannocks were being fried in cast-iron pans. The scents of grilled meat and baked bread were mouthwatering.

But despite the cheerful atmosphere of the games, the incredible Highland landscape, and the blue sky overhead, James couldn't seem to enjoy the day like everyone else. Something hung in the air, menacing and inevitable.

Where was this feeling coming from?

He looked around, seeing nothing that indicated danger.

Right now, the caber toss was taking place on the main green. Angus, probably the biggest and tallest man around, was holding what looked like a 120-pound log vertically braced against his shoulder. Then he ran forward, stopped, and heaved the caber upwards.

The crowd held their combined breath as the log spun end over end. Then one end hit the ground, and the log fell away from Angus. The crowd erupted in cheers and congratulations.

"'Twas a perfect toss," said a voice by James's side.

Tadhg stopped to stand next to James. He hadn't needed to use his crutch for several days now, and looked much better than James had ever remembered seeing him.

"Yeah?" said James.

"Aye. A perfect throw is when the caber lands straight away from the thrower. Look. It lies almost like a mast on a ship."

"Right."

Tadhg turned to James and looked him over. "Dinna ye want to try it?"

James chuckled. "No. I'm not a Highlander."

"And yet ye want a Highland lass, dinna ye?"

James met Tadhg's hard blue stare.

"I'm not sure what I want is any business of yours," said James.

"'Tis if it concerns my bride."

Shock slapped James. "Your bride?"

"Aye."

Had Tadhg proposed during the last three days while James and Catrìona had been busy with the preparations for the games? Had she really changed her mind, after all?

Was it possible that Tadhg had convinced her to change her mind while James couldn't?

Jealousy ate at his insides, corroding him. Everything within him screamed that he didn't want Catrìona to be with anyone but him. But he was a rational man. And as a rational man, he knew this must be for the best—best for her, at least.

"Well," James said. "You better make her happy, then."

Tadhg crossed his arms over his chest. "Or what?"

James clenched his fists. He'd hate to let her go without a fight. But that was what would be best for her, he reminded himself.

Before he could say anything, he saw David heading towards them, his eyes ablaze. "I need a man for the tug-of-war. James, come on, join my team, man."

James glanced at the farther corner of the Highland games meadow, where in a small clearing, two rows of men stood opposite one another, holding a long, thick rope loosely.

Raghnall, who was apparently on the other team, curled his hands around his mouth and yelled, "I need a man, too!"

"Come on, James," said David. "Highlanders against...well non-Highlanders."

"I'll join ye!" said Tadhg to Raghnall and raised his hand, then marched that way, wobbling slightly on his injured leg.

James saw Catrìona standing by the field with Ualan in her arms, feeding him a piece of pastry. His chest ached as he remembered the day they had gone out into the woods with the baby. That had been one of the best days he remembered in a long time.

"Sure," he said to David, and they strode towards the two teams waiting for them. "Who are the other non-Highlanders?"

"Well..." He chuckled. "There's a guy from France. The other two are Highlanders, actually, so...I guess, the logic doesn't work exactly... But still. Meet Craig and Ian Cambel."

James was greeted by two men. One of them, Craig Cambel, was tall and dark-haired, with the clear stance of a leader about him. Craig looked him up and down and narrowed his eyes, and James had the impression of being scanned by an X-ray machine. The other one, a red-haired man, probably as big as Angus, with muscles like tree trunks, grinned at him, and James thought that as long as Angus wasn't on the opposite team, David's team would definitely win.

"Yer accent..." said Craig. "Where are ye from?"

"Oxford," said James.

Craig's eyebrows knitted together for a brief moment, and he glanced quickly at a woman who was standing by Catrìona's side. She had red hair and held a toddler in her arms. On Catrìona's other side was a curvy blonde. They chatted with Catrìona, throwing happy glances at Craig and Ian. Unlike many medieval women, these three didn't cover their heads, and James thought briefly that they were probably quite modern for these times.

Craig opened his mouth to say something, but David interrupted. "Let's go!"

The teams lined up. Somehow, James ended up the first on his team, and Tadhg ended up the first on his. James stared into Tadhg's face, noting the animosity written there. The obvious reason was the competition, but they both knew it was not about that at all. James saw Catrìona watching them, lines of concern on her forehead as she bounced Ualan on her hip.

Then Iòna, one of Angus's trusted men, raised his arm. "When I put my arm down, begin."

He threw his arm down and the rope jerked and tightened in James's arms as both teams leaned back and began tugging. James's muscles screamed as he dug his feet into the ground, bracing his legs and pulling the rope with all his strength. The six warriors of the opposite team grunted, faces red, muscles in their shoulders and thighs bulging like swells in a storm.

The sinews on Tadhg's neck were as taut as the rope they were tugging. James was impressed that Tadhg, who'd been thrown off the wall not that long ago, could actually do this. To James, it felt like he was trying to pull a lorry.

And Tadhg was pushing against the ground with his injured leg as though he wasn't in any pain at all.

But he'd been using a crutch until recently, and he'd just fallen from fifteen feet...

And now he was holding this rope and—

The answer hit James hard, and he let go of the rope for a

split second. The image of Tadhg, holding on to the rope as he hung from the wall—or rappelled down its face like a mountain climber—flashed through his mind. Using the rope to get down from the wall would have saved him ten feet, and that would be a much safer fall than fifteen feet.

The poisoning had started when Tadhg had arrived.

Was it possible that Tadhg was behind all of this and, at the same time, pretending that he was injured and being attacked and poisoned? Being a victim would keep him from becoming a suspect, and had...

It made perfect sense, and finally the missing piece of the puzzle was falling into place. Because while harming Laomann made sense—he was the laird and cutting him down would weaken the clan—there was no reason for Tadhg to be poisoned or murdered.

These thoughts flashed through James's mind in a split second, but the moment he had let go of the rope was enough for the opposite team to gain momentum, and after a few strong pulls, James's team was thrown off their feet, and Tadhg's team was announced the winner.

While James watched Tadhg, Raghnall, and the rest of their team throw their fists in the air and yell jubilantly, cold sweat poured down his spine. Because he now knew that there was a snake that lived in clan Mackenzie. A snake that looked harmless but whose venom was deadly. A snake that was about to bite.

And it was up to James to stop it.

CHAPTER 29

Catrìona wiped the damp cloth against Rogene's forehead.

The shadows of the trees swayed on the surface of the tent, which was for the head family of clan Mackenzie. Laomann was still in the castle, too weak and in too much pain to move, even the short distance. But the rest of the family was here to participate and greet their guests.

To allow Rogene to take a rest whenever she needed, the tent was situated a little away from the arena of the Highland games. Rogene was lying on a makeshift cot and holding a linen cloth to her mouth. Poor pregnant thing, she was exhausted.

Studying Rogene's pale face, Catrìona wondered about the future. About the life that Rogene and David had left behind. The life that James had in Oxford.

She hadn't had a chance to ask much about it, with the Highland games being prepared.

Catrìona had just witnessed the tug-of-war where the two men she'd been thinking about more than she should had competed against each other like two roosters. But before they could finish, Rogene had doubled up, vomiting by a tree, and without seeing the outcome, Catrìona had handed Ualan back to Mairead and taken her sister-in-law into the tent.

"Are ye feeling better?" asked Catrìona.

"Yeah." Rogene sighed out. "Thanks, hon."

Catrìona held out a cup for her. "Ginger tea?"

"Oh, yes, please."

As she took the cup and sipped the tea with a satisfied sigh, Catrìona noticed the movement of a shadow on the canvas of the tent. The next moment, the opening moved and James came inside.

"Here you are," he mumbled, almost unhappily. "I've been looking all over for you. I have to talk to you right away."

Catrìona squeezed water out of the linen. "What about?"

Rogene sat straighter on her cot. "Is everything okay?"

James drew his hand through his short hair. "I know who the murderer is."

"Really?" said Rogene, her eyes burning with curiosity. "Who?"

Catrìona frowned at him. James was looking at her with a guilty and careful expression, as though he was about to kill her favorite dog. "It's Tadhg."

Catrìona let out a long sigh. "'Tis nae Tadhg."

"I figured it out. The night when he and I talked on the wall and he fell, or, as he claims, someone pushed him. He could have easily died in that fall, right? But all he had were a couple of bruises and a cracked rib."

"He had broken ribs," said Catrìona firmly. Anger was beginning to boil within her. How dare he blame Tadhg for something he couldn't have done.

"I found the rope down by the wall. Right under where we stood."

Catrìona frowned. "That doesna prove 'tis his."

"At tug-of-war, he seemed to be pain-free. He pulled on the rope with full force and put pressure on his leg like it was fine—and they won. How sure are you that his wounds were serious?"

"I havena checked on them since we got back from the convent. But he was also poisoned."

"I think he may have poisoned himself. Think about it. The murderer's only victims were Laomann and Tadhg. Why would someone try to kill Tadhg?"

Rogene grimaced thoughtfully. "Yeah, James, sorry. I'm with Catrìona on this. The rope doesn't prove much. And who would throw themselves off the wall?"

"Someone who really wants to appear a victim. Someone who doesn't want to be suspected."

Both women stared at him doubtfully.

"Have faith in me," he said.

Catrìona chuckled. "'Tis a big word to use for a man who only wants facts and information."

"All right. You're right. I need more proof." His jaw muscles worked. "Please tell me you didn't say yes to his marriage proposal."

Rogene gasped. "Tadhg proposed to you?"

Catrìona blinked. "How did ye ken?"

"He told me. He said you were going to be his bride."

Catrìona cleared her throat. "Aye, he did say that he wanted me to marry him, but I havena given him my answer... In truth, I said that I was still set on being a nun."

"So why does he think you'll be his wife?" asked Rogene.

Catrìona looked at James and there was pain in his dark eyes. "I dinna ken. Perhaps he still hopes I'll change my mind."

James's nostrils flared. "He surely wants to avenge his father's death. That must be why he's trying to kill Laomann. He has a motive."

Catrìona shook her head. "Nae. He's a good Christian man. He kens 'tis a mortal sin to kill..."

"But he's a warrior, Catrìona," James said softly. "He's killed before. This wouldn't be his first sin."

Catrìona shook her head, her mouth dry. "Nae. I refuse to believe—"

"I'll prove it." He turned and walked out of the tent.

Catrìona exchanged a glance with Rogene, who was as wide-eyed as she.

Her mind raced. What if folk believed James and tried to harm Tadhg? Or, even more likely, they would turn on a Sassenach who was making accusations against one of them—a Highlander.

Nae. Catrìona couldn't let that happen. Darting out of the tent, she ran after him. In the distance, James was talking to a few men. As she came closer, she realized he was asking if they'd seen Tadhg.

David, who was eating a piece of roasted boar, looked up at him and said, "I saw him leave in the direction of the castle. He said something about getting more blankets as there are more people than anticipated staying overnight."

Catrìona came closer to him and tugged at his sleeve. "James, ye must stop!"

James turned to her, pale. "I don't think that's what he's doing, Catrìona. I think he's going back to Eilean Donan because Laomann is practically alone."

A stab of worry pierced her gut. If he was right about Tadhg, that would give him an opportunity like never before to kill Laomann.

"Tell your men to come with me," James urged. "We must stop him. We must prevent Laomann's death."

She swallowed a knot that felt like a rock. Part of her was worried and wanted to say yes... But no, she couldn't believe Tadhg, the lad she'd known since childhood, the lad who'd proposed marriage to her—twice—could at the same time plot to kill her brother.

"Nae," she said. "Tadhg would never do that. Ye're wrong."

Hope died in his eyes. He looked at David. "David? Will you come with me?"

David winced. "Tadhg? The murderer? Sorry, man, I'm with Catrìona. I just don't see how."

James turned to Raghnall. "I suppose you don't believe me, either?"

Raghnall sighed. "The man saved my life, James. He canna be the one. Can it be that ye're jealous?"

James's jaw worked under his beard. His chin protruded with resolve. "Well, I can't let him kill Laomann. So even if you don't believe me, I must stop him."

Without another word, he raced into the woods towards the castle. As his broad back disappeared among the trees, Catrìona hugged herself, wondering if this was God's test for her.

To trust the man who should be right for her but wasn't.

Or the man who shouldn't be right for her but was.

CHAPTER 30

James couldn't see Tadhg.

The woods gave him the illusion of seeing Tadhg's blond head in the shadows of the trees or around the next twist in the trail. Leaves and branches rustled, masking any cracks of a snapped twig.

He needed to find Tadhg and prove that he was the murderer. Or at least make sure Tadhg didn't try anything else.

As James walked up the hill, he realized the worst thing about the likelihood that Tadhg was the murderer was that he was so close to Catrìona. And James had no idea if Tadhg wanted to hurt only Laomann...

Or if he intended to harm everyone in the Mackenzie clan, picking them off one at a time.

Including Catrìona.

And it was strange, perhaps, but the thought of her being hurt was what made him realize a simple truth he'd been denying.

He loved her. He knew he loved her, and he knew now he'd never loved a woman before. There was no one like her. Not in the twenty-first century. Not in the fourteenth.

But he didn't want to mess up her life, make her change her

mind about the convent and regret it. He'd already caused enough mayhem. And he was about to cause more—by proving the man she'd once loved, and maybe still did, was a would-be murderer, and by disappearing from her life forever.

He'd been walking for a while now. Below, he saw a valley flanked by rolling hills that grew into mountains. The combination of yellow, olive, and ochre moss, stone, and earth was breathtaking. How would it feel to stay here for the rest of his life? Breathe this air, live in harmony with nature.

It was so different to his life back in Oxford. Even though it wasn't a big city, life there was busy. Bikes, cars, lorries, and pedestrians clogged the streets. University conferences as well as all kinds of cultural events meant a lot of activity and noise.

The faint smell of petrol on the busy streets mixing with the aromas of coffee and vanilla from bakeries and the odor of stale beer near student pubs.

None of that had ever made him happy.

Here, life was simpler. Part of him wanted this life, connected to the elements, away from technology, from the hectic pace of the twenty-first century.

But he had his sister there, and his future niece or nephew. He had a responsibility to her, and he wouldn't leave her alone. He was the only family she had left.

Suddenly, something caught his eye. Behind one of the hills, far below, several gray and brown dots appeared and moved. He went completely still, watching. The dots grew closer and soon he could see hundreds of them, moving in his direction.

When the sun glistened off metal, he realized what he was seeing. An army!

An army was moving in this direction, light glinting from their swords. The flying standards made his stomach drop: red flags with three white lions. He'd seen them in the battle with the Ross clan.

The enemy was making another move. He had to run back and warn Catrìona and the others.

Something sharp and cold bit into his neck.

"Dinna move," said a male voice.

Tadhg. James would recognize the voice anywhere.

James froze, a slight shiver of fear running down his spine. He slowly raised his hands up.

"Ye bastart," Tadhg spat. "Ye wilna bring me trouble nae more."

James slowly turned around to face the man.

Tadhg was changed. The mask of a good man, a loyal and God-fearing servant gone. Instead, his handsome features were distorted in a mask of menace.

James chuckled. "Always a noble thing to cut the throat of an unarmed man. Your father would have been proud."

Tadhg's face went white. "Dinna dare speak of my father. Dinna dare to blacken his name with yer filthy mouth."

"Is that why you're trying to kill Laomann, to avenge your father's death? Laomann was the one who discovered you and Catriona. He was the one who got you expelled from the clan, wasn't he?"

Tadhg took a slow, deep breath and relaxed. Clearly, he knew he had won. The only thing James had were his fists, and he knew how to use them.

But he also knew he was now face-to-face with a murderer. All bets were off and Tadhg had no reason to lie anymore. No one would know the truth but James.

And Tadhg wanted to gloat.

"Sit on the ground," said Tadhg, pressing the tip of the knife deeper into James's throat. "Back to this tree."

James glanced back at the tree Tadhg must have been hiding behind. The army was coming closer. The field below was full of people and horses.

Bugger. He had to warn the Mackenzies or it was going to be a slaughter.

"Do you see that?" said James.

"Oh, I see that," said Tadhg. "Sit down, or I will make ye."

James dropped to the ground.

"Hands behind the tree."

James glared at Tadhg. "I thought you wanted to kill me?"

Tadhg smiled. "I wilna have to." He nodded to the army. "They will."

James's blood chilled.

"Hands behind the tree," Tadhg repeated.

James needed to keep Tadhg talking. He put his hands back and Tadhg crouched behind the tree and began tying James's hands with a rope. His arms ached from being twisted unnaturally.

"Is that the rope you used to shorten your fall from the wall?" James asked.

Tadhg kept tying him. "How do ye ken about the rope?"

"I found it. I'm very impressed with your ability to hide your tracks, though that rope was one oversight. Why didn't you hide it?"

"I didna want to cause suspicion by going out of the castle while my leg and my ribs were healing."

"They look mighty fine now."

"They are. Just a wee bit of exaggeration goes a long way. Had to be done. Ye were suspecting the uisge. And uisge would lead to me."

James couldn't help but admire the man's determination to achieve his goal, to cause himself such harm.

"Is that how you gave mandrake to Laomann, the uisge?"

"Aye. It wasna just mandrake. I also added monkshood. 'Tis what caused him to lie unconscious for days."

"When were you able to do that?"

"Catrìona was busy stitching me up and Laomann gave me his waterskin of uisge. While he was distracted, I poured in my poison. I had to drink a bit of it, too, though. Nasty stuff, but it doesna taste like much. I was wrong about the quantity. Clearly. He's still alive."

"And did you plant the knife in my things?"

"Aye. Of course. I hoped with ye out of the way, I'd finally be able to finish the job. But then Angus showed up and saved yer sorry Sassenach arse for some reason."

As the harsh fibers of the rope bit into his wrists, James stifled a groan. "So you're with clan Ross? How?"

Tadhg stopped fiddling, gave a final tug, and then went on to tie James's legs.

When James kicked at him, he put the point of the knife to James's ankle. "Stop moving or ye will stab yerself."

James let out a groan of helplessness. If he wanted Tadhg to keep talking, he needed him to feel victorious.

Tadhg wrapped a piece of rope around James's ankles. "I have lived with clan Ross for years. I serve Lady Euphemia, in all ways that she wishes. All."

He finished tying and stepped in front of James, looking smug. "I was pleasing Lady Euphemia when Angus arrived to convince her to marry him after all. And I stood right before him, and he didna even recognize me. And when he betrayed Lady Euphemia for the second time, rejecting her as she stood at the altar and marrying Rogene instead, she made a plan. She'd send someone unnoticeable, invisible, and trustworthy, and kill them all. Everyone he loves. Everyone but him. And he'd have to watch, helpless."

James's pulse raced. "What about Catrìona?"

Tadhg's Adam's apple moved up and down as he swallowed. "Nae her."

"But why did you agree to murder for her?"

"Because Euphemia will help me become a baron. I'm nae worse than the Mackenzies, and had Catrìona marrit me, she'd have kent I'm better than any nobleman because no one would love her like I do."

"Do you still intend to marry her?"

"Aye. Of course. I realized I never stopped loving her the moment I saw her. I'd thought she'd marrit a nobleman instead of me. But she didna."

"She wants to be a nun."

"I'll change her mind. She loved me before. She'll love me again."

He looked down the hill, triumph on his face. "They'll be here soon."

"You know you'll burn in hell for this, right?" growled James.

Tadhg stared into the distance, his eyes empty and dull. "I ken. But I'll spend this life with the woman I love."

"She'll never forgive you."

He came to James and crouched before him. "Let me worry about that." With pure venom in his eyes, he threw his fist back, about to slam it into James's face.

Instinctively, with his hands tied back and no possibility of protecting himself, James closed his eyes tight, bracing to absorb the hit.

Instead, there was a small thud, a grunt, and the weight of a grown man fell on him, knocking the air out of him.

He opened his eyes. Catrìona was standing above Tadhg, who was now sprawled facedown over James's legs.

As Tadhg scrambled to face her, trying to get back to his feet, Catrìona cried, "Ye bastart!" She kneed him in the face, and the man staggered and fell backwards to the ground.

And didn't move.

Catrìona sank to her knees before James and cupped his jaw.

"Oh, God's bones, are ye all right, James?"

He looked into the most beautiful eyes in the world, the blue of the sky and the sea, lit up as heaven must be if it existed. Highlanders really were like cats, because two of them had come up on him without him noticing a thing.

"I am now," he said.

"I'm sorry I didna believe ye before," she said and planted a sweet kiss on his lips. "I caught up with ye when Tadhg was tying ye up and hid behind a tree. I heard everything. Let me free you, tie this treacherous snake up, and let's go save my clan."

CHAPTER 31

"At arms!" yelled Catrìona as she and James hurried through the trees. "Ross is attacking!"

The Highland games clearing wasn't even visible yet, but James could already smell the acrid scent of smoke. Screams and yells sounded, and James's heart slammed hard in his chest.

Once they came into sight of the clearing, he saw that they were too late. Tents were burning, Ross warriors were fighting with Mackenzie, swords and axes glistening as they slashed.

Catrìona turned to him and planted such a hard, passionate kiss on his lips, it was almost violent. Her eyes weren't those of a nun. Or a compliant woman. They were the blazing eyes of a lioness under attack, who was not going to let anyone harm her family.

"Ye must stay alive," she said. "Ye must. Promise."

James felt a hard knot in his throat and swallowed it. He just now realized how slim their chances were against hundreds of men armed with swords and axes and bows.

He inhaled. "I promise."

Well, the Middle Ages were definitely rubbing off on him because he felt like a Highlander making a vow to his laird.

Or in this case, his lady.

"Promise you will, too," he said, clutching at her shoulder.

Her eyes glistened as she inhaled. "I promise."

She nodded, then ran into the battle. Someone handed her a sword, and she took it and swung it surprisingly masterfully.

Was there a limit to the surprises this woman would bring to him?

Bloody hell!

I promise to stay alive...

How was he supposed to honor that promise?

But somehow he knew he had to.

For her.

He looked around, quickly, and his eyes fell on one of the tents—the Mackenzie tent. Fire blazed all around it, coming from a circle of firewood, branches, and twigs. From inside it, people screamed.

Angus thrashed and yelled, as several men held him by the arms. With cold shock, James realized Rogene must still be in there. He also didn't see David, or Raghnall, or Mairead with Ualan...

With ice freezing his veins, he moved. He had to help. He had to save them.

A shadow moved to his right, and he ducked, avoiding a glistening sword. Tadhg was there, of course, swinging the sword, his face distorted in a furious grimace.

Tadhg kept attacking, and all James could do was keep backing up, ducking.

"Very honorable," he yelled between the attacks. "Yet again trying to kill an unarmed man. Seems to be your specialty—to backstab."

"Shut up!" roared Tadhg. "Ye should have killed me back there, but the Ross men freed me."

As Tadhg swung again, James stepped back, stumbled on something, and fell flat on his back.

"So I will kill ye now," added Tadhg, fury ringing in his voice.

With both hands, he raised the sword like a stake above James's chest. Death flashed across James's eyes, but as he stared up at Tadhg, a sword pierced through the man's shoulder.

He stopped and gurgled something.

With astonishment, James saw David, his hair burned, missing eyebrows and eyelashes, and a nasty burn across one cheekbone.

Tadhg turned.

"You fucking son of a bitch," roared David. "You tried to kill my pregnant sister!"

But Tadhg wasn't done yet. Despite his wound, he hefted his sword and swung it at David. Their swords clashed, then swung and clashed again. Even wounded, Tadhg was still a dangerous enemy. Years of battle experience meant more than whatever training David had had during his short time in the Middle Ages.

James scrambled to his feet as they fought. He saw a bow and a quiver of arrows leaning against a tree and hurried to take them. With the once-again familiar movement, he lifted the bow, pulled the string, and aimed the arrow at Tadhg.

He was going to help David. He was an officer of the law, and he'd just caught a medieval criminal.

"Tadhg MacCowen," he yelled. "I arrest you for attempted murder."

Tadhg turned to him in surprise, and in that moment, James shot the arrow. It pinned Tadhg's sleeve to a nearby tree. Unable to move, Tadhg jerked his arm. Raghnall marched up to him, just as singed as David, with nasty burns that showed through the tunic on his shoulders.

With murder written in his eyes, Raghnall pressed his sword just above Tadhg's collarbone.

"And I sentence ye to death for treason against clan Mackenzie," said Raghnall. And just as James threw his hand out to try to stop him, Raghnall pressed his sword into Tadhg's neck.

The man made gurgling sounds as blood spilled from his mouth and his face became a mask of terror and pain.

"Die, ye shite," spat Raghnall as he retrieved his sword, and Tadhg's body slumped down, hanging by the cloth where James's arrow pinned it to the tree.

"You didn't have to do that," said James, though part of him wasn't sorry.

Raghnall removed the arrow and handed it to James. "Aye, I did. 'Tis my fault. I brought the snake to our home. Now get to work, Sassenach. Help us protect our people and land once more. Are ye with us?"

James looked at David and Raghnall and then into the field of the Highland games, which had now become a battlefield.

As his eyes found Catrìona, who was swinging her sword like a Celtic goddess of war, he nodded.

"I'm with you."

He turned to the wall of Ross men and let his arrow fly.

CHAPTER 32

Catrìona stilled, gasping, as she saw her brother pierce Tadhg's throat. The man she'd just killed lay under her feet with a gash through his stomach.

And the man she'd once thought she loved, the man who'd betrayed her and her family, fell like a sack of stones onto the ground. Her chest contracted as the onslaught of sadness, guilt, and relief flooded her.

She should have seen through him. She shouldn't have trusted Tadhg as she had. She should have trusted the man she truly loved.

James.

Still alert with enemies all around, she moved her gaze to James, whose face grew worried, and she saw him shoot an arrow somewhere behind her.

He was so handsome, so graceful with the bow in his hands, and her heart bloomed.

But when she turned to see where his arrow flew, her heart sank into her feet, because a wall of Ross men were coming through the woods. And right behind that wall, sitting straight-backed atop her horse, was Euphemia of Ross.

As Catrìona assumed her fighting position, holding her sword high up by her shoulder, arrows flew from James's bow, finding their targets among the Ross warriors one by one.

Euphemia cried out, and her troops gave a roar and launched. They clashed with the already ragged but determined Mackenzie forces, and two men came right at Catrìona.

Here she was again, taking more lives, sinking deeper into darkness. Would God ever forgive her for feeling powerful as she sinned? Would she forgive herself?

She swung her claymore, meeting the swords of her enemies with loud clangs. She felt woozy, her body weakened from her fasting and the men she'd already fought today, whereas both her opponents were fresh, strong warriors in their prime.

But what she lacked in physical strength, she made up for in agility and the power of her faith. God must be with her because she was fighting for her clan and for her family. She was fighting for the man she loved.

The Ross warriors fought because their mistress was greedy and wanted revenge.

Catrìona pierced one man between his ribs and cut the other man's throat. As they fell, spilling blood onto the meadow of the Highland games, she noticed Angus cutting his way through the Ross forces like a knife through butter. Raghnall was whirling and turning, his claymore like the wind. David, his face determined, fought another warrior, though he was stepping back, clearly overwhelmed by the attack. James's arrow struck the attacker in the side, and he fell, clutching at the wooden shaft.

There were the Cambels, and the Ruaidhrís, and the MacDonalds, all fighting for the Mackenzies.

So many lives were being lost on both sides—for what? A bruised ego?

She could stop it if she got to Euphemia. Euphemia had sent Tadhg to kill her whole family. Euphemia wanted them dead.

Catrìona had taken so many lives already. She could take one more. One more that would help to stop the spilling of so much blood.

A man ran at her, his sword at the ready. She didn't hesitate. *"Tullach Ard!"* she roared and ran to meet him.

She deflected his slash, but the man was so huge and his blow had so much impact that he knocked her back. She brought her claymore up and across, almost cutting his arm off, but he stepped back in time. She caught her breath and pulled both of her arms back with the sword to thrust it into the man's abdomen, but he stepped aside in time, bringing his fist back and smashing it into her chin.

"Och!" She gasped, staggering back, momentarily disoriented.

She commanded her blurry vision to go back to normal and in time, because his blade was headed for her neck. She ducked, but not enough, and a small blast of pain bit into her shoulder.

The warrior brought his sword up, clenched in both hands, for the deadly executioner-like slash.

She didn't have time to move aside.

But just as the giant warrior was about to swing, an arrow hit him straight in the chest and knocked him back. He gasped and staggered, clutching at the wooden shaft, and fell, eyes wide.

Catrìona looked over her shoulder and saw James sprinting towards her. Around him, men kept fighting, and he had to step aside for a moment when a warrior fell in his path.

He came to her and hugged her around the shoulders, making her wince of pain from the scratch. "Are you all right? Did he wound you?"

She turned and looked straight at Euphemia, who was glaring at Angus as he fought, her eyes wild. "Dinna fash," Catrìona said. "I'm perfectly fine. I just have to get her."

James frowned, his eyes narrowed at the woman. "Is that Euphemia of Ross?"

"Aye."

His hand went into the quiver and took out his last arrow. "I can do this for you, take this death on my conscience." He nocked his arrow, then pulling the string back, found his sight and released.

Catrìona's heart rammed against her rib cage as she saw the arrow fly. Time stretched. She loved him for doing this for her, for taking the sin on his own soul. She'd have done the same for him.

Euphemia's horse moved and the arrow flew past her into the woods.

"Damn," James cursed. "I'm out of arrows. I need to gather some."

"'Tis all right," Catrìona said, rolling her shoulders back and ignoring the ache.

She called upon all the strength that was left in her body. Her tired muscles were burning, sagging from the exhaustion of the battle. And there were still many warriors between her and the woman who had brought death to their celebration. The clatter of swords, the hisses, and groans of pain, and thuds of falling bodies pressed against her ears.

She squeezed her claymore tighter in her fist.

James took a step towards her. "Catrìona, no..."

"I have to."

She wrapped her arm around his neck, and kissed him, tasting blood and dirt on her tongue. The kiss gave her strength, gave her power like a gulp of fresh spring water. She looked into the handsome brown eyes, then turned and walked straight into the battle.

Ignoring James's cry, she pushed, and ducked, and whirled. From the corner of her eye, she saw him dart to gather arrows that were stuck in the ground and in the bodies of fallen warriors.

She scythed her claymore in a dance of death, bringing it over and over into the bodies of her enemies. Soon, she sank into that bloodlust state of a warrior unleashed. Strength surged through her, strangely spurred by the bone-deep fear of death that followed her like a shadow the color of dried blood.

Distantly, she knew she'd been wounded, too. Superficial, hollow scratches. Bruises. Her ribs might have been cracked. One strong kick in her left kidney had left her breathless.

But she made herself forget. Made everything fade away but the woman with golden hair sitting on a warhorse.

And then, centuries later, she reached her.

Euphemia's blue eyes locked on her in outraged surprise, as though she saw a dirty mouse that had just escaped the trap.

Catrìona's fist clenched around her claymore. The handle was sleek and slippery with blood.

"Ye come to kill my family?" she roared. "I dinna think so!"

Euphemia's mouth opened in a gasp. Catrìona grabbed a fistful of the woman's dress and pulled, but Euphemia clenched the horse's mane, managing to stay in the saddle. Her horse neighed and stepped away. One of the Ross men noticed Catrìona and ran at her, his ax dripping with blood.

To her surprise, he slashed low, and she barely managed to jump back. But the movement brought her closer to Euphemia, and she felt the stab of cold steel at the back of her neck.

"Now where are ye going, wee lass?" murmured Euphemia. "Ye think you can just come and take me? As ye say, I dinna think so. Kill her!"

The man's eyes fell on Catrìona, and she knew, just as she had in the tower of Delny Castle, that he wouldn't hesitate. He stepped forward, raised his ax, and scythed it downwards, aiming for her neck. Something thunked, and he was knocked back.

An arrow protruded from his eye. Catrìona looked to where most of the battle was still raging, and saw James, aiming a bit higher than her.

Aiming at Euphemia.

"One word," he called, "and I'll shoot her."

"One movement," warned Euphemia, her blade digging deeper into the back of Catrìona's neck, "and her pretty head rolls from her shoulders."

Catrìona locked her eyes with James's. If she died today, she'd die a woman with no regrets but one.

That she hadn't known what it felt like to be in his arms. What it felt like to be intertwined body and soul with the man she loved. To have him buried inside of her, deep, and dissolve in him.

If she lived through today's battle, that would be what she'd want to do the most.

Their eyes still locked, she mouthed soundlessly, *Do it.*

In the next moment, his arrow flew, and there was a momentary pressure from the blade and sharp pain burned her. Then there was an outraged gasp from behind her, and the blade was gone.

Catrìona stepped back, taking her sword into both hands. Euphemia was holding on to the arrow that protruded from her right shoulder. Her eyebrows drawn together, her eyes wild, her mouth curved downwards, in a mask of absolute rage, she yelled, "Retreat! Retreat!"

She turned her horse back and galloped into the woods.

Catrìona looked at James. "Again! Shoot her again!"

But he showed her the empty quiver.

As Catrìona watched the Ross men following their lady commander back into the woods, she realized the battle was over, at least for today.

Her legs weak, the ground slipped from under her feet as she collapsed. The last thing she felt was strong arms catching her.

CHAPTER 33

Catriona sighed as James put her into bed. He'd held her all the way to Eilean Donan after the battle, as they rode in a cart, exhausted and spent.

They'd won.

At the price of dozens of Mackenzie lives, and the lives of their ally clansmen, they'd won. Would Euphemia's wound stop her? Catriona wasn't sure.

With only superficial scratches and bruises, and one gash in the shoulder that had been sutured properly, Catriona had stayed on the battlefield, tending to the wounded. When everyone was taken care of, they were all invited into the castle, into safety, in case Ross attacked again while they were vulnerable.

They'd returned late into the night, and she could barely keep her eyes open from physical exhaustion. Now that they knew Finn was indeed innocent, he'd been released from the dungeon, and he'd offered to help take care of the wounded.

Catriona had seen him tend to Bhatair, the guard who'd claimed Finn had thrown Tadhg off the wall. As Finn was re-dressing the man's wound, he'd croaked, "I am sorry for blaming ye. I had really thought I'd seen ye. I'm nae afraid of a sword, but magic...witchery...terrifies me to the bone. I had thought ye were the source of our clan's misfortune."

Finn had nodded. "God be with ye. I'm just a healer."

And now James stood by her side, watching her like a solemn statue. Immobile, dependable.

"Ye fought well," she said.

He sank to his knees to be at eye level with her. Gently, he brushed the hair from her forehead. "I had to. You forbade me to die."

She sighed out and eased her face into his palm and closed her eyes. She bathed in the sensation of security and peaceful joy that he gave her. Contentment with herself. With life. A sense of fulfilled duty.

Again, she'd taken lives. She knew the guilt would crush her later like a boulder, but now she was just empty. Empty, but glad her family was alive.

James's hand slipped from under the side of her face. He stood up and, panicked, she caught his hand.

"Dinna go," she said.

"Don't you want to sleep?"

"Stay with me, my angel," she said, and he blinked, as raw need and anguish dampened his eyes. "Guard my sleep."

"Catrìona, I'm pretty sure in your time, it's not proper or something..."

"I told ye last time, I dinna care. Please."

He hesitated for a moment, then gave a curt nod. He walked around the bed to the other side, climbed onto it, and stretched out behind her, wrapping one arm around her waist. His body was muscular, and warm, and strong, and she relaxed in an instant.

"Dinna go," she whispered again as she drifted into an exhausted sleep. "Dinna leave me..."

But as she sank into the sweet oblivion, she knew she wasn't just talking about tonight. She was pleading for him to stay with her in this time forever.

When she opened her eyes, darkness still clung to the room; she could make out only the faint outline of him between shafts of moonlight. They'd twisted in sleep, so she faced him now, and even removed from the circle of his arms she felt a deep peace.

Catrìona had spied men before in various stages of undress. But James was different. An uneasy need to see every inch of him beat through her. She couldn't look away from the dark hair on his bare chest. For once in her life, she didn't restrict her desires. She reached out and ran her fingers through the wiry curls.

His hand caught hers a heartbeat later, trapping it. "What are you up to, Catrìona?"

She blinked, meeting his eyes now that hers had adjusted to the darkness. "I dinna ken. But I want ye so fiercely everything in me aches for it."

The grip around her fingers tightened for a moment and then, almost reluctantly, he released her hand, setting it on the rumpled bedding. "You don't want me. You're probably just in shock."

She shook her head and shifted closer on the bed, the linen of her undershirt tangled around her hips. "'Tis nae from fighting. It seems in the dark, I'm brave enough to take what I want."

"Take? Hmm...what do you know about taking things from a man?"

His gentle challenge raised her hackles, and she scooted close enough to him to shove him flat on his back.

A gentle *oof* fell from his lips, which morphed into a strangled groan as she climbed on top of him and straddled his thighs. He grabbed her hips, she assumed to keep her small form from toppling off his much wider one.

"I ken plenty about taking a man."

What she didn't know, outside of animal husbandry, was what came next. Not that she would confess that to him.

His big hands molded around her hips, as his eyes traced the shape of her body through her thin undershirt. Her nipples were hard points jutting from the fabric. She wanted him all right, and by the heavy length of him between her thighs, he didn't want to turn her away.

"Really, Catrìona, what do you know? Tell me."

A wash of heat stung her cheeks, and she was glad he couldn't see her blush in the dark after her bold words. "When a man and woman care for each other or...or when they are marrit, they join together."

His voice took on a throaty timbre. "Tell me why?"

"Children, but 'tis for pleasure, too."

At the word "pleasure," a tiny tremor passed through his body, and he arched his hips up into hers. It was barely a pulse of action, but the friction his body caused along hers shot a sizzling wave through her. Like a lightning strike of pure undiluted joy.

She leaned forward to brace her hands on his chest, suddenly breathless. By his wide-eyed stare he'd felt it, too. Before she slid from the heat of his body, he gripped her tight in his arms and spun them into the bed so she lay below him now. Her thighs opened wide without consideration as his heavy weight pinned her into the mattress. It wasn't uncomfortable; it felt more right than a prayer.

"Do you feel that?" He punctuated his words by driving himself into her hips. Even with his weight, he did so gently, reverently, and she hissed out an exhale. He brushed her face with his knuckles. "When a man wants a woman, he first gets her ready for him. He makes sure she gets pleasure."

Why was he telling her all this when he could be doing it?

She licked her suddenly dry lips. "And then?"

"Then, when she's hot and wet and dripping for him, he'll slowly slide inside her to bring her to pleasure all over again. It can hurt the first time, but you probably know that."

She nodded. Other women talked of such things, after all, but not what he said, not the... It was then she realized she was wet and hot between her legs where they made contact. It had already begun between them.

"I'm already wet for ye."

He pressed his forehead between her breasts and muffled a groan into her dress.

She raised her head. "Are ye in pain? Can I—"

He shook his head. "It's not a groan of pain."

When he lifted his eyes to hers, the indignity faded to something darker, achier. She squeezed her thighs around his hips, and he swallowed. Shaking his head, he leaned in like he might kiss her, but stopped a breath away from her lips. "I'm not going to take your virginity. I can't do that and live with myself."

She didn't care about her virginity, not right now. She wasn't going to marry anyone... Well, anyone but James—but that wasn't an option. And she'd have her whole life to pray this sin away. She arched into him, wanting, aching, needing him. The need for him to ease the heady thrumming ache in her body with his own was unbearable.

"Please." She wasn't above begging, not for him. Not for how she felt right now in his arms. She trusted him. It went beyond her body and deeper than her heart. The knowledge was in her blood and in her soul: whatever had brought them together— magic or God or a simple coincidence—he was like her. Just as she wouldn't hurt him, he wouldn't hurt her, either. Inside that soul of his was the unstoppable need to serve and to help and to protect.

He did it following logic and mind.

She, following her heart.

And when they were one, like now—intertwined, entangled, open to each other with no reservations—they were complete.

As though reading her thoughts, his dark eyes flashed and shone with meaning. Slowly, he leaned closer and sealed his mouth with hers. But surprisingly, the kiss wasn't gentle. It was as though the last of his restraint had broken, and he could finally have what he wanted. He was demanding, taking, owning her. She took his tongue into her mouth, and scorching heat flowed through her body as he began lashing and licking.

Her mind went blank. She was all fire and tingles and need. He traced his lips down her throat, then stopped at her breasts and cupped them both with his hands. She gasped as his mouth took one nipple and sucked at it right through her dress, while his fingers circled and played with her other nipple. Desire raged within her like a wildfire. Something primal, animalistic roared within her.

Pleasure was building, pushing her somewhere she'd never been before. Somewhere in the kingdom of bliss. But before she could reach it, he lifted the warm, sensual weight of his body from hers, and she stifled a cry of protest.

He went farther down her body, kissing her stomach through the fabric of her dress and her undershirt. His hands traced the length of her thighs, reached down to the skirt of her dress and lifted the hem up to her belly, exposing her to his sight. She should be mortified, she should be covering herself, but she didn't want to, not with the hungry look in his eyes as his gaze roamed her naked flesh.

If this was what man and wife did with each other—naked and open and bare in front of each other, then so be it. She took ahold of the boldness she'd embraced when she'd straddled him and opened her legs wider, letting him see all of her.

"You're so beautiful," he whispered.

The gentle awe in his tone threatened to stop her heart.

He nudged her knees wider and positioned himself flat on his stomach, his face by her most intimate places.

She held her breath and raised her head. "J-James... What are ye doing?"

He smiled up at her, a dark promise in his gaze. "Loving you."

She barely had time to consider what he'd said, when he hauled her knees across his shoulders and delved his tongue through her aching flesh.

Her entire world narrowed and contracted to the feel of his body against hers. Everywhere they touched, pleasure danced across her skin. He'd fisted his hand in her dress, holding it above her belly. He used his other hand to hold her open for him. After that first lick, he'd taken another pass igniting a whole new wave of pleasure over her.

Soon, it became too much. She dug her fingers into his hair, not allowing herself to consider whether or not men and women were permitted such things. Whether this was sinful or whether God intended for a man and woman to have this joy.

He groaned into her skin, shooting a vibration up her body. Then he focused his tongue on a spot at the top of her cleft, and she arched up into him as his tongue found a rhythm that made her body sing hymns. Not just hymns, a prayer of pleasure so fierce her skin hummed with it, her limbs shook from it.

She clutched his hair tighter. "What are ye doing to me?" It was a moan, a plea, a song of praise.

He lifted his face to look up the line of her body, a roguish grin on his damp lips. She helplessly gazed back at him. "Worshipping you."

Her reply was a soft gasp, and he redoubled his efforts. Then he took the hand he'd been holding her dress with down to prod her opening.

When she jolted against him, he murmured soft, indiscernible words against her skin, and then so very slowly inserted one finger into her body. It stretched her, opened her up almost till it ached—but pleasantly. It didn't hurt.

Then he lowered his mouth again and the sensation changed. Her body clamped around his finger with every swipe of his tongue and the pleasure took on an ebbing flow, like the waves on a rocky shore. Retreating and gaining with the tide. Except, this tide felt like a breaking. Like at any moment she might shatter on the rocks of pleasure and not recover.

"Let go, love," he said, between long licks. "Don't be scared."

With anyone else, she might fear giving herself to this. But not with him.

It wasn't the steady pressure of his tongue that drove her to the edge of oblivion, but the wanton rocking of his own hips into the mattress. As if he wanted her so fiercely, he was reduced to rutting the bedding to keep her safe from him.

She imagined what it would feel like, to have his hips splaying hers and rutting into her with that same intensity. It shattered something inside her, broke it open.

The power of her pleasure brought out a long moan and every inch of her body quaked. He lapped at her faster, harder, until the pleasure began to recede, and his ministrations became too much for her overly sensitized skin.

She didn't have to tell him to stop; he could feel it and slowed, carefully removing his finger from her body. When she reached down, determined to have him, or to at least give him the same sort of pleasure he'd bestowed upon her, he shook his head and eased her hand away.

"No, Catrìona. You have no idea what it costs me not to throw myself at you. If you touch me, I won't be able to control myself. I won't be able to stay the honorable man you believe me to be."

She shook her head. "Dinna deny me, James. I want ye more than anything."

He pressed his forehead to hers and shook it. "No, not more than anything. Not more than your dreams, even if it feels like that now."

Gently, he rolled onto the mattress, pulled her dress back down, and tugged her into the warm strength of his arms. As she sighed into his embrace, listening to the hard beat of his heart, she knew nothing would ever be the same after this.

Because she'd never want to let him go.

CHAPTER 34

S he lay in his arms, sweet and pliable, and so beautiful, James's heart hurt. His erection still throbbed, needing her, excited by her arousal and her release. It had been one of the hardest things he'd ever done, not to take her and make her his.

But that would have been irreversible, and he wouldn't do anything to make her regret this.

He wanted to hold on to this moment forever. Never to leave her side, never to wake up a day without her.

But that wasn't possible.

He pressed her into his arms and kissed her forehead. "Are you sure you'll be fine going to the convent after this?"

She hid her face against his chest and her sigh tickled his heated skin. "I'm nae going to be a nun."

He rose on his elbow. Her tangled hair was silvery in the darkness of the room. An angel that had fallen from the sky. "What?"

She smiled, her face serene. "I've changed my mind... Well, ye've changed my mind. I dinna want to be a nun nae more. I want..." She bit her lower lip, and a cheeky smile touched her face. "I want ye."

James closed his eyes and shook his head. "No, Catrìona, don't change your mind on my account."

The smile fell. She sat up, covering holding the blanketto her chest. "Why nae? I swear to ye, James, only a man from another time, from another world altogether, would be able to change my decision to be a nun... To change me."

James's throat contracted. "Catrìona, I should have never done any of this."

"What?"

"Kissing you, making love to you... God, I just couldn't stay away. You're like a part of me that I lost long ago, that aches to come back to me. No matter the century. No matter our destiny."

She cupped his face. "See, 'tis how I feel, too. Like I've been asleep in a bad dream my whole life. Believing blindly I wasn't worthy. Believing I didn't deserve happiness. I will never abandon God, but I havena become a nun yet, I havena taken the vow. And now ye've come and changed everything. I dinna want to be a nun nae more. I want to be the woman ye wake up with every morning. The woman that loves ye. The woman ye crossed time for."

He hung his head and shook it.

Bloody hell, he was going to hurt her and himself—pierce his chest with a jagged knife and turn it good, wrenching his own heart out.

And hers.

"I never should have become close to you," he whispered.

"James..." Her whisper was full of urgency.

He raised his head and looked into her eyes. Taking her hands in his, he gathered them and kissed them. How could he make the blow as soft as possible?

"I just wanted you to open your eyes," he said. "For you to make the decision for yourself. For you to know you're worthy, and beautiful, and for you not to be brainwashed by religion like my mother was. For you to see reality for what it is. And know that you can have a man who loves you—hell, you can have any man you want. Anyone would be so lucky to have you."

Tears welled in her eyes. "I dinna want just anyone, James. I want ye."

"I can't..."

The words were like a detonation. She closed her eyes for a moment and exhaled sharply. She looked like he'd just hit her.

Bloody hell, he hated himself.

"Why?" she said. "'Tis because ye must take care of yer sister?"

He nodded. "Did you think I could ever abandon her? I have stayed here far too long already."

"Nae, I just thought ye'd find another way."

Something ached in his gut, like a fist twisting his insides. "I don't believe there's another way."

She chuckled. "Belief. Didna ye tell me to stop blindly believing and open my eyes?"

He knew she may be right. But there was more. "I'm also an officer of the law. I came here to find two lost people, and I have to take David back as he wants to return to the twenty-first century."

She nodded, breathing heavily and looking at him from under her lashes.

"You haven't vowed yet to be a nun, but I have vowed to defend and protect. I can't just abandon my work."

"Yer work..." she whispered.

"Yeah. My work."

She stared into his eyes for a long time, as though she was trying to take in his face, to remember every crease of skin and every detail. She nodded firmly and stood up, leaving James feeling empty, sad, and angry. And he hurt as if someone had cut off one of his limbs.

She turned to him, solemn and resolved, loss deep in her eyes. "I had thought...stupidly...ye'd change yer mind if I did. I was clearly wrong. Why would ye?"

Hell...

James rose onto his knees and moved across the bed to take her in his arms and make all the hurt in the world disappear like a puff of dust.

"Catrìona..."

But she took a step back.

The little sparrow was spooked and flew away.

She'd never come back and trust him enough to sit on the palm of his hand.

"I wilna stand between ye and yer vow, Sir James. If anyone understands the strength of one, 'tis me."

Tear his heart out and stomp on it, why didn't she?

"I wish it were different, Catrìona. I wish I could stay."

His mouth went dry, and he swallowed around what felt like a rock in his throat. "But you could come with me."

She blinked. "What?"

"You could come with me. If you're not going to be a nun, come with me to the future."

She kept silent for a while, her eyes shining. "Ye want me to be with ye?"

"Very much. Can you leave everything for me?"

The light in her eyes died. She looked down at her feet. "My clan needs me, James. They need a healer, and I need to help them. A bigger war is coming, I can feel it. We will need to raise our swords against Euphemia again. I will ask Rogene to teach me to read and write. I will borrow books from Abbess Laurentia. I finally have a chance to be independent, and strong, and needed. I had hoped I could be all of that and be with ye. But I canna live with my soul if I abandon my clan in a time of need. And it seems, ye canna live with yers if ye abandon yer sister and yer work."

James felt as if his chest were being crushed between two grindstones. "The faerie was wrong. Duty is stronger than fate, for the both of us. I'm not your destiny and you're not mine."

He felt empty, scraped clean from the inside.

"Ye helped us find the murderer," she said. "Ye helped to protect my clan. I believe yer mission here is accomplished, Sir James. Isna it?"

He held her eyes for a long, long moment. Then he nodded. "I believe it is."

"Then I let ye go," she said in a broken whisper.

His gut churning, he nodded and got out of her bed. He felt as if something was drawing him to her, but he resisted the urge to pull her into his arms again.

"Goodbye, Catrìona Mackenzie," he said, his voice rough.

Was this it? Was this the last time he'd see her in his life? God, he wished he could take a picture of her so that he could look at it in the future and still feel like she was with him in some way. She nodded, tears welling in her eyes, chin protruding in what he guessed was a stubborn resolution not to cry. He made an effort to memorize every small detail—every eyelash, every fleck of gold in her blue eyes.

Then, when he knew it wouldn't get any easier, and she wouldn't say anything more to him, he turned and walked away. The floor dragged at him, glued to the soles of his shoes. She didn't follow, and he told himself it was for the best. The farther away from her he went, the harder it was to keep going. And he knew the longer it took, the more seductive it was to forget his life in the twenty-first century and stay.

He went down the stairs, through the storage room on the ground floor, through the dusk of the Highland morning, and into the barracks to change his clothes. As he entered, he saw David's sleeping figure on one of the beds. The other men, most of whom had fought at the Highland games yesterday, were sleeping, as well.

James sat on the edge of David's bed and shook him slightly. David turned to him at once, sleepy, his eyes wild. His shoulder was bandaged as he had a deep cut from the battle. His face was decorated with bruises and cuts and blisters from the burns.

"James," said David as he massaged his eyes.

"I'm leaving," said James.

David sat up, his eyes bright with hope. "You are?"

"Yeah. You coming?"

"Fuck yeah," David exclaimed as he hung his legs off the bed.

A couple of grunts came from both sides of the room, where sleeping men had been disturbed by David's exclamation.

"Sorry," whispered David as he began putting his shoes on, wincing from pain.

As James stood up and went to his corner to change, he wondered if he'd be as happy to leave as David if he hadn't fallen in love with Catrìona.

"I need to see Rogene first," said David. "She'll never forgive me if I don't say goodbye."

"Sure. Go tell her. I'll meet you by the stone."

David wobbled enthusiastically out of the barracks. As James was changing, he felt like he was dragging his limbs through wet sand.

Finally, he left his medieval things behind and threw a last glance at the barracks. He silently thanked the men who'd fought by his side for helping protect the clan, the woman he loved, and himself from the enemy. Walking through the bailey, he marveled at the fact that he'd fought for his life alongside medieval warriors.

As he descended into the underground, he took the torch and lit the way. It didn't take long to hear footsteps behind him, and agitated voices.

He stood by the stone, staring at it like it was a window into an abyss he had to step into. His heart throbbed as though it was a raw wound and someone had just poured vinegar on it.

As the door opened, he looked up. Several torches appeared in the doorway, and there they were. David came first, his face lit up with excitement. Rogene, in her nightgown, was behind him, Angus after her.

"...and don't forget to call your aunt and uncle," Rogene was babbling. "They're still family...the only one you have. And don't you dare screw up your studies! Don't party and don't sleep around. Ever heard of venereal diseases and unexpected pregnancies?" She glanced down at her growing stomach, then seemed to soften.

"Rogene, calm down," murmured Angus.

"I'll be fine," said David. "You don't have to lecture me."

He gave the torch to Angus and took his sister in a bear hug and held her for several seconds. She dug her fingers into his tunic and wept into his chest. When he let her go, she cupped his face. "God, how did you grow up so fast?"

He squeezed her hand.

"I love you," she whispered. "I love you so much!"

She sniffed, and Angus wrapped his arms around her, pretty much swallowing her in his hug. She was weeping, shaking into his chest.

David stood, lost and wide-eyed. He sniffed. "I'm sure it's the hormones, Rory," he said, blinking. "I'll be fine."

He reached out and squeezed her hand once more before finally turning away and striding to James, his face hard with resolve.

"Goodbye, Rogene. Goodbye, Angus," said James, his heart sinking. "Take care of Catrìona for me, will you?"

Angus nodded, and Rogene only shook more.

James looked at David. "Ready?"

David nodded. "This better work this time."

Loud footsteps sounded behind the door, it opened, and James's heart leaped.

Catrìona hurried in, a torch in her hand illuminating her face in a golden-orange light. James had a sudden memory of the moment she'd found him locked in the darkness of the underground—the image of an angel who had opened the doorway into light and saved him. Their eyes locked, and he felt as if he were sinking into the ground.

A sudden hope blossomed in his chest. Had she decided to

come with him? Had she found some other way for them to be together?

"I'm nae too late," she whispered. "Thank God."

She came to him in quick, broad steps. "I couldna stay away. I had to..."

Come with him?

"...say goodbye," she finished.

It was like a hit to his solar plexus.

"Yeah," was all he could say.

She reached for the string on her neck, pulled it up and over her head, and gathered it in her hand. It was her simple wooden cross, and she held it out to him.

"For you, Sir James," she said. "May ye take my blessing and God's blessing with ye wherever ye go."

He stood, senseless for a moment. Her cross would be the only part of her he'd have. She was giving him her mother's cross.

"This means more than I can say," he managed, his voice cracking.

One more second and he'd change his mind. He'd drop to his knees and beg her to come with him, or for her to take him back.

But both choices would mean the end of their souls, his and hers.

He leaned forward and took her into one last hug, trying to imprint her memory into his body, inhale her scent for the last time.

Then he let her go, stepped back, grabbed David by the shoulder, tugged him to the rock, and slammed his hand into the handprint.

The familiar buzzing intensified, the air vibrated and shifted, and the cool rock disappeared from under his palm.

He was falling.

When he looked back at Catrìona, she wasn't crying, but he saw the eyes of a woman who'd never be whole again.

Darkness consumed him, and when he opened his eyes, a single electric bulb was illuminating the underground space with scaffolds and supporting beams. The pile of rocks and rubble was hiding the Pictish rock.

He was lying on the ground.

He sat up and looked around.

"David?" he said.

But he was alone.

CHAPTER 35

F*ive days later, 2021*

A BABY'S SQUEAL MADE JAMES JERK IN THE CHAIR, PULLING HIM out of his dream of rolling Highland hills, the gray walls of Eilean Donan, and the bright-blue eyes of the woman he'd never see again. He blinked in the harsh reality of hospital lights and white walls, disoriented.

The sight of his newborn niece, Lilly, lying swaddled in the transparent plastic cot of the hospital birth room filled his chest with warmth and chased the aching emptiness in his heart away. James stood up from the armchair and came to stand by Lilly.

"I'll get her," he told Emily.

His sister pressed the button on her hospital bed, and it gave out a mechanical whirring sound as the mountain of pillows rose. Poor thing—after eight hours of labor, she was exhausted and could barely lift her heavy eyelids.

He picked up the mighty seven-pound-and-fifteen-ounce Lilly, who kept producing sounds as alarming as a police siren.

"She must be hungry," said Em, rubbing her eyes.

James brought Lilly to his sister, who took her into her arms. Before she opened her gown to let the baby nurse, James turned around to give her privacy. He'd waited outside during the labor itself, as Lilly's grandmother, Harry's mum, had been there for her birth itself. She'd gone home for a short break now but would be back when it was time to take the baby home.

"Want some tea?" James asked, walking over to the door. "I can get some in the ward kitchen."

"No, just water would be fine," said Emily.

The screaming stopped, and James assumed Lilly was nursing. As he poured water for Em, he thought for probably the fiftieth time how easy and convenient it was in the twenty-first century to boil water, and how good it was that women could give birth in the safety of hospitals.

Even after five days, he still caught himself thinking he should go fetch water from the well to wash his hands.

Yesterday, he'd submitted the report on Rogene's and David's disappearance. Although the investigation wasn't officially over, there was a finality to his report.

He knew it would now probably stagnate and go into the pile of unresolved cases. At some point, they'd be assumed dead, and their friends and family would come to terms with their deaths.

It warmed his heart that those two were, in truth, alive, and at least one of them was happy.

He wrote in his report that he hadn't found any trace of Rogene and David beyond Eilean Donan and also hadn't found any evidence of foul play. He'd let Rogene and David off the hook and let them live their lives in peace. Though, why David wasn't able to come back with him to the twenty-first century, James didn't understand.

"How are you feeling?" James asked.

"I'm fine," she said and yawned. "Hungry. You?"

"Me, too." He chuckled.

Since he'd returned from the fourteenth century, he'd started a list of things he wouldn't have been able to enjoy had he stayed there. His sister's spaghetti bolognese was on top of the list, along with warm homes, electrical light, ibuprofen, and cars.

Cigarettes weren't on his list anymore. He was relieved that his cravings had diminished, and he'd decided since he had such a good head start to quitting, he should just stick with it.

But the list was there to remind him of all the reasons why it was a good thing he was here, walking around like a depressed zombie.

He took the cup of cold water to Emily. He'd seen her every day since he'd come back. He'd explained that his investigation had led him to unexpected places and he couldn't talk about it because it was police business. He'd apologized that he hadn't gotten in touch and for worrying her.

All this was better than the impossible explanation of time travel, which he still had a hard time believing himself. As it turned out, when he got back, she and the baby were fine, although she had been worried about him. He'd been gone for about two weeks, after all.

After a while, Lilly fell asleep and Emily gave her to James, but instead of putting her back into her cot, he cradled her in his arms and sat back in the armchair by Em's bed. The little girl made a sweet noise, and James rocked her a little, and she settled.

"She kind of looks like Mum," said James, unable to take his eyes off the wrinkled face. "Don't you think?"

Emily sipped her water and lay back against her pillows. "Kind of, yeah." She threw a careful glance at him and frowned. "Is that a cross?"

He looked down at his chest. Catrìona's wooden cross had come out of his dress shirt. He wished he could hide it, but his hands were full. "Um...yeah."

"Since when do you believe in God?"

"I don't."

Her eyebrows rose to her hairline. "Then why are you wearing a cross?"

"It's more a souvenir than a symbol of my faith."

"Souvenir of what?"

Of the only woman he'd ever love. Of the part of his soul he'd never get back. Of the happiest and the best days in his entire life. Of the biggest adventure he'd ever had.

"Just something I don't want to forget."

"My enigmatic brother, ladies and gentlemen." She shook her head with a smile. "Some things never change."

They were silent for a while, both unable to look away from Lilly.

"You know," she said. "You're so different since you came back from Scotland. You wear a cross, you don't smoke, you have this haunted look about you. What happened to you there?"

He stilled, his heart breaking all over again, like it did every time someone said the word "Scotland."

He wished he could tell his sister everything. They'd shared this darkness, this tragedy in their life, being raised in a cult, but it was still hard for him to open up to her. To anyone.

But who else would he open up to if not Emily?

"Something did happen."

His sister was his family, the closest person he had in this world. And he knew, just like him, she was going through a loss. Her fiancé had died, and she had just given birth to his child.

"I met someone," he said.

"Oh," she said, surprised. Then, enthusiastic: "Oh!"

Lilly gave out a noise of complaint and he rocked her.

"Well?" Emily said. "Who?"

Oh bloody hell, now there'd be a hail of questions. How could he tell his sister about what had happened? Should he tell her the truth or create some sort of a believable lie? Rogene had told David and look where it had gotten the poor lad. The hell James would let his sister and niece come with him...

Well, he was not going anywhere, anyway. No matter how much he wanted to.

Still.

He didn't see any purpose in testing Emily's ability to suspend disbelief.

"She's a Scotswoman," he said quietly. "Beautiful, and kind, and so incredibly brave..." He chuckled as the memory of Catrìona tightened his chest and made his eyes water.

"Is that her cross?" Emily asked gently.

"Yeah."

"Is she religious?"

"She is."

"Uh-oh. What did you do, James Murray?"

"Not enough. Too much. Take your pick."

"Well, are you still together? I mean, based on your puppy eyes, I don't think you are, but I'd like to hear it from you."

"We're not. And we'll never be."

"Why? You can always ask her forgiveness. If she loves you, there's nothing...well, almost nothing you could have done to completely ruin it."

He gasped. "Why do you think it's my fault?"

"Is it hers?"

His shoulders slumped. "No. You're right. It's mine."

Emily took a long sip of water, studying him thoughtfully.

"I just want to know," said James. "How do you do it?"

She placed the cup on the bedside table. "How do I do what?"

"How are you okay?"

She pulled up the blanket to her chin and looked at him with different eyes—sad and full of light at the same time.

"I'm not doing anything, Jamie. I mean, missing him hurts like I'm being bathed in boiling water. You know?"

He knew and he nodded.

"There are days I think I'd give everything to get him back. Like, anything. Bargain with the devil. Rob a bank. Plead and pray and eat no meat for the rest of my life. And you know how much I love my meat."

He chuckled and she smiled sadly.

"But then I realize he's still with me, you know?" She looked out the window. Wind moved the branches of a tall tree and soft shadows played on the wall. Birds chirped and cars buzzed in the distance. "He's looking out for me. He won't leave me or Lilly. I remember the good times. Our first date, our first kiss. How he said he loved me. How he proposed. I know this isn't the end. And even if I meet someone, he'll be okay with it as long as it's a good man."

James blinked at her. "You're thinking about meeting someone?"

"Well, not now! But after some time, once I'm ready, yeah. I mean, I'm not going to hunt for a man, but if I meet someone, I know Harry will be okay. He'd want me to be happy. I can't be a single mum forever."

"You're not going to be a single mum," James said firmly. "I'm going to be there for you every day."

She snorted. "No, you're not."

"Yes, I am. That's why I'm here. That's why I came back."

The words were out before he could stop them. Emily widened her eyes. "Excuse me? You came back to be here for me?"

"For both of you. You can't do this alone."

She threw the edge of the blanket to her knees. "Excuse me? I can't do this alone? Are you kidding me? I'm not some kind of damsel in distress, man. I have a good job and I can provide for myself and my baby."

"That's not what I meant. Taking care of a baby is hard."

"I'm not a stranger to that, James. The first few years will be hard, but I'm a fucking lioness. I just pushed a human being out of my body, and I really don't need you to take care of me."

"I didn't mean you're not capable," James said, thinking of another woman who reminded him of a lioness. "I just don't want you to feel like you're alone. Like you're abandoned."

"What makes you think I feel abandoned?"

"I'm the only family you have left."

She lay back on the pillows. "Jamie, I appreciate your concern, really. And I know you're doing it out of love. But I'm fine. You don't have to worry about me. You're not the only one who wants to help. Harry's parents have been calling every day. As you know very well, his mum was with me for the labor and she even took the birth course with me."

James flashed a smile and nodded, something in him lifting. Little Lilly would have a family. Not just him, but also Harry's parents and other relatives.

"But what did you mean you came back for me?" she insisted. "Did you break up with her because you thought you needed to come back to Oxford?"

"Yeah. You're my sister."

"Okay." She sat up straight. "I have so many questions about this. Why did you feel you had to make the choice between me and that mysterious Scottish woman? Why couldn't she move to Oxford if she loves you so much?"

"It's...um...hard to explain. It's not my secret to tell, but let's just say that it's impossible for her to come to Oxford. I'd have to move to where she lives."

"And you think you can't because I need your help?"

"Of course you need my help."

She leaned towards him and flicked his forehead. "You idiot!"

"Stop it! We're not kids anymore." He rubbed his forehead.

"Then why do you think I am one?"

"I don't."

"Yeah, you do, if you're basing your life decisions on thinking I can't make it without your help. I'm not going to be responsible for ruining your happiness."

"What? You don't want my help?"

"No! Not at the price of your happiness."

James stared at her, both furious and stunned, blinking. "I hadn't considered you might think this way."

"Look, I know you. You have never been in love. All you did your whole life was take care of me and Mum. I'm a grown woman. I'm a mother. You will not be my husband—sorry, I know it sounds weird, but you know what I mean. And I will not be the reason you're unhappy."

"Em—"

"Why can't you just move to Scotland and visit us every couple of months or something?"

"Because I can't. If I move there..." He cleared his throat, and Lilly stirred, rubbing at her cheek in her sleep. Goddamn. He understood now what Rogene was dealing with. "I'd never be able to see you again. Or my niece."

She frowned. "So it's not Scotland, is it?"

He sighed and kept silent.

"Why is it such a secret?" Her face straightened and she leaned down to him and whispered, "Wait...is it about MI6?"

The British Secret Intelligence Service...but usually, the agents still had normal lives, families.

"Um...what if it was? What if, for a reason that I couldn't tell you, the only way for me to be with Catrìona would be to never see you or Lilly again, never to talk to you, never come back here? Would you still want me to choose happiness?"

She blinked and tears welled in her eyes. "Yeah, I would, Jamie." She gave him a sad smile. "I'd have done it for Harry and never regretted it for a second."

He swallowed hard, his chest tightening with heartache. It hurt to hope.

"But what if..." He exhaled sharply. "I don't know if she wants me back. I don't know if it's too late. If she took that vow..."

"What vow?"

"She wanted to be a nun."

Emily's jaw dropped. "James Murray, when I asked what you

did, never in my life did I expect you'd seduced a nun! You can't disrespect religion that much!"

He winced. "Shh, you'll wake up Lilly. I didn't seduce a nun. She was still deciding if she wanted to be one. And now that I left, I don't know if she's already become one. If it's too late."

Emily took a deep breath. She looked pointedly at the cross around his neck.

"Well, then, brother dearest, you'll have to have the one thing you've always rejected."

"What?"

"You'll have to have faith."

CHAPTER 36

F*ive days later, 1310*

LAOMANN RAISED HIS CUP OF FRENCH WINE. "HEAR ME, everyone."

Catrìona looked up, grateful for the distraction from the dark, aching longing in her chest for the man she'd never see again. The core family of clan Mackenzie were all gathered at the table in the lord's chamber. The faces of those who were dearest to Catrìona were lit with the warm orange glow of the candles placed along the length of the table—real, expensive wax candles, not the smelly tallow ones.

The lord's chamber was filled with the scents of food that sat along the table. To cheer everyone up, Rogene had organized a special dinner. Yes, they were preparing to defend against clan Ross, but Rogene had suggested they forget about the enemy for one evening and get together as a family and enjoy life before they'd need to fight again.

Catrìona wondered if this was partly for David's sake. He

hadn't been himself after his failed attempt to leave with James. Anger and helplessness had been clearly simmering in the lad, although he was hiding them behind a stern mask. He caught Catrìona's eyes on him and she smiled with reassurance. He responded with a sad smile.

"Well?" said Raghnall, who, for once, had accepted the family's invitation to join them. "Do continue, brother, before we all die of old age."

Everyone around the table chuckled and Laomann cleared his throat.

"I think ye'll be pleased with my news, Raghnall," he said. He took his wife's hand and she squeezed it with a supportive smile. "I resign as laird."

"What?" Angus boomed.

Confused, surprised gasps went across the table.

"Why would it please me?" Raghnall asked.

"I'd like Angus to be laird in my place," said Laomann. "And Angus likes ye more than I do."

Angus shook his head. "What are ye talking about, Laomann?"

"Brother, ye're a good laird," said Catrìona. "We all love ye and dinna want ye to give up."

Laomann shook his head and looked into his cup. "Frankly, sister, Tadhg's attacks left my health weaker than I'd thought. I... I'm nae longer myself. Our people need someone strong and capable, someone they respect and can rely on, especially with the Ross army at our door. We all ken Angus has been unofficially laird all this time. 'Tis time to make it official."

Silence fell on the table as everyone considered his words, looking at one another. Catrìona couldn't disagree with Laomann's statement. No one could. Every word was true.

"'Tis very selfless of ye, Laomann," she said. "And noble."

Angus scratched his beard. "I ken ye're nae doing it because ye're afraid, but what will people think?"

Mairead sighed. "'Tis what I said to him, but Laomann is

bigger than worrying about what others think when it comes to the safety of the clan."

Laomann nodded. "Aye. Our clan stands a better chance under yer leadership, Angus. I dinna care if I seem a coward."

Silence hung in the room.

"Are ye certain, brother?" said Raghnall.

Laomann nodded solemnly. "I never should have been laird in the first place. 'Twas only so because of birth order, nae ability. Angus, 'tis yer role now. If ye accept."

Angus looked at Rogene and she smiled at him. "Is that what history has planned for me?" he asked her.

Catrìona frowned. She knew now what it meant, with Rogene being from the future. He was asking if this would be what happened. But everyone else was watching them with confusion.

She nodded. "Yes."

"Do ye agree, then?" Angus said. "Being a laird's wife has all kinds of new responsibilities. We'd need to live here and ye'd need to help with the management of the castle."

She squeezed his hand. "I really don't care if we live on a farm or in a castle. As long as I'm with you."

Catrìona's eyes filled with tears. She wished she could be with James now. She'd tell him the same thing.

Raghnall snorted. "Enough. My arse cheeks will stick together from all the sweetness that seeps through ye two."

Angus rewarded him with a hard stare as cold as stone. "I accept, Laomann. I will be laird of clan Mackenzie, and I even ken what my first ruling will be."

The smirk fell from Raghnall's face. "Why are ye looking at me like that?"

Angus kissed Rogene on the cheek, stood up, and walked with his cup in his hand to Laomann. "I thank ye for this honor, Laomann, and for yer trust." He hugged his brother and clapped him on the shoulder. "I wilna let ye down, I swear on my life."

Laomann raised his cup to the whole table. "To the new laird of clan Mackenzie, Angus! Slàinte!"

Everyone raised their cups and echoed him cheerfully. "Slàinte!"

Laomann clapped him on the shoulder and went to sit on the far side of the table. He gestured at the chair at the head of the table.

"'Tis yers now," said Laomann.

Angus nodded and held the back of the chair, looking around the table, strangely solemn and serious.

"We have a grave time ahead," he said. "I ken and I apologize, Rogene, for bringing this up, because ye didna want to, but 'tis important nae to lower our guard. There will be battles and we will lose many men. But I promise ye, I wilna let Euphemia take our happiness away. We will win, but we must use caution."

He looked sternly at Raghnall. "Ye've been away from yer clan long enough and Father was wrong to chase ye away. As long as I'm laird, ye'll always be my clansman and have never been anything less than that."

Catrìona reached out and squeezed Raghnall's hand. He squeezed hers back without looking at her till it hurt. He blinked, wide-eyed. Was she wrong, or were his dark eyes watering? He nodded one quick, sharp nod.

"But to be yer best, ye need a home." Angus paused, then said carefully, "Ye need a wife."

Raghnall frowned. "I need a what?"

"A wife," said Angus. "I will give ye back the estate that belongs rightfully to ye once ye prove to me ye're ready to settle down. Once ye're marrit and ye're a serious man."

Raghnall's face fell. "Angus, what is this nonsense?"

Laomann looked at Raghnall with an amused smile. "I hadna thought of that, but I agree. Having a wife, a family to care for will be good for ye. Will ground ye, make a man of ye."

Raghnall's upper lip curled into a snarl. "I am a man."

"Ye're still a lad the way ye behave," said Angus. "I love ye, brother, and I ken 'tis nae what ye want, but because I care about ye, I think it will be best for ye. So, prove to me ye're serious and take a wife and the estate is yers."

Raghnall stood up so fast, he knocked down the chair. "I wilna be forced into anything."

"But it would be good for ye," said Catrìona softly.

Raghnall glared at her. "And ye would talk, sister? Ye, who still wants to be a nun? Why dinna ye insist she finds a husband, Angus?"

Everyone stared at her, and Catrìona felt like she wanted the floor to swallow her. Rogene knew exactly what she was going through. The moment James had disappeared forever, Catrìona had collapsed to the floor. Rogene had held her for only God knew how long, rocking her, until Catrìona had cried out all her tears. Angus and David knew Catrìona loved James, but she wasn't sure if the rest of her family knew.

Angus's eyes softened as he looked at her. "Catrìona has had enough people in her life telling her what to do. I wilna be one of them."

The sob of relief that burst out of her mouth surprised everyone, including herself. Rogene stood up and moved to her side, holding her hand.

"It's okay, hon," said Rogene.

"I...I'm sorry, sister," said Raghnall. "I didna want to make ye upset. If ye want to be a nun, ye should do that."

"Do you still want to, though?" asked Rogene softly.

Catrìona clutched at the cross on her neck—only to find the space empty. Her cross was in the future, with James.

"I dinna ken... I like to be useful and I like to serve people."

"Ye can do all those things here," said Raghnall. "Dinna ye ken that?"

"I..." Did she? Her whole life, she'd felt unwanted, unlovable. And when she'd imagined herself being a nun, healing people and caring for the poor and the sick, praying to God, writing, reading, painting, making fabrics, growing plants, she'd thought she'd finally feel useful.

Appreciated.

Lovable.

Only, James had changed everything. *For someone who believes so fiercely, you have surprisingly little faith in yourself.*

And if she had that unconditional faith she'd given to God, the members of her family and her friends, she could give it to herself, also. Believe in herself. Know she was all right. Know she was loved.

She looked around at the faces of her family, and each and every one of them looked at her with nothing but love. How could she not have seen this before? Why did she think that because her father had treated her like an object, every man would? Yes, Tadhg had been a traitor, but Sir James had treated her with nothing but respect and appreciation. Even though he didn't believe in God, he cared for her soul.

He'd even saved her virginity, much as she'd wanted him to take it.

If this wasn't what being lovable meant, she didn't know what was.

And they were right, she wouldn't need to be a nun to care for people and be useful.

And if Angus allowed her to have all the freedom she wanted, she wouldn't need to go to the monastery after all.

She could stay with her family, even though she'd never be completely happy without the man she loved.

"Ye're right," Catrìona said, smiling to every member of her family. "I dinna need to be in the convent to serve people. And if ye promise to nae marry me off without my will, and allow me to live here, I wilna be a nun."

Rogene squeezed her hand. Angus nodded and the corners of his eyes wrinkled as he smiled warmly. "Of course ye can stay here. Ye'll always be cared for."

Catrìona knew what this meant. An unmarried woman was

often a liability, a mouth to feed, which was one of the reasons noblewomen were sent to monasteries. So her brother promising her she'd always be cared for and protected meant everything to her.

She wished this could be different. She wished women didn't need men to protect them, like in the future where James and Rogene and David were from.

"Thank ye, brother," she said.

Rogene looked at her. "Does this mean you can start eating like a human again and not a bird? And can we get rid of this brown burlap sack you're wearing and make a proper, beautiful dress for you? Please?"

Catrìona smiled through a sigh. "Aye, sister. 'Tis what we'll do."

The only thing lacking in her life now was James. Because no matter how much time passed, she'd never love a man as she loved him.

CHAPTER 37

ne week later, 2021

JAMES GLANCED BACK AT THE SECURITY CAMERA IN THE UPPER corner of the hall of Eilean Donan Castle. What were they going to think? Would they send one of the Oxford cops here to investigate his disappearance? Poor Leonie, one more person would be gone on her watch.

But, perhaps, the MI6 explanation would satisfy his colleagues. It certainly had been enough for his sister.

She'd cried into his shirt as though he'd told her he were dying. It broke his heart to leave her and Lilly.

But she told him he was doing the right thing and she'd tell his niece everything about her uncle, the secret agent. And, maybe, one day when he retired, he could come back to them.

James told her that was exactly what he'd do, only he knew it would never happen.

He'd resigned from his job as a policeman and had spent some time considering what to do about the rest of his affairs.

He understood now Rogene's meticulous and practical preparations to leave. He wished he could leave all his money and things to his sister, but that would probably be pretty suspicious, and he didn't want to do anything to make the police suspect her.

Part of him still wondered if he were insane. If he'd gotten his mother's gene for believing in things that didn't exist. What proof did he have that he could even go through the stone for a third time? That he would end up in the same year? And what would he do if by the time he got there, Catrìona had entered the convent?

But he kept squeezing her cross and repeating to himself to have faith like she did.

To have faith in her.

To have faith in his love.

And that she loved him back.

And so, with one last glance at the security camera and at the empty corridor, he pushed the door marked Staff Only and went down the narrow stone stairs. As he marched down the steps, he shifted his rucksack on his shoulder.

Like Rogene, he had prepared to stay in the Middle Ages forever. Whether Catrìona would be his or not, he felt sure this time he would be stuck there.

But his faith in her told him to take an engagement ring to propose with, which was his grandma's. He also took a roll of soft, fine blue woolen fabric from which he'd thought Catrìona could have a very pretty dress made. It was embroidered with patterns of flowers and leaves in silver thread, and when he imagined how the colors would highlight her eyes, his heart threatened to stop.

He took books, knowing he'd miss good novels, and he'd thought he could use them to help Catrìona with her reading. Plus Rogene and David could borrow them.

And he took an electric torch, and no cigarettes. He was now officially a nonsmoker, and couldn't believe how much better he felt.

He also took an excellent bottle of whisky with him to see if he could get Angus to make the stuff out of the moonshine they called uisge. Real Scotch whisky would be first made around the fifteenth century, and James thought if he could speed up progress a little, there was nothing wrong with that.

The door was approaching, and with it, his heartbeat was galloping faster and faster. When he pushed it open, he froze because unlike every time he'd come here before, the large space wasn't dark and it wasn't empty.

Beaming like a streetlamp, there stood Sìneag. The scent of lavender and grass reached him, and he knew she was real.

"James Murray!" she exclaimed and clapped her hands together. "Oh, dear lad, I kent ye'd be my biggest victory of all."

With his pulse thundering in his ears, he closed the door behind him and turned to her. "Um. Hi."

Emotions were battling within him. Anger that Sìneag had put him through the craziest experience of his life, gratitude for having met the love of his life, confusion at why she was here again, curiosity at how she did all the time travel, and fear...

Fear that for an unknown reason, she wouldn't let him pass.

"Hello!" she said and giggled. "Ye came prepared."

"Well...yeah. You were right. She's the love of my life. She's love beyond my life. She's everything."

The smile fell from Sìneag's face and suddenly there were tears. She blinked and touched under her eyes, then looked at her wet fingertip. "Gods, I am becoming more human the more time I spend like this... Look at me. I'm just so glad ye opened up to love. I'm so glad ye are going to get her."

"Yeah... You won't stop me...will you?"

"Ah," she said and smiled mischievously. "Ye're smart, are ye nae, Detective. It wilna be as easy this time."

Bugger...

"Ye need to buy yer passage."

"Sure. Do you accept credit cards?"

She tilted her head and laughed. "Nae, I dinna. But I do accept something tasty."

James blinked. "Tasty? Like food?"

"Aye. Food!"

"Really?" James put down his rucksack and rummaged inside. "I brought a pack of tomato paste and some basil to make pizza —I know Rogene and David would love it—but it's not very tasty uncooked. Would you like some chocolate?"

"What is that?" Her eyes sparkled.

"It's a dessert... It's good. Women usually like it. I brought some for Catrìona, but if it's the price for my passage, please take it." He took out a box of chocolate pralines.

"Mmmm..." Sìneag stretched out her hand and grabbed the round chocolate ball with a little lemon top.

She studied it with a frown, then put the whole thing in her mouth. As she crushed it, her eyes rolled back in bliss.

"Mother Nature..." she said through a mouthful. "What is this delight of sun and stars?"

James couldn't stop a smile. For someone who changed people's destinies without their consent, she was way too charming to stay angry at.

"So," he said, putting the rucksack on his back. "Does this count as payment?"

"Oh, aye," she said as she put another chocolate in her mouth. "Especially if ye allow me to keep the whole box."

"Sure. Keep it. Enjoy."

"Thank ye! Ye may go now, but I always warn everyone, 'tis yer last time, aye? Ye wilna be able to go through time again."

Though he had suspected this, knowing it for sure weighed heavily on his chest. He looked at the door leading back to the castle, his last chance.

But no. It would only be a half-life. Part of his soul was back in the fourteenth century with a Highland woman who had hair the color of gold and the eyes like a turquoise sky. A woman who had taught him to believe again.

"Yeah," he said. "I won't want to go back, anyway."

The rock started glowing, and as he stepped towards the rubble, the familiar pull made his stomach drop in anticipation. But there was still one question he had to ask. He turned, and had to chuckle at Sìneag's chocolate-smudged face.

"Is this payment enough for David? Or can I offer you something else for him to be able to come back?"

She stopped chewing and her eyes became sad. "That poor lad. He isna supposed to come back to this time."

"Right. Well, bollocks."

"Well, nae until he meets the woman he's destined for. Then the tunnel of time will work for him again."

James frowned, not understanding her meaning at first. "Wait...there's someone for him there, too?"

Sìneag beamed, her teeth dark with chocolate. "Oh, aye!"

James shook his head. "Poor mate. Well, cheers, Sìneag. Please, stop sending people through time. The police have enough to do already without investigating disappearances they'll never be able to solve."

Sìneag giggled. "I'm nae nearly done."

And then she was gone. James approached the stone and put his fingers into the handprint.

He opened his eyes in the complete darkness. It smelled like mold and wet dust and earth. At first, he was disoriented. Then after a while, he realized this was good. The lack of electrical light and the tomb-like silence meant he was back in time.

Oh, good Lord! What if the door had been locked again?

He sat up with a jerk and felt around until he found his rucksack. He retrieved the torch he'd brought with him and switched it on.

Yeah. Same familiar room. The rock. The walls.

The door.

He scrambled to his feet, still a little dizzy. Taking the longest steps of his life, he reached the door and pulled.

It moved. Cool air scented with a hint of metal and wood wrapped around him.

Oh, thank God!

He pulled the rucksack higher on his shoulder and grasped Catrìona's cross with his free hand. He didn't pray. He didn't think he'd ever prayed, even back in the compound with his mother.

But he prayed now.

Please, let her not have taken the vow yet. Please, let her be free.

Please, let her still want me.

Exhaling, he marched through the dark space of the underground, towards the narrow stairs. He climbed them quickly, barely catching himself as he slipped on one step. When he opened the door, there was no one in the ground-floor storage area. He walked out into a world ablaze with the pink and golden light of a sunrise. There was no wind, no noise of a busy castle around him. Only birds chirping cheerfully, greeting the new day.

The buildings were still dark against the glowing sky.

Catrìona must be sleeping. He sighed out. He hadn't realized how tense he was, unsure if he'd make it to the right time, if she'd still be here. He might as well go for a walk while he waited for the castle to wake up. Putting his rucksack against the wall, he walked to the sea gate. A sleepy guard opened the gate just enough for him to slip through.

The world outside was glowing with pale pinks, oranges, and blues that reflected in the completely still water of the loch. The hills and mountains were a black landscape in the water.

But none of that beauty mattered. None of it compared to the absolute bliss his soul sank into when he saw a slim, long-haired figure standing on the jetty and looking out at the sunrise.

The world shifted under James's feet. Right away, he was calm and peaceful. Right away, just from seeing her, without knowing whether she'd be his or not, the cracks in his soul glued back together. He didn't even need her to say anything or love him. Just breathe somewhere in the same world, in the same time, and he'd be complete.

He didn't move or say a word.

She turned over her shoulder and, like him, went completely still. And yet there it was, that pull between them that always drew him to her. Her hand shot to her mouth and her muffled whimper made his heart stop.

Now he could say thanks to God—any god. She was here. She hadn't become a nun.

"Hi," he said.

She moved. Walked to him first, then ran, then rammed into him at full speed like an Olympic sprinter, knocking all the air out of him. He wrapped his arms around her, crushing her to him, as though she'd disappear like a dream if he didn't catch her.

"James?" she whispered as she leaned back and took his face in her hands. Her eyes glistened with tears. She looked his face up and down as though to make sure he was really here. She was wearing only her nightgown and had a blanket on her shoulders that now slipped to the ground.

"Yeah." He laughed out. "It's me."

"Ye came back?"

"I came back."

"Oh…" She hid her face in the crease of his neck, and he closed his eyes, inhaling the herbal, angelic, feminine scent of her, drinking it in, making it part of his system.

"Am I too late?" he asked. "Did you take your vow?"

She shook her head and looked at him, a huge smile on her face. "If ye're asking about me becoming a nun, I didna. And I wilna."

He sighed out loudly. "Good. I didn't know what to do if you had. Because…well…" He reached into the pocket of his jeans and took his grandmother's ring and held it out between his fingers for her.

Her eyes widened. "What is this?"

"I realized your faith gives you strength and helps you through difficult times. Something I could use, too. My faith in you, in us, gave me strength to come back to you. It gives me the strength to offer you my vow."

She swallowed, and tears welled in her eyes.

"This is my vow," he said. "To love you till the end of days and till the end of time. Love you beyond life and after death. Love you even when I can't speak or see or hear. My vow to be your loyal husband...if you agree to be my wife."

She covered her mouth once more, and a tear streamed down her face.

"Do you accept my vow?" he asked, love blooming in his chest.

She nodded. "Aye. Of course. I will marry ye, James." She took the ring and put it on her finger. "Ye're the love of my life, an echo in my soul, and the only one I'll ever love."

"God you're so beautiful," breathed James.

"I will give my vow to ye, James. I vow to forever have faith in me, in ye, and in our love."

He felt it in his bones. Somewhere deep inside him where he couldn't reach and couldn't touch, and couldn't even explain. The vow resonated there, and he knew they were bound now like he'd never been bound to anyone or anything. It went deeper than his police officer's oath to serve the queen and protect the people. And deeper than the need to breathe.

Like a deep rumble somewhere beyond. Longer than time. Bigger than life.

It was love.

And then she kissed him.

EPILOGUE

 *ne week later...*

WHEN THE WEDDING FEAST DEVOLVED TO DRINKING AND ribald jesting, Catrìona gave James a knowing look. To which he immediately finished his ale, slammed it on the table, and scooped his bride into his arms.

The shouts grew in intensity, and a few brave, younger revelers followed the newlywed couple to their bedchamber door. She couldn't stifle her laugh as they climbed the stairs to the landing, face burning at the jokes from those escorting them to their threshold.

James delivered a sound kiss to his bride and slammed the door in their faces.

Catrìona giggled all the way to the bed, and then sobered at the heat in James's face as he looked at her. Not that she feared this night—she'd been longing for it. But now, perched on her marriage bed, she shivered under the intensity of his gaze.

As if he could sense her anxiety, James stepped into her,

gently opening her thighs from on top of her heavy skirts to give him better access. She reached up to drag his face down to hers.

He kissed her like this would be their very last kiss and so he needed it to be threaded through with everything he felt in that moment. And by the urgency of his lips on hers, Catrìona knew he felt everything, and wanted her to feel it, too.

When he swiped his tongue against the seam of her lips, she opened to him. Allowing him to sweep in and claim her mouth like he would soon claim her body. He tasted of ale, and the rosemary and fennel that had seasoned the meat served at the feast. It tasted even better from his lips.

She broke away with a gasp, but he wasn't content to let her get away so easily.

He brushed his knuckles against her cheek. "Let me help you out of this dress."

A smile split her lips, and she stood and turned so he could access the laces of her gown. "Aye, husband, undress me."

Mumbling curses, he began working on the laces of her cornflower blue wedding dress. Catrìona giggled. It took him so much longer than any woman—from a lack of experience undressing medieval women, surely. Finally, he pulled her woolen gown up and over her head, and she stood before him in nothing but her undertunic and stockings.

She turned to him and looked him up and down. "Yer turn."

A soft smile played across his mouth, and with a nod, he undid the belt on his tunic. He pulled his tunic over his head, then the undertunic and his braies and stockings, then shoes, until he wore nothing save a smile.

All humor fled her mind as she took him in. The long muscular lines of his body. Soft hair on his chest and torso, his bare skin glowing in the firelight and candles illuminating their bridal chamber.

Thinking she'd never be more brazen than she felt in this moment, she quickly removed the rest of her own clothing and added it to the mounding pile at the end of the four-poster bed.

"Look at you," he whispered. The reverence in his tone made her feel beautiful, worshipped by him. She'd gained more weight, and she felt more like the woman in her dream, fuller and more feminine, and free.

"I think ye're beautiful, too," she offered, unsure of what she should do now that they were both naked. She knew what she wanted to do. Explore every inch of him, toes to scalp, and learn what would make him as breathless and needy as he often made her.

But he had plans of his own and scooped her into his arms. Covering her body with his own, he said, "Tell me what you want, Catrìona."

The hard length of his erection already pressed into her wet center. If he meant right in this instant, she wanted him inside her, but she couldn't *say* that. "I want you to do what you did the last time." She was proud her voice didn't waver on the end of her request.

A mischievous glint entered his eyes, and the corner of his lips tipped up. "Happy to oblige. But this time, we won't stop after you achieve your pleasure."

She was ready for everything he wanted to give her and more. "Good."

He eased down her body, slowly, trailing gently nibbling kisses. When he got to the curve of her breasts, he drew one nipple into his mouth.

She arched off the bed, gripping his head to her harder. After he finished with one, he delivered his attentions to the other, sucking the nub gently and then releasing it with a tiny *pop*.

All she could do was stare down at him in awe. "What was that?"

He didn't answer, only gave her another grin, and continued his trek down the flat curve of her belly. Every so often, a small lick or bite would mark his passage until he reached her thighs. He stopped to nibble along the seams of her legs, and then spread them wide, exposing her to him completely.

She swallowed the shame that washed across her skin. No, she needn't fear this. James was her husband, and she couldn't ask him to stop anyway, not with his eyes locked on her very center. Not with the needy look in his gaze as he memorized the lines of her intimate flesh.

He braced himself on his elbows and used his fingers to part her gently. Then he quickly ducked his head and laved her with his tongue.

Catrìona reached out to grasp the coverlet, digging her fingers into the fabric to give herself something to hold on to. Another ministration like that and her soul might depart her body from the pleasure of it.

"No, love, hold on to me, not the sheets," he whispered.

She realized she'd clenched her eyes shut as surely as her fists. It took a moment to depart the haze of pleasure to look at him. Then she followed his instructions, releasing the bedding and entwining her fingers over the top of his head.

He hummed his appreciation into her skin, sending even more pleasure spiraling through her.

But he wasn't content there. He gently positioned her knees so her thighs rested against each of his cheeks and his face lay flush into her. Then he added a finger, gently easing his middle digit into her channel.

"You're ready for me already," he whispered.

She could only nod at the statement, words having fled her mind completely with every new sensation threatening to drag her into an abyss.

When she didn't respond, he carefully eased a second finger inside her and circled his tongue over the bundle of nerves near her mound. Every swipe of his clever mouth there left her breathless. Her heart already felt like it might beat out of her chest and escape.

"First I'm going to show you the stars, then I'm going to sheath myself in your heat and take us both to the moon," he whispered, more to himself than her.

She nodded, not understanding some of his words but happy to do anything he asked as long as he didn't stop touching her.

He ducked his head again, lapping at her with more intensity, each stroke causing her to lift her hips in the rhythm he somehow set for her.

From the last time, she knew not to fight it, but to let the pleasure wash over her when it broke. And it did, hard enough to shoot stars behind her eyes. She clutched his hair between her fingers, wrapping her thighs around his head, and rode out her peak until she stopped shivering.

When she finally opened her eyes, he stared up at her with a predator's gleam.

She opened her arms to him, and he crawled up her body to settle between her legs. The hard length of him pressed against her belly at this angle, the tip sticky against her skin.

"Are you ready?" he asked.

Catrìona nodded. "Yes. I want ye more than anything. I always have."

He dropped a kiss to her lips, gripped himself between her legs, and gently eased himself into her opening.

It wasn't painful, more of an ache that shouldn't quite alleviate. She held on to the broad strength of his shoulders while he slowly pushed inside her the tiniest bit at a time.

His jaw was clenched tight as he fed himself into her body, his eyes locked on their joining with an intensity he got only in battle. Oh, and she loved him for it.

With each new bit of her he breached, she allowed herself to loosen, to relax underneath him, and trust it wouldn't all be discomfort in the end.

Once he sat wholly inside her, she was full and felt deliciously invaded, and she clenched around him. He resettled squarely into her hips, framed his forearms around her shoulders to hold some of his bulk off her body, and stilled. "Are you all right, love? I'll stop if it hurts."

She shook her head frantically. "Dinna stop." It didn't hurt, not really. Even now the ache gave way to a heady sort of pleasure she knew she could get lost in. No wonder they called fornication a carnal sin. In this moment, she'd never felt more inside her own body. And him with her.

He nodded and carefully eased out of her. The movement ignited sparks inside her, breaking the discomfort completely and making way for something better.

"I don't know how long I'll be able to last. You feel so good," he murmured against her lips.

She wrapped her legs around him, crossing them below his backside. "Then dinna last. Give yerself to me, too."

He dipped his head and kissed her hard and fast. Then he pulled away to stare down into her eyes as he gently eased from her body and ebbed back inside. He set a soft, gentle rhythm. For her, no doubt. She could see by his clenched jaw how much effort it took to control himself.

"James, dinna hold back because ye think I'm too weak to take this. Ye could never hurt me."

With her permission, he surged out of her, dragging himself from her body almost completely, then arched his hips and plunged back inside. The force of it drove her up the mattress and wrung a gasp from her lips.

Oh. This wasn't the gentle lovemaking they'd started with, and now that she felt it, she didn't want to go back.

She dug her nails into his shoulders, urging him to do it again. And he gave her everything. Using his knees to give himself leverage, he pounded into her body.

Each pass of his cock through her channel drove her spiraling towards her end again. Wave after wave of pleasure crashed over her as he plundered her body with his own.

Wolfish groans were coming out of his throat. "Come with me."

She was already so close to the edge it wouldn't take much to toss her over.

He moved faster, sheathing himself inside her over and

over, the pace brutal and unrelenting. And then like a tidal wave undeterred by a seawall, he crashed into her. That wave of pleasure took her over, possessed her as surely as he did now.

He moaned into the hollow of her neck, jerking his hips but slowing, stilling as he pressed into her. His entire body shook around hers and her own shivers matched his.

It took several minutes for her to find her way back into her own skin. A dull ache had taken root inside her, and she knew she might feel that tomorrow.

Right now, she only had eyes for her husband. Sweat beaded along his brow, catching errant pieces of hair she'd mussed with her crazed fingers.

"I'll be gentler next time, I promise," he said, eyes closed as he laid his head beside hers.

Then he eased out of her, and she flinched as he slipped free of her body. "Dinna ye dare. I may be sore now, but I want all of it, every time."

He turned her to face him and scooped her into his embrace. "What about my heart? Do you want all of that, too?"

"I already have it, my love, as you have mine," she said, entwining their fingers.

Suddenly, his eyes were dark and serious. "Do you promise?"

She traced the side of his face with her fingertips and smiled. "I dinna just promise. I vow so."

"So do I."

And as her husband covered her lips with his, his kiss told her everything that he felt towards her. She was loved. She had found joy by his side. Her purpose was clear to her—to help her clan and her husband in the way only she could—with her knowledge and her faith and her passion. She was a free woman, even though she was married. That was what she'd wanted from being a nun.

To be loved, and needed, and free.

She knew now that she deserved the love that was all around

her. Love she felt most strongly in James's arms. Love and faith that had brought them together across time.

THE END

Loved Catrìona and James's story? Get excited for Raghnall's story next in **Highlander's Bride.**

ALSO BY MARIAH STONE

CALLED BY A HIGHLANDER SERIES (TIME TRAVEL):

Sìneag (FREE short story)

Highlander's Captive

Highlander's Hope

Highlander's Heart

Highlander's Love

Highlander's Christmas (novella)

Highlander's Desire

Highlander's Vow

Highlander's Bride

More instalments coming in 2022

CALLED BY A VIKING SERIES (TIME TRAVEL):

One Night with a Viking (prequel)—grab for free!

The Fortress of Time

The Jewel of Time

The Marriage of Time

The Surf of Time

The Tree of Time

CALLED BY A PIRATE SERIES (TIME TRAVEL):

Pirate's Treasure

Pirate's Pleasure

A CHRISTMAS REGENCY ROMANCE:

Her Christmas Prince

JOIN THE ROMANCE TIME-TRAVELERS' CLUB!

Join the mailing list on mariahstone.com to receive exclusive bonuses, author insights, release announcements, giveaways and the insider scoop of books on sale - and more!

Join Mariah Stone's exclusive Facebook author group to get early snippets of books, exclusive giveaways and to interact with the author directly.

ENJOY THE BOOK? YOU CAN MAKE A DIFFERENCE!

Please, leave your honest review for the book.
As much as I'd love to, I don't have financial capacity like New York publishers to run ads in the newspaper or put posters in subway.

But I have something much, much more powerful!

Committed and loyal readers

If you enjoyed the book, I'd be so grateful if you could spend five minutes leaving a review on the book's Amazon page.

Thank you very much!

SCOTTISH SLANG

aye – yes

    bairn - baby

    bastart - bastard

    bonnie - pretty, beautiful.

    canna- can not

    couldna – couldn't

    didna- didn't ("Ah didna do that!")

    dinna- don't ("Dinna do that!")

    doesna – doesn't

    fash - fuss, worry ("Dinna fash yerself.")

    feck - fuck

    hasna – has not

    havna - have not

    hadna – had not

    innit? - Isn't it?

    isna- Is not

    ken - to know

    kent - knew

    lad - boy

    lass - girl

    marrit – married

nae – no or not
shite - faeces
the morn - tomorrow
the morn's morn - tomorrow morning
uisge-beatha (uisge for short) – Scottish Gaelic for water or life / aquavitae, the distilled drink, predecessor of whiskey
verra – very
wasna - was not
wee - small
wilna - will not
wouldna - would not
ye - you
yer – your (also yerself)

ABOUT THE AUTHOR

When time travel romance writer Mariah Stone isn't busy writing strong modern women falling back through time into the arms of hot Vikings, Highlanders, and pirates, she chases after her toddler and spends romantic nights on North Sea with her husband.

Mariah speaks six languages, loves Outlander, sushi and Thai food, and runs a local writer's group. Subscribe to Mariah's newsletter for a free time travel book today!

f facebook.com/mariahstoneauthor

⊙ instagram.com/mariahstoneauthor

BB bookbub.com/authors/mariah-stone

⊙ pinterest.com/mariahstoneauthor

a amazon.com/Mariah-Stone/e/B07JVW28PJ

Made in United States
North Haven, CT
10 November 2022

26520759R00181